A DEAD WITNESS IS NO WITNESS

GIACOMO GIAMMATTEO

Inferno Publishing Company

TITLE PAGE

GIACOMO GIAMMATTEO
INFERNO PUBLISHING COMPANY"

INTRODUCTION

Gino and Ribs are investigating what appears to be a routine drug murder when things get out of hand. A prominent citizen is killed, then a priest, and those killings are followed by more drug murders. After the priest's murder, the Chief of Detectives and the mayor—both Catholics—put pressure on Captain Cooper to solve the murders.

It's now up to Gino and Ribs to do just that. The problem is, all the witnesses are dead.

Chapter One

TROUBLE IN PARADISE

Monterrey, Mexico

Raul got up early, had breakfast, then took a walk with the kids. They climbed the steep, narrow path behind the house until they reached the peak of the mountain.

"Look how far you can see," Amarida said.

"That's almost forever," Nuño said.

Raul reached down and tousled Nuño's hair. "It's pretty far, but it's not quite forever."

"I'll bet you can't throw a rock that far."

Raul laughed. "You're right. I don't think I can. But now that we've resolved that, how about we go back down and eat breakfast. I bet your mama's got it waiting."

Amarida ran down the path ahead of them. "And I'm hungry too."

When they got back, the kids ran to the kitchen and Raul took a seat on the patio. Renata, his wife of many years, served him an espresso. "I'll make sure to keep them inside now so you can have your meeting."

~

Raul sipped his espresso and waited patiently for the rest of the men to show. After the last one arrived, he signaled for the door to be locked, then he stood at the front of the patio and faced them.

"I'm happy to see everyone made it today," Raul said. "But it remains to be seen how many of you will be happy when we're finished."

"Why shouldn't we be happy?" Rodrigo asked. "I heard reports from most that regions were up, and I *know* my territories were good."

Raul nodded. "There were good reports, *si*, but there were also reports that weren't so good."

He glanced around the patio. "And one of those reports was from Dallas TX, which should have been good. If you read the news coming out of Dallas, drug use is up. But you wouldn't know that from looking at our numbers. Our market share lowered, and the information I received is that it lowered due to a neighboring cartel, not infiltration from the Italians, Colombians, or any other source."

"I'm sure it's temporary," Rodrigo said. "Whoever is trying to move into Dallas must not know we have claimed it."

Raul walked from one side of the patio to the other, staring at the men seated before him. "Do you truly believe that, Rodrigo? Or are you just that stupid? Or worse, are you working with our competition?"

Six tables were seated on wobbly legs that sat atop the flagstone covering the patio. Rodrigo looked about nervously, an attempt to gather support. "Raul, you know I would never do such a thing. How could you say it? I'm married to your sister."

Raul pointed his finger at him. "Being married to my sister means nothing—other than you like unattractive women."

He drew laughter at that, but his glare silenced them quickly. "You can show me it wasn't you, by doing your damn job and increasing our territory *and* our market share. Our target was to not only cover the Dallas market by now but the nearby suburbs as well. If you want to prove your worth, I expect you to blanket Houston with our product, then move into Dallas and reclaim our position there. You said you were good. Let's see how good."

Tito spoke up in defense of Rodrigo. "Excuse my saying so, but when dealing with a product that generates profits such as this, it invariably draws heated competition, and there is little to be done in the way of stopping the competition, only staying ahead of them. Dallas is a big market, and if you think it's another cartel, I'm sure they are putting a lot of money into the market, not to mention soldiers to support it."

Raul sneered. "Did you learn that strategy while taking your lessons in English? If so, the learned professors don't know much about our business." Raul sat on the edge of a chair near the front of the room and turned sideways. "By the way, amigos, I'm impressed with how much English all of you have learned so far. It's imperative for us to speak well while penetrating the market; however, don't imagine the professors can teach you much more than language because their knowledge of how our business works stops at profits, and the need to launder the money."

"Perhaps you'd care to enlighten us," Tito said. "My territories in the southern districts have all increased significantly, and in no small part, due to following the suggestions and teaching of the professors."

Raul shook his head. "Tito, you have a different situation, and if you had the brains to realize that, you'd know that smaller territories often do well where larger territories don't. Your territories—which have indeed done well—are Brownsville, the Valley, and north to Corpus Christi. The population of Corpus Christi, the densest in your territory, is about 440,000 people. The populations of Dallas and Houston—when surrounding areas are included—are almost seven million each. A significant difference."

Tito lowered his head. "Sorry, Raul."

"There is never a need to be sorry for offering a suggestion, Tito, or for asking a question. Only excuses deserve punishment." He turned to Rodrigo. "Do you have any of those excuses?"

Rodrigo stood. "No excuses. Simply saying that Pablo didn't deliver what was expected in his territory and neither did Juan in his, and his was a quickly growing district. And we don't have the competition in Houston. Neither do we have pressure from the cops."

Raul shook his head. "So, no excuses, you say, but then you offer excuses."

"My apologies, Raul. It won't happen again."

"What won't happen, Rodrigo? The excuses or the bad reports?"

"Neither one, Señor."

Raul glared. "I'll forgive your slip of the tongue this one time. Do not address people as señor or señorita. Use American terminology—U.S. American terminology."

Rodrigo relaxed. "Yes, sir. And the reports next month will be better. I guarantee you."

"Good, Rodrigo. I like guarantees. They give me comfort. Now, if I were you, I'd see to it that Pablo and Juan are made examples of. People learn best by example."

"What kind of examples?" Rodrigo asked.

"The kind that people learn from, my friend. I think you know what I mean."

Chapter Two

A DRUG DEAL GONE BAD

Houston, Texas

Rodrigo dressed in his finest suit, packed his briefcase, then headed to the airport in Monterrey. He boarded the eight o'clock flight to Houston, and after arriving, drove to the western territory to observe the day's activity. He called Jorge as soon as he settled in.

"How did the meeting go with Raul?" Jorge asked.

"Not as good as it should have," Rodrigo said. "Raul expects us to take over Dallas in no time, but he doesn't understand that Ortega is a smart man. A *very* smart man; in fact, when it comes to distribution, he may have an edge on Raul."

"Does that mean we back off on Dallas for now?" Jorge asked.

"No, Jorge. Not at all, but it *does* mean we need to approach it more carefully."

"We'll be ready when you are, Rodrigo."

"Jorge, let's forget about Dallas for now. Today, I want you to take someone with you and observe Pablo. Don't take your eyes from him, but don't let him see you watching either. Am I clear?"

"I'll take Ranza. He's here now, so we can leave in five minutes. Do you know where Pablo is today?"

"Sage Street," Rodrigo said. "Remember, make sure he doesn't spot you. And keep your phone on. I'll be calling you."

"You're back in town?" Jorge asked. "Back from Monterrey?"

"I am. I just got in, and as I said, things could have gone better."

"You decided to come to Houston instead of Dallas?" Jorge asked. "Is that because of what you said?"

"I need to establish complete control in Houston, before moving to Dallas. When I get to Dallas, it will require my full attention, and I can only give that if Houston is secure."

"I understand, Rodrigo, but we can control Houston."

"It's easy to claim you can do something, Jorge, but it is much more difficult to accept responsibility for it. Will you step up and have your hands chopped off if something goes wrong?"

Jorge said nothing.

"I thought so. If you're not willing to do that, you're not ready to control Houston or anywhere else."

"Si, señor."

"English, you must speak English. I heard enough of that from Raul, so now I'm passing it along to you." Rodrigo issued Jorge a scolding rebuke.

Jorge recognized his mistake immediately and tried correcting it. "My apologies, Rodrigo. It won't happen again."

"Be thankful I'm an understanding man, Jorge. If you had

made that mistake with Raul, he would see to it that you had no tongue to make the same mistake again. Now take Ranza to where Pablo does business and observe what he does. And stop and get a car he won't recognize. I don't want him to know anyone is watching."

"Yes, sir. Right away."

"Jorge, you might want to bring a couple others in case we need them. But have them take a different car as well."

"Yes, sir."

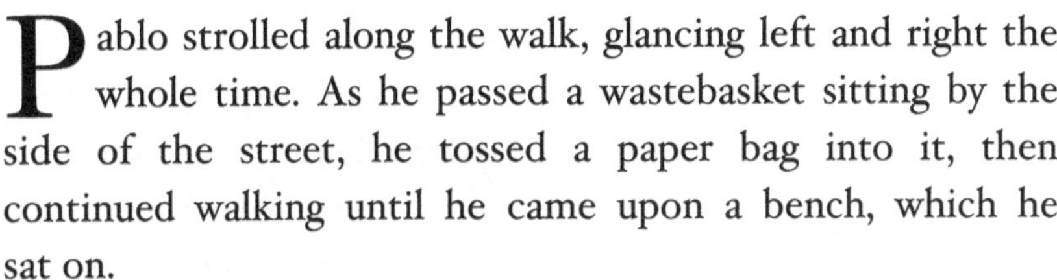

P ablo strolled along the walk, glancing left and right the whole time. As he passed a wastebasket sitting by the side of the street, he tossed a paper bag into it, then continued walking until he came upon a bench, which he sat on.

Fifteen minutes later, an older blue pick-up truck pulled alongside the curb, and a man in his thirties got out and approached. "Got anything for an old friend, dude?"

"As long as that old friend has something for me," Pablo said.

The man handed him a handful of crumpled up bills. "Should be enough for two tastes," he said.

Pablo slowly unfolded the money, counting as he did. When he finished, he smiled and patted the man on the back. "If you look in that trash can down the street, you'll find a paper bag that you might want to take with you. Just so happens, I think it contains two tastes."

The man smiled, showing teeth rotted from meth.

"And remember," Pablo said, "If anybody asks, you didn't

get that shit from me. And we won't be meeting here next time. Meet me over on Richmond, by Fondren."

"You got it," he said. "Thanks."

The man walked to the trash can, reached in, and removed the bag which he stuffed inside his jacket, then he got into the truck and drove off.

Jorge's phone rang when the man in the truck drove off. "Send the others after him," Rodrigo said. "And let me know what was in the bag. While they're doing that, invite Pablo inside your car to talk."

Jorge and Ranza walked up to Pablo slowly. As they approached, he displayed increasing signs of nervousness: shifting on the bench, tapping his foot on the ground, and more. By the time Jorge got to the bench, Pablo was trembling. "*Buenos dîas,* Pablo."

Pablo flashed a quick smile. "Ah, *Señor Jorge. Buenos dîas. ¿Cómo está?*"

Jorge looked at Ranza and smiled. "You see what I mean, Ranza. Pablo can't even speak English."

Jorge then reached down and pulled Pablo to a standing position before walking him toward the car. "Maybe the three of us should chat. Does that sound good to you?"

Jorge opened the back door and pushed Pablo inside, then Ranza got in the other side next to him. Jorge then squeezed in, pushing Pablo to the center, between him and Ranza. Just then, his phone rang. "Jorge."

"Ask Pablo if his sale was a good one."

Jorge held the phone against his chest, turned on the

speaker, and said, "Rodrigo wants to know if that was a nice sale. In other words, how much was it?"

Pablo faked a laugh. "What? That bum. It was nothing. In fact, I gave him a few bucks to help him out."

"And the trash basket? What did he take from there?"

"Trash basket? I don't know, Jorge. I didn't notice."

"That's odd, Pablo, because he took the same bag I watched you place in there on your way to the bench."

"Pablo shrugged. "Probably just one more bum searching for garbage."

"That's one explanation, Pablo. But there are others, and the others are not so innocent."

"What do you mean?"

Jorge put the phone back to his ear. "Are you getting all this, Rodrigo?"

"I heard," Rodrigo said. "Search him. I'm going to have Diego and Miguel stop the truck."

~

"Do it," Rodrigo said. "And make sure he buys nothing again. From no one."

"All right," Diego said, then he turned to Miguel. "Stop the truck at the next light."

Miguel pulled in front of the truck, then Diego walked back and opened the door. "My name is Diego. We work for Rodrigo."

The man looked confused. "What—"

Diego laughed. "Don't worry what we want," he said. "Just turn left, then pull over into the parking lot on the right."

Miguel parked alongside the truck. When he opened the door, he and Diego both stabbed the man numerous times.

Miguel reached down and took hold of a package of drugs that was sitting on the seat in a canvas bag.

Diego grabbed his elbow and shook his head. "I wouldn't do that. Rodrigo didn't say to take the drugs, so I wouldn't do it. Not worth it."

"But that's worth a lot of money."

"Is it worth your life?"

~

Jorge and Ranza searched Pablo and came up with a handful of crumpled bills—the ones he'd just received moments earlier. "And where did this come from, Pablo? It looks like ten or twenty thousand. Didn't Rodrigo teach you to keep your money neat and organized?"

"Yes, but I—"

Jorge chuckled. "Pablo, Pablo. You know what Raul says: there are no excuses. I thought you at least learned that."

Jorge got out of the car and behind the steering wheel. As he pulled away from the curb, he glanced in the rearview mirror. "Pablo, are you really going to stick with that story?"

"It's not a story."

"Really? Let's see if it is or not." He dialed the phone and waited.

"Yeah, Jorge?"

"Did you stop the truck, Diego?"

"We did."

"And what did you find?" Jorge asked.

"We found about ten thousand worth of heroin wrapped up and inside a canvas bag. And it doesn't have our marking on the wrapper."

"Whose marking does it have?" Jorge asked.

"El Lobo is written below a large wolf's head stamped on the outside."

"Many thanks," Jorge said, then he turned to Ranza and nodded. "It seems as if Pablo likes working for Ortega. Maybe he needs to learn a lesson. Make it one that others may learn from."

Ranza pulled a long, thin-bladed knife from his waistband and stabbed Pablo between the ribs. Almost simultaneously, Jorge reached to the back and shoved a knife into Pablo's leg just above the knee. Blood gurgled from Pablo's mouth and dripped down his chin. He coughed, spit blood, then coughed more, but Ranza continued stabbing him.

It didn't take long for Pablo to die, and when he did, Jorge pulled close to the nearest curb. Before he reached the corner, Ranza opened the door and pushed Pablo's body into the street.

~

The squealing tires grabbed Arlen Langer's attention, and he turned his head to look. Jorge's car pulled away from the curb and increased speed rapidly, barely missing Arlen, who jumped to the sidewalk to avoid being hit.

Arlen lifted his head and stared as the car passed. He noted the make and model of the car, then committed the license plate to memory.

The car turned at the next intersection, tires once again squealing, then it disappeared. Arlen stood and brushed his clothes off, then typed the license plate number into his phone, along with what he recalled of the description.

"Arlen, good morning to ya."

Arlen looked up to see Father Burns standing in front of the church, waving at him and yelling loudly.

Arlen drove his car over and up the street and parked in front of the church. He got out and walked up the sidewalk to meet Father Burns. "Good morning, Father. Did you see what happened?"

"I didn't see it happen," he said, "but I walked out in time to see you were almost run over. Are you all right? You're not hurt are you?"

Arlen panicked. "Did you call an ambulance? They pushed a man from the car. I don't know if he's dead or not, but they dumped someone out of the car and in the gutter before almost hitting me."

Father Burns nodded vigorously. "I called for the police *and* an ambulance; they should be here momentarily, although I doubt they'll be in time to do that poor soul any good. I'm guessing he was dead before he hit the street."

Father Burns blessed himself, then said, "And thank the Lord for watching out for you, my son." Father Burns then repeated the sign of the cross.

Arlen used a handkerchief to wipe sweat and grime from his forehead, then he put the cloth in his back pocket. "I need to get this reported before I forget what happened."

Father Burns placed his hand on Arlen's arm. "I don't know if I'd do that. Wait and see if the police think it's a drug killing."

"What difference does that make?" Arlen asked. "A killing is a killing. It doesn't matter who did it or why they did it."

Father Burns shook his head. "Arlen, I think you know it does. Being a witness for any crime is bad enough, but if you give information to the cops on a drug killing, you're likely to end up the same as the dead man."

Arlen paced. "I don't know, Father. I feel as if I should report it."

"Did you get the car's make and model? Or the license plates?"

"I got all of it, why?"

As he was about to respond, the sound of footsteps alerted Father Burns. He turned to see another priest approaching. "Good morning, Father McLaughlin. It's a fine day, isn't it?"

Father McLaughlin shook his head. "Not for that poor soul across the street. Has anyone called it in?"

"I did," Father Burns said. "Just after it happened."

"Then I guess I don't need to do the same," McLaughlin said, then turned and walked the other way.

Father Burns waited for him to get out of earshot, then spoke to Arlen. "Maybe you should give the information to me, and let me be the one who turns it in. I doubt even the drug people would go so far as to kill a priest."

"I doubt it too, Father, but I could never risk your life that way. I wouldn't do it."

Father Burns rested his hands on Arlen's shoulders. "My life is my people. If I can't help them, I have no life. You should go home and rest, then think of what you want to do, but I would strongly advise you to do as I suggested, and let me contact the police. I've already told the police it was a small gray car, though that's all I could tell them. I'm not very good telling the model or make of cars."

Arlen patted Father Burns on the shoulder. "All right, Saint Burns," he said, exuding sarcasm. "I'll think about it, though I doubt I'll see it your way."

Arlen began to walk away, then turned. "By the way, you'd

make a terrible witness. It was *not* a small, gray car; it was a Chevy Impala—four-door."

Father Burns laughed. "And I suppose you have the license number too?"

"Of course, I do," Arlen said. "It's PRK 7425."

"I've played cards with you, Arlen. I know your memory isn't that good."

"You're right, Father, but I jotted it down in the phone, just in case."

Father Burns lost his smile and grew concerned. "Arlen, you need to get rid of that. If anyone knew you had the license number, your life wouldn't be worth a darn."

"Nobody knows but us, Father, so don't worry so much."

Father Burns shook his head. "I still say you should let me turn it in. Text me the plate number, and I'll call it in. It'll be safe coming from a priest."

"I'll think about it," Arlen said.

"Do that, my son. Go home and think about it. I'm sure you'll see it my way. And talk to that darling wife of yours; she's the one with brains and common sense. You'll see. Things have a way of working out."

Father Burns genuflected as he reached the center of the aisle, then he blessed himself and continued on his way.

As he crossed the brick sidewalk on his way to the rectory, Father McLaughlin hailed him. "Father Burns, wait up."

McLaughlin caught up to him, though he was winded from running. "Did you get all that reported this morning?"

"If you mean that horrendous crime, yes. I already told you, Father. Are you showing signs of age?" Father Burns asked, then laughed. "Besides, I'm sure it was another drug-related crime, and you know what that means."

McLaughlin scowled. "I know all right. It means nothing will get done, and we'll have lost another soul to satan."

"It's a pity that more of these crimes aren't prosecuted," Burns said.

"I agree with you on that, but with you giving them the license plate number, they should have a good start finding out who did it."

"Let's hope so," Father Burns said. "Let's hope so."

Arlen Langer finished dinner, shared a drink with his wife, then went for a stroll around the block, and all the while, he thought of what to do.

Half an hour later, he entered his condo, went into his office, and texted the license plate number to Father Burns. When it was acknowledged as received, he deleted the text. *That's done. Now let's hope they catch the ones who did this.*

Chapter Three

THOSE AREN'T RAUL'S DRUGS

Houston, Texas

"Ribs, have you heard about the body found in the pickup off Westheimer? That makes two bodies now, and both of them are within spitting distance of St. Michael's on Sage, so what the hell is going on? Why are people being killed? And who's doing the killing?"

"I was looking into that already, cuz. When I heard Harris and Langkon caught a case within two miles of us, it set off an alarm—a coincidence alarm. But coincidence, or not, the murder was drug-related as well."

"Which means we need to speak to Harris and Langkon because there isn't any way another drug-related body went down the same day in the same vicinity, and it wasn't related to ours."

"That settles it then," Ribs said. "Let's call Harris and Langkon and see what they've got to say."

~

We caught Harris as he walked into the station. "Harris, you no-good son of a bitch, we need to talk about your case."

"I can make that happen, Cataldi, but you're buying, and I'm not talking at Starbucks either."

"All right, where the hell do you want to eat?"

"I'm talking a nice steak and somewhere good too. Somewhere like Pappas or Killens."

"You're out of your fucking mind," Ribs said. "I wouldn't take you to Killens if you let me fuck your wife; in fact, I wouldn't take you to Killens for both your wives. The best you're going to get is Outback. If you don't want that, we'll read your reports."

Harris stared for a long time, then he smiled. "Okay, asshole. Outback it is. We'll be there at seven."

~

At seven o'clock, Ribs and I walked into the Outback. Harris and Langkon were already seated, and they stood and waved us over. "Sit and talk," Harris said. "Or sit and ask."

I sat across from Harris and next to Langkon. "All right, tell me about how you caught it, and what you found when you got there."

"Shit, the first part's easy," Langkon said. "We caught it the same day you caught the case on Sage. It wasn't half an hour later."

Harris sipped his drink and nodded. "Got a call from a

citizen who saw a man slumped over the wheel in his truck, and blood was all over the seat."

"But that ain't all that's on the seat," Langkon said. "There was ten or twenty grand worth of drugs in a canvas bag, and the bag was wide open. The mystery is why didn't whoever the hell killed him, take the drugs? They were visible just from looking through the window. It's been bothering us ever since."

"It's been more than bothering us," Harris said. "I'd have considered snatching that shit myself. I mean, that much dope . . ."

"Who did drugs belong to?" Ribs asked.

"What the hell do you mean who did the drugs belong to?" Harris asked. "Do you think somebody stopped by and dumped drugs in his front seat? They belonged to the damn dead man That's who."

"You idiot. If you don't get smarter, you'll be paying for your own meal. What I meant was, which cartel did they come from? What label did they have on them?"

Harris and Langkon looked at each other, then Gino said. "All the cartels have labels. It's usually an animal like a wolf or a boar or a cobra."

"No shit, Cataldi. Like we didn't know that," Harris said "It was a wolf, a goddamn wolf, and it said El Lobo under it. If I'm not mistaken, that puts it squarely into the hands of Ortega from Juarez."

I stopped eating and looked at Harris. "You're right about that, but the problem that brings up is location. This is Raul's territory, so if Ortega's selling his dope here, we've got a problem, and a couple of dead men are just the beginning of it."

Langkon finished off his meal and leaned back. "You know,

I always love those damn onion things. I swear, some day I'm gonna come here and order nothing but that."

"And I'm sure you've sworn that before, Langkon. Now tell us something that contributes to the case."

"I don't know how much we can count on it, but one of our witnesses said the pickup came from Sage Street about fifteen minutes prior, and another witness wouldn't swear to it, but said they thought so. If that's the case, it would put the truck on Sage about the time of your murder."

"Which would fit," I said. "Our body was a known dealer, and he was found with a pocketful of money and some of Ortega's drugs as well. And the amount of money aligns with how much you found in drugs, so if our guy sold Ortega's drugs to your body, it would work."

"Then who killed them?" Harris asked. "I'm guessing it had to be Raul."

"That makes sense too," Ribs said. "If it *is* Raul, he's not taking the drugs, but leaving that as a message for anyone else thinking of selling Ortega's product."

"I agree it's a definite message, and a strong one—sell Ortega's shit and die."

"That's the kind of message people listen to," Harris said. "At least those kind. I haven't met many brave drug dealers."

"To be sure the drugs match," Langkon said, "we need to have the M.E. do a comparison. I'd feel better if we did."

"I'll call in the morning," Harris said, "but I'd bet another steak dinner they match perfectly."

"The question we need to be asking is why are Raul's dealers suddenly selling Ortega's product? Is the product better? Is Ortega paying more? Does he offer better protection?" I held each of them fixed for a brief moment. "It's something. And we need to find out what."

"I'll call a detective I still know in San Antonio," Harris said. "Ortega's big there, so if anybody knows anything about him trying to move into Houston, it might be Burks."

"All right. Let us know if you find anything, and don't think you can weasel another dinner out of us."

Harris laughed. "Next time it'll just be coffee."

GINO AND RIBS GET A BODY

Houston, Texas

The call came in to Charlie, a.k.a. 'Fat Charlie,' and he routed it straight to Captain Cooper.

"We've got a body on Sage," the officer said. "I just left there, and it's a mess."

"You just left there? Was someone else on the scene?" Coop asked.

"Harris and Langkon had just pulled up. They took over, so I left."

"Shit. Do me a favor. Go back and tell Harris that I'm giving this to Cataldi and Delgado, then stay there until they arrive."

"Will do, Captain, but I hope you don't mind my saying, sir. You know they won't like that."

"I know that, officer. And if they say anything to that effect, you can politely tell them I don't give a shit."

"Yes, ma'am," he said, and hung up.

Coop dialed Charlie's extension. "Charlie, when you see Cataldi or Delgado, have them report to me immediately."

"Yes, sir, Captain."

I drove down the freeway listening to music, or should I say *trying* to listen. It was difficult when your partner talked nonstop about anything and nothing.

"Cuz, if you'd turn that garbage music off and listen to me, you might learn something. *Might*."

"The only thing I'd learn by listening to you is how to piss people off, although, I'll admit, you're very good at it—pissing people off, that is. Not to mention talking nonsense."

"Now that you've gotten that off your chest, let's talk about something important."

"Like what? You haven't brought up an important topic since you adopted Little Marissa," I said.

"How about the annual shooting contest? Tell me that's not important."

"Of course, it's important, but it's also a foregone conclusion. Tip will win it like he does every year."

"Two years ago, he didn't win," Ribs said.

I almost laughed, but just shook my head, instead. "Ribs, he wasn't in the contest that year. He was out of town."

"He still didn't win."

"Why the hell are you so interested in it anyway? You think you're going to win? In order for you to win, you'd have to have Tip and about fifty others drop out. Then you might have a chance. *Might*."

"Hell no. I doubt I'd have a chance then, but it would give me a good clue of who to bet on. There should be some good odds floating around."

I reached over and turned up the radio. "I'll tell you what, Ribs. When you figure out who you think will win, tell me, and I'll bet on someone else. Now can I please listen to at least a few songs before we get to the station?"

I couldn't find a place to park, so I dropped Ribs off at the door while I searched for an open spot.

Ten minutes later, I parked the car, went inside, and up the steps. Ribs stood at the top, holding a cup of coffee. "It's about time you got here, cuz. I've been waiting for days."

"If you've been there more than a minute, you're more stupid than I imagined." I reached for the coffee, but Ribs pulled away.

"What the hell makes you think this is for you? Other people drink coffee, too, you know?"

"But other people aren't one of your many cousins—or your only partner."

"Which is another reason why you're not getting it," he said, then we headed toward our desks.

We had barely passed Julie's cubicle when Fat Charlie hollered to us in his raspy voice.

"Hey, Gino. Coop wants to see you and Ribs, and she said to get your asses down there immediately."

"Thanks, Charlie," I said, then Ribs and I turned and headed toward Coop's office. When we were out of earshot, I said, "You know, Ribs, his voice always reminds me of Chill Wills, that old Western actor from back in the thirties and forties."

"You mean the guy with the deep, raspy voice and the Texas twang?"

"That's him," I said. "Sometimes he sounds just like him."

"I agree," Ribs said. "By the way, what do you think Coop wants? Think we've got a case?"

We turned the corner and approached Cindy, who sat at her desk guarding the cave. "Good morning, Cindy," I said.

She raised her brows. "It depends," she said, providing an indication of what awaited us in the cavern.

"We got a case?" Ribs asked.

Cindy shrugged. "I can only guess, but why else would she summon you? It's sure as hell not because she likes you."

"Damn, but you're nasty," Ribs said. "See if I bring you any more flowers."

Cindy laughed. "Ribs, you've *never* brought me flowers, and if you did, I might pass out."

"If I'd have known that, I would have," Ribs said, then he opened Coop's door and went inside.

Ribs entering first showed just how unintelligent he was. "Good morning, Captain. How are you this fine morning?"

"Shut the hell up, Ribs. You too, Cataldi. Sit down and

listen, and please don't say anything. We've got another body in the Galleria area, and you know that's going to piss off the new mayor. And before you say anything, know that I don't like pissed-off mayors even if they are new to the office."

"This another drug deal gone south?" Ribs asked.

Coop removed her glasses and rubbed her eyes, as she was wont to do. "I can only guess, Ribs, but that's what you two are going to determine. And you're going to do it quickly and quietly. I do not need, nor do I *want* anyone breathing down our necks on this one."

"Or crawling up our asses," Ribs said.

Coop shook her head. "To put it more crudely—yes."

"Captain, let's agree to ignore my partner for now. How about telling us what we have?"

"What we have is an apparent drug dealer who was stabbed multiple times and dumped from a moving vehicle in broad daylight. And right on Sage Street. Not to mention within shouting distance of St. Michael the Archangel's church."

"Any witnesses?" I asked.

"That's for you to determine," Coop said. "We haven't heard anything as yet, so it looks as if you'll have your work cut out for you."

I stood up and grabbed Ribs by the elbow. "Come on, cuz. We've got work to do."

We rode toward the Galleria with Ribs talking non-stop. Not that his incessant talking presented a different scenario than normal, but it was amazing that he had so much to talk about. Most people just remained quiet if they had nothing to say, but not Ribs. He simply found something else to talk about, and he never seemed to run out of topics.

"Hey, Ribs, do you *ever* stop talking?" I asked.

"What the hell, Gino? Riding in the car and not talking is like riding on the bus and not saying anything to the person sitting next to you. *Dios mio.*"

"Ribs, you can spout that Mexican charm bullshit all you want, but I know better. You're no different than the rest of us, and the truth of the matter is, you'll do us a lot more good if you focused on what we are working on, and forget about chatting with people who don't know shit and wouldn't tell us if they did."

"So damn cynical," Ribs said. "It's a good thing we're at the scene so I don't have to listen to your negativity."

"What the hell, Ribs? Now you're turning into some damn hippie guru?"

"It wouldn't hurt for one of us to be aware," Ribs said, but he laughed when he did.

I pulled to the curb south of St. Michael the Archangel's church, and we both stepped out of the car.

"Looks like everyone is still here," I said, and gestured to the other side of the street where the crime scene unit appeared to be processing the scene.

They had several people working on the curb where the body was, two more on a nearby bench, and one digging through a wastebasket by the side of the road.

Ribs tapped one of the techs on the shoulder and held out his badge. "Got anything to report yet?"

The guy stood up and removed a mask he was wearing, then took off his goggles. "Multiple stab wounds in the lungs, and oddly enough, the legs. The ones in the lungs are what killed him, of course. From the blood pooling, he may have been dumped while still alive, but he didn't stay that way for long."

"Any drugs on him? Or money?" I asked.

The tech nodded. "A pocketful of crumpled-up bills, mostly fifties and hundreds, but it amounts to quite a bit. And he had three or four packs of Mexican Brown on him. I'm amazed whoever killed him didn't take it. Or the money for that matter."

"Any markings on the packages?" I asked.

The tech nodded again. "An image of a hooded cobra. That means it belongs to the cartel in Monterrey. La Cobra, it's called, which is odd because that's a feminine name in Spanish. Most of them use names like El Lobo or El Jabato. Something like that. La Cobra is a little unusual."

"But you're sure it's tied to the Monterrey cartel?"

"Positive," he said. "Check with your guys in Narcotics. They'll tell you."

Ribs moved a few feet away and dialed his phone. "Randy, you got a minute? I need a heads up on some drug activity."

"Shoot."

"We're looking at a body by the Galleria, and he's carrying a wad of crumpled up bills, plus a couple packs of

Mexican Brown tagged with a cobra image. Mean anything to you?"

"Hell yeah. It means he was working for Raul out of Monterrey and some dumb-as-shit rival probably took him out. It was a dumb thing to begin with, and even dumber if he didn't take the dope or the cash."

"So Raul runs the heroin up here?"

"Yes, and no," Randy said. "Raul is the top dog, but his man, Rodrigo, runs things up here. And he's a slick son of a bitch. We've been after him for a long time."

"You think this is a turf war? Anyone trying to move in?"

"I don't know, but if it is, there's gonna be a lot more bodies, so be ready."

"Okay, Randy. Thanks."

Ribs hung up and rejoined Gino. "I just talked to Randy in Narcotics. He confirmed the label, and he basically said for us to keep our fingers crossed that it's not a turf war, because it'll get bloody if it is."

~

"All right," I said, "Let's see if we can round up any witnesses while CSU finishes up."

~

We struck out at the crime scene, but that wasn't surprising because the good witnesses usually left the scene early. The last guy we talked to said he'd seen someone talking to a priest at the church across the street. Ribs gestured to the church. "Let's check it out. You can't get a better witness than a padre."

We skipped the church entrance and walked around to the rectory. A knock on the door brought a youthful-looking priest within moments.

"May I help you?" he asked.

I showed my badge, whipping it out before Ribs showed his. "Detective Gino Cataldi, and this is my partner, Detective Delgado. We're here about what happened this morning."

"This morning? You must mean that horrible incident across the street."

The priest stepped aside and motioned us inside. "Come in, detectives, please. I'm Father Robert Burns, and I witnessed the incident."

He grabbed a pitcher of water and brought it to a small sitting area. "Here I go telling tales again. I didn't actually witness the event, but I did catch a glimpse of things at the end. I saw a car speeding away from the curb on the other side of the street, and when I looked, I saw that a body had been dumped there."

"Did you get a good look at the car?" Ribs asked.

"I wouldn't call it a good look, but it was a small gray car, light gray."

"Do you know the make or model?" Ribs asked.

"I'm sorry, Detective, but I'm not very good with cars. If you get much beyond big or small and what color it was, I'm lost."

"How about the guy you were talking to?" I asked.

"I'd like to help you with that, Detective, but I'm prohibited from speaking about it."

"Prohibited? It wasn't a confession. As I understand it, you were talking to him right outside the church entrance," I said. "If that's the case, I can't see how the confessional policy applies."

"I don't want to state in any absolute terms that it does or doesn't," Father Burns said, "But he had asked me if I was open for confession when I saw him. When I said *yes,* he said,

'Then let's go. I've got a lot to say.' At that point, we walked toward the confessional, and he told me what he'd seen."

I wrote down what he said, then put the notepad away. "It sounds to me as if you weren't in the confessional yet."

Father Burns nodded. "You're right about that, but it doesn't mean it wasn't protected conversation."

"I think you better check with a higher authority, Father. As far as I'm concerned, it wasn't protected, and I'll be pursuing that line of thinking, even if it means pressing charges."

Father Burns patted my hand and smiled. "In that case, perhaps we both should consult higher authorities. But now I have to prepare for mass, so please forgive me."

"Be a little late, Father. Tell us more of what we need to know. You want us to catch the people who did this, don't you?"

"Of course, I do, but I don't know if I can."

"Father, I don't like to call bullshit on a priest, but I'm doing it. You can tell us what we need, or at least a lot more than what you've said so far. Let's start with the plates. Did you catch the plates? Or any part thereof?" I asked.

Father Burns shifted his weight from one foot to the other. "I've already told you what I know for sure. It was a small gray car. I did not see the plates, and I do not know the make or model of the car. If I can tell you any more, I will."

I started to say something, but Ribs handed him a card, and said, "Father, call us if you remember anything helpful." After that, he grabbed my arm and led me away.

Chapter Five

MAYBE CONFESSION ISN'T SO SACROSANCT

Houston, Texas

I was working at my desk when Sandra buzzed me. "You have a call on line two," she said.

"Gino Cataldi."

"Detective, this is Father Burns. We met yesterday."

"I remember, Father. Did you seek advice from above yet?"

Burns chuckled. "Not yet, but I *have* reconsidered what we spoke about, and I've arrived at the conclusion that what the parishioner told me did not meet the requirements of protected conversation."

"I'm still listening," I said. "And I'm glad we're on the same page."

"Not on the phone," Father Burns said. "Perhaps we can meet tomorrow. I have an early morning mass to say, and I have a funeral service to perform, but I could meet by noon."

"Noon is fine. Where do you want to do it, the church?"

Father Burns laughed. "It might surprise you to know, Detective, but even we priests like to get out once in a while, no matter how trivial. How about we meet at Starbucks up on Westheimer by Fondren."

"Sounds good, Father. You've restored some of my faith in the sanity of the church, or at least, in some of its members. Let's plan on meeting at Starbucks around noon."

I got to the coffee shop a few minutes before noon and went inside. Ribs was good enough to stand in line while I secured a table that seated four.

I read the paper, and when Ribs came back, he set the drinks down, then glanced about. "No Father Burns yet?"

"Unless priests can now turn invisible, no, he's not here yet. I shouldn't have had to explain that, and I wouldn't have had to if I had a normal partner, but religious wackos like you may believe in that shit."

Ribs tore a bigger hole in the lid of his cup, to allow more room to drink. "I see what you're doing, asshole, and it won't work. I know you're a sacrilegious sort, but you'll not convince me to abandon my beliefs, you atheist."

I laughed. "By the way, why do you tear a bigger hole in the lid? They've already got an opening that works. A lot of people did research to determine the size of the opening that was needed."

"Damn, but you're an irritable sort. Besides, they didn't ask me, and if they had, I'd have told them they needed a bigger hole. And by the way, do I ask you why you're so damn grumpy all the time?"

I set my coffee on the table and stared. "You ask five times a day, you ass."

Ribs never even looked up. "But do you answer?" he asked. "No need to respond because the answer is *no* you don't. And I'm going to keep asking until you provide a good answer."

Father Burns walked in, saving me from further conversation regarding the subject. I stood to greet him. "Father, nice to see you've come to your senses."

"My senses were never in question, Detective. It was my morals and ethics that concerned me."

"Then I'm glad to see that those have aligned," I said. "What will you have to drink?"

"Coffee is fine," he said, and scooted a chair over from the table next to us.

He leaned forward and spoke softly. "Now what is it I can tell you?"

"You can start by telling us who you spoke with, and what he said."

Burns turned my way, sipped his coffee, and said, "Detective, I already told you all I know about what I saw. As to what he saw, you'll be much better off asking him, however, I can tell you he got a license plate number."

"A plate number?" Ribs asked. "What is it?"

Father Burns wrinkled his brows. "I'm surprised you don't already have this. I called it in anonymously yesterday."

"Called it in where?" I asked.

"To the hotline," he said. "The number they've been announcing all over the news."

"And you gave them the plate?" Ribs asked.

Burns nodded. "I told them it was a small, gray car, and I told them the plate number, which was PKM 7428." Burns seemed to give it thought. "I'm fairly certain that was the number."

"Anything else?" I asked. "How about the name of the witness?"

Burns hesitated a long while, then said, "I'm going to give this to you, but I want you to proceed with all caution. Treat it as if he were one of the people in your witness protection program because if this is as I suspect—a drug killing—I don't want this man placed in danger."

"That's the last thing we want too," I said. "We treat all witnesses the same. All of them are protected."

Father Burns snickered. "Detective, forgive me if I'm unable to contain my laughter, but I've seen how some of your witnesses are protected. It's not something I'd want for my family."

"All right, Father. I give you my word, he'll be safe."

Burns nodded. "I'll take your word, Detective. The man's name is Arlen Langer, and he lives on the top floor at Montebello."

Ribs whistled. "Montebello? That costs a fortune to live there."

"Nonetheless, he does," Burns said, then he tossed his coffee cup in the trash and stood. "Now, detectives, I must go. I have a busy day ahead of me."

"Does he attend St. Michael's?" Ribs asked.

Burns nodded. "He does. In fact, Arlen and I are good friends."

～

Ribs and I remained at the table after Father Burns left. "We need to discuss how to handle what we got from the priest," I said.

"We didn't get anything to speak of," Ribs said.

"*I* know that," I said, "but Langer doesn't. Let him think Burns told us everything he said, and we'll see if we learn anything different."

"Cuz, you know I'm not in agreement with you on that, but what the hell, this is a murder case. Let's go. You handle the questioning though. I'm a religious man."

I laughed. "You're a religious man, my ass. You're only religious when you want to be. If it benefits you, you're the furthest thing from it."

"Think what you will," Ribs said. "I'm on my way to Montebello."

"I don't know if they'll let you in," I said.

~

Ribs told the doorman we were there to see Mr. Langer. He looked us over, almost as if judging our suitability, then buzzed him.

"Mr. Langer, two gentlemen here to see you."

"Who are they?"

I stepped up and held out my badge. "We're detectives," I said. "Homicide."

"Show them up, please."

~

We rode the elevator to the top and were met by a young man with an accent I didn't recognize. It may have been Nigerian, but I wasn't sure.

We stepped to the end of the hallway and were admitted to Langer's condo. He greeted us with a warm handshake and a smile. "Detectives, nice to make your acquaintance. Have a seat, please. And would you care for a refreshment?"

"We're fine," I said. "We just have a few questions."

Langer sat in a chair across from us and placed his elbows on his knees. "I'm ready to be grilled," he said.

I started off with only a white lie. "Mr. Langer, we spoke to Father Burns, and he said you told him you witnessed the killing of that man on Sage Street."

Langer smiled. "Detective, I know Father Burns. He is one of the more strict followers of Catholic rules, and that includes the sanctity of the confessional; in fact, that may be at the top of his list."

"Two things about that," I said. "First, this wasn't confessional, and secondly, Father Burns said you okayed him telling us."

Langer laughed. "Detective, you could probably get away with telling most people that lie, but I know Father Burns too well. He wouldn't have told you that, nor would he have said anything other than what he and I spoke about. But today's your lucky day because I have no qualms about telling you myself."

Ribs smiled and leaned forward, taking notes. "I'm glad to hear it, Mr. Langer. Please go on."

"First, it's Arlen, not Mr. Langer. Second, what I saw was a body being dumped from a new—maybe brand new—Chevy Impala. It was light gray, and it was a four-door, of course. It sped away after dumping the body, and, in fact, it darn near ran me over."

"That's good information," I said. "Are you certain about the make and model?"

Arlen nodded. "Pretty certain. I've always had an interest in cars, so I can usually identify a car with no more than a glance."

"Father Burns said—he really did—that you got the license plate number."

Arlen scrunched his nose. "Forgive my confusion, Detective, but I'm at a loss. I gave that plate number to Father Burns; in fact, I texted it to him."

"May we see the text, please?" I asked.

Arlen shook his head. "I wish I could show it to you, but I erased it. Father Burns and I decided that it may not be wise to keep it on my phone just in case the wrong people came looking. I even spoke to Rita, my wife, about it, and she agreed it was the thing to do as well."

"Do you remember the plate?" Ribs asked.

Arlen seemed to think, then he shook his head again. "Definitely not all of it. I'm pretty sure it began with a 'P,' and I know it had a '7' and a '4' in it, but other than that, I can't say. I'd only be guessing."

We finished talking to Arlen, then rode down the elevator and walked back to our car. "I say we stop by and chat with Burns again. I'd like to know why he didn't mention receiving a text of the plate number."

"It's not far from here," Ribs said. "Let's do it."

We parked in front of the church and walked out back to the rectory. Father Burns was walking along by himself when we approached. "Father Burns," I called.

He turned and greeted us with a smile. "Detectives, how nice to see you so soon. Did you get to meet with Arlen?"

"We did," Ribs said, "And that's why we're here. Arlen told us something that sparked our interest."

"What would that be?" Father Burns said.

"Arlen mentioned he had texted you the license plate number for the car," I said.

Burns nodded. "He did. I thought I gave you the number."

Ribs pulled out his notepad and flipped through it. "You gave us what you *thought* was the number: PKM 7428. Is that the number Arlen texted you?"

"I'm sure it is, Detective. I can't verify it because I deleted my text, but if you check with your tip line, they should have a record of what I called in."

"And why did you delete it?" I asked.

"For the same reason, I suggested that Arlen delete his copy—so that one of the drug people doesn't take revenge against us."

"All right, Father. Thanks for your help," Ribs said.

As we drove away, I glanced at Ribs. "Did you buy that shit he was dishing out?"

"I didn't *like* it," Ribs said. "And I thought it could have been handled differently. But I can't see why he'd lie, so I guess I'd have to say *yes,* I bought it."

"I'll reserve judgment until after I talk to the people who

handled the tip lines. Let's go see if we can find out who took the call."

~

After speaking to half a dozen people who had manned the lines, we had nothing. "That son of a bitch didn't call it in," I said.

"Don't jump the gun," Ribs said. "Ten or twelve people who answered phones aren't here. It could have been any one of them."

"And if it was, why didn't it get turned in as a viable lead? If someone calls in a plate, that shit should go to the head of the line. But I don't see it anywhere."

"We'll check it tomorrow," Ribs said. "I'm sure it's here."

Chapter Six

A DEADLY CONCERN

Houston, Texas

Arlen Langer returned from his morning jog, took a shower, then joined his wife for tea.

Rita took a bite from her bagel. "Did you have a nice run, dear?"

"It's a jog, not a run, dear, but yes, I did. I'm now ready for a hot shower."

"And then what? Have any plans for the day?"

"I didn't before, but after those detectives visited, it got me thinking. They said Father Burns hadn't called them with the information I gave him, but I was sure he said he had."

"He may have gotten busy. I'm sure he will. You know Father Burns stays on top of things. He wouldn't let something like this slip his mind."

"No, not Burns, but usually he would have done it right away. I think he's doing it to protect me. I'm going to talk to Father McLaughlin about it and see what he says. Maybe he can talk some sense into him. I'd call it in myself, but I erased the damn text I had with the plate number."

Rita finished chewing the mouthful of bagel she had, then said, "I wouldn't worry too much over it. Give Father Burns a call, and I'm sure you'll get it straightened out; besides, we're dealing with drug dealers. How much difference does it make?"

Arlen put his teacup in the dishwasher, then turned to Rita. "You might be right, but I can't believe you said that. Either way, I'm going past the church today anyway, so I may as well drop by. If Father Burns is there, I'll talk to him, and if not, I'll talk to McLaughlin. No matter what, it will be done with today."

"Excellent idea, dear. And don't forget to bring home some of that delicious wine we had at the Parker's house last week."

"Good thing you reminded me," Arlen said. "I'd forgotten all about it. Do you remember the name?"

"I don't," Rita said, "But if you call Joan, she'll tell you. If you can't reach her, call Richard at work. Just make sure you get the right one. I loved that flavor."

～

Arlen drove the few blocks to St. Michael's, then parked and went into the church to find the priest. Father Burns wasn't there, so Arlen went to the rectory and knocked on the door. Father McLaughlin answered.

"Hello, Father. Is Father Burns in?"

"Father Burns isn't here, Arlen. May I help you with something?"

"Possibly so," Arlen said. "Remember that killing on Sage

Street? I witnessed a lot of what happened, and right afterward, I told Father Burns about it. He convinced me to let him report it for safety reasons, but now I've found out he hasn't done so, and I feel sure it's his way of protecting me. I'm concerned, though, because that information needs to get to the police."

McLaughlin leaned against the open door and scratched his beard. "Now I'm confused, Arlen. I know Father Burns reported that. It was the license plate and description of the car, if I recall. But if the detectives are saying they don't have it, something has gone wrong. Father Burns will be gone until tomorrow, but I'll look into it right away. I'll let you know what I find out."

"Fantastic," Arlen said. "I appreciate it, Father. We need to stop this kind of thing from happening."

Father McLaughlin dialed the number he'd seen advertised for the tip line. He was placed on hold, so he put the phone on speaker and worked while he waited. Almost ten minutes later, someone picked up the line.

"May I help you?"

"This is Father McLaughlin at St. Michael the Archangel's church. We're on Sage Street right across from where that man was killed a few days ago."

The lady on the phone seemed to perk up upon hearing this. "Yes, Father. What is it?"

"One of our parishioners reported the crime and provided a good description as well as a license plate, which Father Burns called in, but the detectives in Homicide said no one has a record of it. I wondered if it may have been misplaced."

"Oh my, Father. I don't know, but I'll surely look around. If he called it in, I'm sure someone recorded it. We've had a lot of tips come in."

"All right, young lady. Please do so, and when you find it, send it over to the detectives in Homicide. I believe their names were—"

"I know who is handling the case, Father, and I'll make sure they get the information. And thank you. We appreciate the help."

Father McLaughlin dialed Arlen's number and left him a message, then he placed a note on Father Burns's desk, informing him of what he'd done. When he finished, he decided he'd go for a brisk walk.

Rita finished setting the table for dinner. It wasn't often she did this herself; it was a chore normally handled by Chalia, but today she had taken off so she could take her son to the doctor.

Rita called Arlen to dinner, and they ate in near silence, then she poured two glasses of the new wine Arlen had brought home. "Good God, this is good," Rita said. "I'm so glad the Parker's introduced us to it."

"I agree," Arlen said. "In fact, it's so good, I'm going to take my run early tonight so I can come home and enjoy some more."

Rita wagged her finger at him and smiled. "Don't you mean, your *jog*?"

Arlen laughed and kissed her cheek. "And that's why I love you, Mrs. Langer." He set his glass on the counter and said,

"You should come with me tonight. I'll take it easy on you and only run a circle around the Galleria. And I'll go slow."

Rita nearly spit out her wine. "You'd have to have an ambulance following us so it could rush me to the hospital."

Arlen laughed and slapped her butt. "Okay. I'll see you soon. And don't drink all that wine before I get back. I intend to beat you at some canasta."

~

It was nearly dark when Arlen left, and by the time he ran south on Post Oak and turned onto Alabama, heading west, it had turned pitch dark. He jogged along, nodding to the few people he passed, and when he got to Sage, he turned north to Westheimer, then east for the final leg of the jog. He was looking forward to finishing up that bottle of wine, and he was strategizing on his game of cards against Rita.

Not ten yards after he turned, a car raced down Westheimer, jumped the curb, and smashed into him. It immediately backed up, then sped off, heading north on Sage.

Several people called an ambulance as well as the police, and it wasn't long before the intersection was lit up with flashing red lights.

"Back up, please. Back behind the line," the officer said. "Give us some room to work here."

A second officer questioned the onlookers. "Did anyone see what happened? What kind of vehicle was it?"

"I saw it," a young woman said. "He was jogging along, and that car jumped the curb and hit him. It looked like it was on purpose too. The man didn't even stop. He just backed up and took off."

The officer took notes. "It was a man driving? You're sure about that?"

"No doubt," the woman said. "It was a gray car, and it had four doors. I don't know what kind, but it was fairly new."

"And why do you say it was on purpose?" the officer asked.

The woman got animated, pointing in the direction the car came from. "Because he increased speed just before jumping the curb, and he turned right into him. Then he backed up and went the other way. He could have definitely avoided him if he wanted."

"Anything else you can tell me about the car?" the officer asked.

The woman shook her head. "Nothing more than what I said." She pointed to a few other bystanders. "Ask some of them; they might know."

By the time the officer finished, he had two reports of the car being white, and one even said it was blue, but four people confirmed the first woman's report of it being gray. And all but one agreed it was a four-door.

The officer wrote everything up, then joined his partner.

"Get it all?" his partner asked.

"I got it. Whether it's right or not, we'll see. It was either white, blue, or gray, and it was either a four-door or a two-door car. But most of them claimed it was a man driving."

"At least you've got no reports of a pickup," his partner said.

The officer laughed. "The night's early. Don't count it out yet."

~

Rita Langer finished her third glass of wine and paced in front of the window. She occasionally looked out to see if she spotted Arlen. From this high up, it was doubtful that she could, but she looked anyway.

She couldn't spot Arlen, but she saw the flashing lights of the ambulance and police cars. Worried now, she rushed to get her phone.

She dialed Arlen and waited while the phone rang. Just as she was about to hang up, someone answered.

"Hello?"

At first, Rita felt relief, but then she realized it didn't sound like Arlen. "Arlen? Arlen, is that you?"

"Who's calling?"

"Who's calling? I'm his wife. Who the hell is this?"

There was silence, then, "Ma'am, this is officer Fresno. We're at the corner of Sage and Westheimer, and there's been a terrible accident."

"Oh my, God. Oh my, God. Is Arlen all right?"

"Ma'am, perhaps you should come down here. I can send someone to get you if you need it."

"No. No, I'm only a few blocks away. I'll be right there."

She parked in the corner of the shopping center, then rushed over to the scene of the accident, fighting her way through the crowd that had gathered. "Let me though, please. That's my husband down there."

She fought her way to the front of the line, then explained to the officer in charge who she was. "I'm Mrs. Langer," she said. "That's my husband!"

The officer lifted up the crime-scene tape he'd put up and let her through. "I'm very sorry about this, ma'am."

"How did it happen? Who did this?"

"We don't know yet, ma'am. We're still gathering evidence."

Rita began crying. She pulled a handkerchief from her purse and wiped her eyes. "Oh, my God. Arlen. Arlen."

The officer took hold of her elbow and led her to the side, where he addressed his partner. "This is the wife. I'm going to drive her home. Be right back."

Chapter Seven

EARLY MORNING BODY

Houston, Texas

I got a call as I entered the freeway ramp heading downtown. "Cataldi."

"Gino, this is Coop."

"Good morning, dear. What's up with you on this lovely morning?"

"Don't bother with anything before you see me—not even coffee."

"Why? What happened?"

I could hear Coop sigh. "Somebody screwed up big, but the bottom line is we've got another body on Sage."

"Son of a bitch," I said. "We're on our way. See you in twenty."

Cindy looked to be in a panic when we came down the hallway. "She's waiting, but not patiently."

I opened the door, and Ribs and I went in. Ribs did the smart thing and sat the farthest away, leaving me to bear the brunt of the shit-storm I knew was coming. "We got here as quickly as we could," I said.

Coop nodded. "Arlen Langer is dead."

She said it somberly, but in hindsight, I guess that was the only way. We hadn't expected this, but here it was slapping us in the face.

"How?" Ribs asked.

Coop sat up straight. "He was run over. Witnesses said it was definitely intentional, and two witnesses claim it was a gray car, but we didn't get much more than that."

"When—"

"Last night," she said. "Right after dark."

"Since the scene's gone, what do you want us to do? Do we need to notify the wife?"

She shook her head. "Mrs. Langer had called her husband's phone, and an officer on the scene answered it. She came right down." Coop repositioned herself in the chair. "I would like you to see her though. I know you won't want to hear this, and I know you don't care, but he and his wife were good friends with Cybil, and even though she's no longer the mayor's wife, she still wields influence."

"What the hell's that have to do with anything? Rusty's not—"

"Hang on to your ass, Cataldi. If you listened before speaking, you would have already heard me say, 'She's no longer the mayor's wife,' but Langer was a friend of Cybil's, and she asked me to pay special attention to it. And it might irk your ass, but I told her we would."

"What's that mean, Captain? Are we supposed to drop everything and focus on this?"

Coop got her pissed-off look and glared. "No, Cataldi, it doesn't, but it *does* mean I want you to focus your *undivided* attention on this case when you're on it. And when you're not on it, do whatever the hell you like. No matter how you slice it, this has got to be related to the other case—even the other two cases. That alone makes it a priority."

After we left Coop's office, I drove over, turned south on Loop 610, and exited San Felipe.

"He lived in the condos about a mile or so from here," Ribs said.

I looked over at him and stared. "Are you an idiot or just dumb? We were just here the other day, remember?"

"I remember, but I was concerned about you. By the way, I've got my money on the wife." Ribs looked at me and asked, "He had a wife, didn't he?"

"Yes, he had a wife, and though it's not fair of me to take such easy money, my bet is on a business acquaintance. A partner or associate—something like that."

"Make it ten bucks," Ribs said.

"Ten it is," I said. "Now do something useful and brush up on the file Coop gave us so we don't look like idiots when we get there."

"Name's Arlen Langer," Ribs said. "Now at least you won't mess up the name."

I shook my head. "I knew the damn name, Ribs. We were *here*."

"I shouldn't have told you the name. I could've won five bucks on that."

"At least the bad part is over with. I despise notifications. I'd much rather go in when the family already knows."

Ribs nodded. "I agree there, cuz. Not much worse than telling a spouse that their wife or husband is dead."

I parked the car in the garage, we entered the building, showed our badges, and took the elevator up to Langer's condo. The door was answered by an attractive woman who looked to be in her mid-thirties.

Ribs stepped forward and showed his badge. "I'm Detective Delgado, and this is my partner, Detective Cataldi, ma'am. We're sorry to hear of your loss."

She opened the door wider and stepped aside. "Come in, please. I've been expecting you."

Mrs. Langer led us to a spacious living room, replete with comfortable sofas and chairs. "May I fix either of you a drink?"

Ribs and I both refused. "We won't be long, ma'am. We've just got a few questions for you, then we'll be on our way."

She returned holding a martini and took a seat in a chair next to Ribs. "Take all the time you need. I'm not unemotional, but I come from a family of law-enforcement officers, so I know what must be done."

"From around here?" Ribs asked.

She swallowed the sip of drink in her mouth while shaking her head. "Dallas. Actually, Dallas *and* San Antonio. I planned on settling down in Dallas until I met my husband. She stopped and corrected herself—met my late husband at a fundraiser. We married six months later."

"Not to pry, ma'am, but how long were you married?" I asked.

"Not long by many people's standards, but it seemed like it to me. We had twelve magnificent years before this."

"I'm so sorry," I said. "I understand the hurt. I lost my wife after twenty years."

She nodded and sat up straighter. "What do you need to know, detectives?"

Ribs took out his notebook and pen. "Your husband was found not far from here. Do you know what he was doing at the time? We don't often see homicides involving cars unless they're the result of road rage or an intentional action. Do you—?"

"Let me interrupt. I have no idea why anyone would have wanted to do Arlen harm. He was pleasant to everyone, and he was beyond generous to those who needed it. It would not have been road rage based on his mannerisms because he was the ultimate gentleman. If it had been me—maybe—but not Arlen. And before you ask, he *did not* have gambling debts, nor did he associate with people like that. And he didn't run around on me or do drugs. Lastly, I didn't do it for money. The money we have was mine; at least, most of it was."

"And his work?" I asked. "Any problems there?"

Mrs. Langer shook her head. "You're welcome to look at his books. I'll give the okay to Bud, his CPA, but his consulting business was doing very well. He billed more than ever last year, and this year started off even better; in fact, it was going so well he started playing golf with some of his friends every Wednesday morning. They did it religiously."

"I'll need those names if you have them, Mrs. Langer."

"Of course, Detective, I'll get them for you. And please,

call me Rita. I already feel old, and people referring to me as Mrs. Langer makes me feel even older."

"No problem, ma'am . . . I mean, Rita. I'd also be grateful for the CPA's contact information." I handed her a card. "You can call this number or simply text the information."

"I'll call," she said as she sat back down. "You might check into the church as well."

"What about the church?" I asked.

"Arlen has always been a religious man, a devout Catholic, but of late he's been more involved than normal."

"More involved?" I asked. "How so?"

"About once a week, he would go to see Father Burns, and he'd spend an hour or so with him."

"And that was unusual, I assume."

"In a sense, it was. It wasn't unusual for him to talk that long to a priest, but he never did it so frequently. Before about six months ago, he might have seen Father Burns once every two or three months. Lately, it's been almost every week, although I'll be quick to add that Arlen has been helping the church with fundraising activities, so that may explain the time."

"We've met Father Burns," I said. "We'll pay him a visit."

"Please don't interpret what I said the wrong way. Arlen and Father Burns are—were—friends, not just priest and parishioner, but *real* friends. They played golf together, went fishing together. Father Burns even played in a few of Arlen's poker games, though I suspect Arlen may have fronted him the cash. So let me amend what I said earlier. Arlen used to see Father Burns once every month or so, but that was aside from the normal get-togethers with his friends."

Ribs stood up as if to leave. "One more thing, Rita. Would it be all right if we looked at your husband's computer?"

"Of course. Wait here, and I'll get it. You can take it with you as long as you return it. There may be things on there I need."

She left the room, returning in a moment, and handed us the laptop. "He did everything on this laptop," she said. "It's the same one he used at work too. If it has a password, I don't know it, but I'm sure Bud will."

She walked us to the door and said to call if we needed anything.

On the way to the elevator, I held out my hand, palm up. "You want to pay now, Ribs?"

"Screw you, cuz. She may still be involved. You don't know yet?"

"In that case, would you like to double the bet?"

"No, asshole, I'd like to go to St. Michael's where *I* will interview a priest since I know that talking to a member of the cloth sends you off the deep end."

"Just make yourself useful and get your shit together because we're only a few blocks away."

"You know, cuz, we're going to have to verify all the stories Goldilocks told us."

I laughed. "Forget about your ten dollars; it's gone. As to verifying what *Mrs. Langer* said, we'll do it, but it won't take long. I believe her."

Ribs mumbled something, then said, "You always had a soft spot for a pretty lady."

"You're full of it, Ribs."

He smiled. "Need I remind you of who you're living with?"

Chapter Eight

HOW WELL DID YOU KNOW HIM?

I turned onto Sage and parked close to the church, then we went around to the rectory and knocked. A youthful-looking priest opened the door.

"May I help you?" he asked.

I showed my badge, whipping it out before Ribs showed his. "Detective Gino Cataldi, and this is my partner, Detective Delgado. We're here to see Father Robert Burns."

The sound of heels meeting tiled floors echoed in the foyer. "Then it is indeed your lucky day, Detective. I'm right here. I just hope whatever crime I'm accused of isn't too serious."

"That depends," Ribs said. "How well did you know Arlen Langer?"

Burns narrowed his eyes, and his body seemed to sag. "*Did* I know him? Has something happened to Arlen? What? When?"

Ribs took Father Burns by the arm and led him to an

empty chair. "Perhaps you should sit down, Father. I assumed you knew. Mrs. Langer told us you were close to Arlen."

Father Burns blessed himself as he sat. "What happened?"

"That's what we're trying to find out," Ribs said. "He was hit by a car not far from his home. He'd been jogging, and it looks as if someone intentionally ran him over."

"Dear God. Arlen was such a good man."

I moved to Ribs's side, knelt, and stared at Burns. "I understand you and Mr. Langer spent a lot of time together—both at the church and away from it."

Burns nodded slowly. "We did. We golfed, we fished. I even played poker with him, though it was more like him putting up with me while he and the others played. I wasn't very good."

"And his weekly visits?" Ribs asked. "Mrs. Langer said his visits to the church had increased of late. What was that about? Was he troubled by something?"

"Those were of a religious nature," Burns said. He shook his head then said, "Let me correct that. Not *religious* as you might think from the way I said it. He was helping me with fundraising events and strategizing on how to more effectively raise money for church projects. Our get-togethers had nothing to do with Arlen's personal life; he was simply helping us out, as I always did. As I said, he was a good human being."

"No matter how you look at it, this is a murder investigation, so anything you can tell us may help."

Father Burns stood, clasping his hands as he did. "I'm sure you know I'll do anything I can to help. Arlen was a good human being, a good parishioner, and a good friend. One of the few I have. Besides that, we have to stop these senseless killings. If they continue, people will be afraid to attend mass or confession."

I patted Father Burns on the shoulder. "We're going to be busy interviewing his other friends. If you think of anything. I mean *anything*. Tell us."

Burns walked us to the door, and we headed back to the car.

"I'm at a loss," Ribs said. "It's not often we get a murder victim who comes up this clean."

"I hear you, Ribs, but just for grins, let's dig a little deeper. We need to check out his poker-game buddies and his golf buddies, not to mention examine his books. I'm not ready to put a halo on his head. Not yet."

We climbed into the car, but before starting it, I checked my messages. There was one from Rita Langer containing the contact information for Arlen's friends. "Ribs, your guilty-as-sin wife just sent us all the contact information. For a master criminal, she's damn efficient. I'll give her that."

"Go to hell, cuz. But out of curiosity, do any of those contacts live near a coffee shop? I'm in desperate need of caffeine."

"Christ's sake, Ribs. You sound like a damn drug addict. And you knew damn right well any one of these addresses would take us by a coffee shop—if that's what you want to call Starbucks."

"And you say I'm the one who talks too much. Just stop, and we'll plan our visit."

We drank two cups of coffee while deciding on what we'd ask whoever it was we got hold of. At this stage of the investigation, everyone had a motive and everyone was a suspect.

"I think we should try Josh Hamill first," Ribs said.

"Any reason?" I asked.

"What if I told you it was because I didn't like his name?"

"I'd laugh because sure as hell I'd know that was the truth. But we don't have anything better to go on, so let's do it."

We drove to the address for Josh Hamill on San Felipe. It turned out to be another high-rise condominium project. It wasn't as nice as Langer's, but it was far more than either one of us could afford. Hell, we couldn't afford it if we moved in together. We parked the car, got out, and headed toward the building.

Ribs eyed the building as we approached. "You know, cuz, I think we need to start accepting more bribes. Everybody's living in a damn luxury condo. Everybody but us, I mean."

"What do you mean by *more* bribes, Ribs? Is there something I don't know?"

"Oh shit, forget I said anything," Ribs said, then laughed like hell.

We were buzzed up to see Josh Hamill and introduced ourselves when he opened the door. It was rare to find so many husbands at home during the day, but I guess with this much money, it wasn't all that uncommon.

"I presume you're here about Arlen?" Josh asked, then quickly gestured to a sofa and several chairs. "Sit, please."

Ribs took the lead. "We are. It's a damn shame what happened, and we're eager to find out why."

"What exactly *did* happen? All I know is he was hit by a car."

"A lot more than hit," I said. "So far, we're fairly positive it wasn't an accident. We believe someone intentionally ran him down."

Josh shook his head slowly. "I almost can't believe it. Arlen was such a damn nice guy. Did it happen while he was jogging?" He then looked up at us. "And how about Rita? Is she okay? Is anyone with her?"

"It was while he was jogging," Ribs said. "As to his wife, I didn't know she had anyone here. I thought her family was in Dallas and San Antonio."

"They are from there. San Antonio mostly, but quite a few in Dallas. I think even a couple in Austin, but I'm sure plenty of Arlen's friends or their wives will be going over to help. I know my wife wanted to go, but she had to leave town on business."

"How well did you know Arlen?" I asked.

"As well as anyone, I guess. We golfed every week. We played cards every week. And we fished when possible. And like I said, he was a damn nice guy. I don't know of anyone who did business with him that didn't come away pleased."

Josh laughed when he said that. "If you know business and politics in Houston, that made him a rarity. And there was more than one reason for that, but the main one was that Arlen made money for his investors, and he more than satisfied all his clients. Oh, and he *never* pissed off a vendor. And trust me, that's a difficult thing to do. But he had an understanding nature and a calming demeanor."

I continued jotting notes as I asked my next question. "If you don't mind me asking, Mr. Hamill, what kind of vehicle do you drive?"

"It's not a gray one if that's what you're asking. I drive a dark blue Mercedes or a red Corvette. And my wife drives a black Porsche 911."

"How did you know we were looking for a gray car?" I asked.

"I watch the news, Detective. At least, sometimes I do. And whenever they mentioned Arlen's death, they never failed to repeat it was a gray sedan that hit him."

"How about the card games?" Ribs asked. "Any big losers or winners?"

Josh laughed. "You won't find motive there either, Detective. We've had the same players for six years, and I doubt if anyone has won or lost more than a few thousand at the end of the year accounting."

I know I must have looked puzzled. "End of the year accounting?"

"Yes, Detective, we keep meticulous records of how much everyone wins or loses each week. At the end of each quarter, it's reviewed, then at the end of the year, it's both reviewed and discussed so we might adjust the betting. We do the same thing with golf. In fact, we bet on damn near everything, even our fishing. We bet on first catch, biggest catch, most fish caught, and more. It makes it more fun."

Josh sighed. "A lot of that won't be the same without Arlen. He almost always won first on the green when we played golf, and he never failed to remind us of that."

"And no one got upset?" I asked.

"Not at all. The amounts we bet may seem large to some people, but it's less than my car insurance for one month."

I looked to Ribs, who shrugged, then I announced that we had to move on. Josh walked us to the exit and said to call if we needed anything.

"You should talk to Marv Hamilton. He may have known Arlen better than any of us. Or at least he knew him longer. Marv lives—"

"I've got his address," I said. "But thanks. I appreciate it."

"That was a bust," Ribs said once we were in the car.

"Not necessarily," I said. "I think Josh gave us enough so we can dish out the rest of the interviewing to another team."

"Good idea, cuz. I like it." Ribs turned the radio off, then said, "You know, it's not that I dislike interviews, but I only like them if we get something to advance the case. I didn't feel as if we got anything from Josh, and worse, I didn't feel as if we'd get anything from any of the others either."

"Which is exactly why I suggested giving the interviews to someone else."

"The only problem I see is that Coop will have your ass for it."

"My ass?"

"Absolutely. Because I'll tell her it was your idea."

"You son of a bitch," I said. "Then let's go talk to Marv Hamilton and hear more good things about Langer."

~

Hamilton didn't live in a swanky condo, but he lived nearby, and I'm sure his house was even pricier than the condos.

He showed us in immediately, and we sat on a patio in the backyard to chat. We all had iced tea.

"Mr. Hamilton, how well did you know Mr. Langer?" I asked.

"Arlen and I went to college together, and we've been damn good friends ever since. He even introduced me to my wife while we were in college. I dated her then and married her shortly afterward. We've been married for twenty years."

"What can you tell us about Arlen and Rita's relationship?" Ribs asked.

Hamilton laughed. "You won't find any nicks in the woodwork there, detectives. They had a good marriage, a happy one. And they both had money. If I had to guess, I'd say Rita had more than he did, but it didn't matter. They were both well off, and neither one of them seemed to care about it."

I sipped my tea, then set the glass on the table. "You'll have to forgive our asking, Mr. Hamilton, but it all sounds too good to be true. Nobody is *this* nice a person."

"Get used to it, Detective. I doubt you'll find anyone with a bad word to say about Arlen. It's what makes it so difficult to believe he was killed intentionally. I've been racking my brains trying to figure out why."

"And you're sure about that?" Ribs asked.

"I'm positive," Hamilton said. "You learn a lot from the way a person handles both winning and losing. I've seen how Arlen handled it for more than twenty years, and it was always as a gentleman regardless of whether he won or lost, and no matter how much it was."

I stood up and shook hands. "Okay, Mr. Hamilton. That should do it. We greatly appreciate your time and your cooperation."

We left Hamilton's house and headed back to the station.

"Hey, cuz, did you ever follow up with the tip-line people about Burns calling in the description and plate?"

"I didn't personally, but I gave it to Julie, and asked her to do it."

"I feel better already. She'll do a good job."

"And I wouldn't?"

"I didn't say that, but . . ."

"Screw you, Ribs. Consider that recent visit to Starbucks, your last stop for coffee."

"Cuz, just get back to the station so we can chat with Julie."

Chapter Nine

TELL ME YOUR SINS

"Go with God," Father McLaughlin said, as the man exited the confessional. A moment later, he peeked out to see how many people remained in line. *Still about half a dozen*, he thought, then sat straight to greet the next penitent.

The man knelt and blessed himself. "Bless me, Father, for I have sinned. It has been three weeks since my last confessional."

Father McLaughlin made the sign of the cross while he finished. "Go on, my son."

The young man confessed his sins, received absolution, then exited the booth and knelt in a nearby pew.

A slightly older man who had been waiting behind him immediately entered the confessional and knelt. "Bless me, Father, for I have sinned. It has been six weeks since my last confession."

"What is it you need to talk about, my son?"

"*I˘n nōmine Pătris ĕt Fīliī ĕt Spīritūs Sānctī.*"

"Your Latin is good, my child, but how may I help you?"

"I'm a little leery of talking, Father. I have a friend who told a priest what he knew, and I heard the priest told others what he said."

"It's difficult to believe that a priest would do that. I don't know of any priest who would break the sanctity of the confessional."

"So you wouldn't do that? No matter what."

"Never."

"That's odd because my friend came to see you, and I heard you told others what he said."

"I don't know who your friend is, my son, but regardless of who he is, I did not, nor would I ever mention what someone told me in the confessional."

"That makes me feel better, Father. I was worried you had broken your vows with my friend. I never worried you'd break them with me."

"I'm happy to hear that, my son, because I never would."

"I knew that before I came here."

Father McLaughlin shifted in his seat. "I'm glad to see you had faith. You can always count on it."

The penitent sighed. "Father, it's a relief to see such undying faith. It gives me hope."

"I'm glad, my son. Now, tell me your sins."

"It's hard to do, Father. They're pretty bad."

"Have no fear. No matter what you say, it will remain a secret with me, and if you are truly remorseful, God will forgive you."

"If you say so, Father. Well, here goes. To begin with, I killed someone."

A long pause followed, then, "Murder is a serious offense,

my son. Have you expressed remorse to anyone or in any way?"

"No, but I am sorry to have to do it."

Another pause. "Have to do it? You said it as if it was already done?"

"It hasn't been done yet. But if you lean closer, I'll tell you about it."

Father McLaughlin leaned closer to the confessional screen which separated them. "I'm listening."

"Good, then you should be able to hear the shot that ends your life." After saying that, the man shot twice through the screen and into the side of Father McLaughlin's head. He fell to the side, then the man stood and calmly left the confessional. No one was in the church, but it wouldn't have mattered. The man had used a silencer on his gun, so the noise was no louder than a balloon popping.

Father McLaughlin slumped over and banged his head against the back wall of the confessional where he bled through the screen and onto the floor.

~

It was another hour before anyone entered the church. Father Burns walked through the side door and called Father McLaughlin's name.

"Father Tom. Father Tom, are you here?"

When he got no answer, he walked toward the confessional. As he got close, he saw blood had pooled on the floor. He quickly looked inside, then dragged Father McLaughlin out to administer first aid. It wasn't until he lay on the floor that he saw it was much too late.

Father Burns dialed 9-1-1 and requested an ambulance, then he reported it to the police as well.

I heard the phone ringing as I exited the coffee shop. I had left it in the car, something I seldom did, and now I remembered why. Someone always called when I left it somewhere.

I raced the last few feet, opened the door, and grabbed the phone. "Cataldi."

"Where the hell have you been?"

"Coop, what in God's name do you want? You know we were supposed to meet the priest. Whatever you wanted could have waited."

"Not today. We've got another body, and the chief is all over my ass about this one."

News of another body didn't excite me, but it didn't do

anything else either. "Where? And do I want to know who?"

"Probably, or maybe not. Why don't you and your partner stop by the station? I want to prep both of you."

"No need, Captain. Just tell me where to go, and we'll be on our way."

"Just stop by. For once—just once—do something I ask without an argument. It will make me feel as if you really *do* work for me."

"Aye, aye, Captain. We'll be there shortly." I turned to Ribs, who was just opening the passenger door of the car. "Step it up, Ribs. The captain summoned us, and she sounds like her normal, sweet self."

"In other words, you did something wrong again."

I laughed. "You're so full of shit. I should have taken Tip up on his offer to trade partners. I think working with Connie may keep my blood pressure lower."

"Cuz, if you're thinking about ditching me, then BP is the least of your worries."

We turned the corner, heading toward the station. "Besides," Ribs said. "I doubt if Marissa would want you staring at Connie's ass all day."

"And what makes you think I'd be looking at her ass?"

"First, I said, 'staring,' not *looking*, and to answer your question about 'why,' it's because you're a man."

"What the hell does that have to do with anything?"

Ribs looked at me as if I were crazy, then laughed. "I think you know why."

"You mean because she's got a nice ass," I said.

"What'd you say, cuz?"

"I said 'she's got a nice ass.' "

"Who's got a nice ass?"

"Who the hell were we talking about—Connie. Connie's got a nice ass."

Ribs laughed and held up his iPhone. "Cuz, you're so damn easy. Threaten me with switching partners again, and Marissa will hear this." Ribs pressed the 'Play' button on his iPhone, and my voice came on.

'Who the hell were we talking about—Connie. Connie's got a nice ass.'

Try getting out of that after I play it for Marissa."

I grabbed for the phone, but Ribs pulled it away. "If you want this phone, cuz, you'll have to take it off my dead body."

I pointed a finger at Ribs. "You ever play that for Marissa, and there will *be* a dead body to take it from."

We made it to the station in record time and headed straight for Coop's office. Cindy sipped a cup of coffee as we approached.

"She's waiting for you, and not with much patience."

"What's up?" Ribs asked.

Cindyi shook her head. "No idea, but her mood tells me it's serious."

Ribs opened the door and took the closest seat. "What's up, Coop? Somebody shoot the chief?"

Coop shook her head and glared. "Why the hell would you even joke about that? Suppose someone had shot him? How would you feel then?"

Ribs laughed. "Captain, find your sense of humor, and while you're looking, you can tell us what you called us down here for."

Coop removed her glasses like she always does when

things were serious. She leaned forward and rested her elbows on the desk. "We've got a dead priest."

Ribs lost his smile. "*Dios mio*. Where?"

"St. Michael's, the one down on Sage near the Galleria. The parish where Father Burns is, and the same one where you just found Mr. Langer close by."

Coop picked up a slip of paper from her desk and read from it. "Father Thomas McLaughlin. He's been there—excuse me *had* been there for fifteen years. Early reports say everyone loved him, but I'm guessing that's not necessarily true."

Coop stood and glared. "One thing's for sure. The chief is Catholic, and I guarantee he'll want this case cleared quickly, especially after this mess with Langer. And don't come back to me with any child abuse stories or parental revenge."

"Suppose that's what we find," I asked.

She shrugged. "I won't tell you to ignore evidence, and I'm certainly not telling you to hide anything, but spread a wide net and dig deep, and make sure what you come back with is the truth."

Ribs got to his feet. "In other words, do a normal investigation."

"Sometimes you piss me off, Delgado."

Ribs laughed. "Just *sometimes*? Damn, I've come up in the world." Ribs grabbed my arm and tugged it. "C'mon, cuz, let's get out of here while I'm ahead."

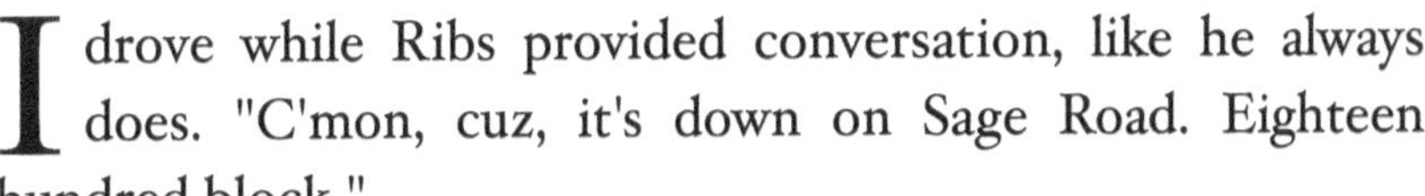

I drove while Ribs provided conversation, like he always does. "C'mon, cuz, it's down on Sage Road. Eighteen hundred block."

"I know where the hell it is. We were just there, remember?"

"I didn't tell you before, but when I was younger, I attended mass there a few times."

"At St. Michael's?"

Ribs nodded. "I didn't know any of the priests though. We only went because we were visiting Rosalee's cousin, who lives near here."

I made a turn off the freeway onto Loop 610. "Regardless of what the captain said, the first thing we need to do is check the good father out and see if he had anyone looking to get even with him."

Ribs shook his head. "Cuz, one of these days I'll cure you of your hatred of the church. I told you when you married Mary you were wrong."

I exited the freeway, heading west on San Felipe to get to St. Michael's. "You can *tell* me all you want, but until somebody *shows* me the church means well, I won't believe it."

Chapter Ten

WE FOUND A LEAD

We parked in front of the church and went inside. I dipped my finger into the holy water and blessed myself—the reverent thing to do—then we quietly made our way to where a small crowd had gathered, including the crime scene unit.

I recognized Debbie from previous interactions and knelt next to her. "Hey, Deb, get anything yet?"

She looked over and smiled. "Not much, Gino. He was shot twice in the head, which is obvious, and he was shot while in the confessional. If you peer inside, that's obvious as well."

"Anything else?"

"The body was moved, but the other priest who was here told us that. He said he came looking for Father McLaughlin and found him in the confessional, so he pulled him out."

"The other priest being Father Burns?" Ribs asked.

Debbie nodded. "I think that was it, yeah. He just left a few minutes ago."

W e waited for Debbie to finish, then stepped inside the confessional and had a look. As Debbie said, it was fairly obvious what had happened—two shots through the screen and into Father McLaughlin's head. The bigger question was *why*. *Why* would someone kill him? That's what we had to find out.

A priest stood in the aisle, leaning on the back of a pew. Ribs approached and spoke gently. "Father Burns, I'm sorry for your loss. I know you and Father McLaughlin have worked together a long time."

Father Burns sat and shook his head. "Detective, it makes no sense. Why would anyone kill him? He never harmed anybody. I've known him for twelve years, and he hasn't done a single thing to warrant anyone doing this. If this is in retaliation for the drug killing, it should have been me they killed, not Father McLaughlin."

Ribs placed his arm across the back of Father Burns's shoulders and spoke softly. "Father, I know this is a bad time, but it's also when we need to act quickly if we're to have any chance of catching these people. I strongly suspect this murder has something to do with the death of the man on the street last week and the killing of Mr. Langer. Do you have *any* idea what connection there could be between the three?"

Father Burns turned to Ribs. "Detective, the way I feel right now, if I had any idea, I might do something about it myself. But the truth is, I don't have a clue. In fact, I can't imagine a more unlikely scenario. A man as wealthy as Arlen, as pious and kind as Father Tom, and a person involved in drugs." He shook his head again. "It doesn't make sense. No sense at all." Father Burns wiped his eyes on his sleeve.

Ribs handed him a handkerchief which Burns used to wipe away the remaining tears that had been building. "I know it's difficult, Father, but can you think of *anyone*, no matter how unlikely, that would have wished him harm?"

Father Burns sat up straighter. "Detective, I've told you. There's no one I know of. He was a good man all the way around. He had the longest confessional line every week because people felt comfortable speaking to him even when it involved confessing their sins."

"All right, Father," I said. "We're going to wrap up here, and then we need to canvass the area to try to find a witness who may have seen anything. If you are in a praying mood, pray that we find someone willing to talk."

"Unless whoever did this looked out of place in an obvious manner, I don't know what good talking to witnesses will be. Confession was open today, so a lot of people would have come in and out of the church."

"Are the lines usually long? Do a lot of people come?" I asked.

He nodded. "If it is just Father McLaughlin, he typically gets seventy or eighty people. If another priest hears confession at the same time, Father McLaughlin's lines drop to about fifty or sixty. Many of the parishioners preferred to see him."

I thought while Father Burns talked. "Would it be safe to say that whoever did this came at the end of the day?"

Father Burns nodded. "Not just safe to say, Detective, but I think it would have had to be that way or it would have been reported by one of the penitents."

Ribs turned to me and gestured to the confessional, or to the floor outside it. "I have to agree with Father Burns. No one is going to ignore a pool of blood on the floor. It doesn't matter if they cooperate with police or not, if they're the type to go to confession, they'd report something wrong with one of the priests."

"I agree with you on that, Ribs. Let's go outside and see if we can find somebody that knows something or is willing to say something."

We canvassed the neighborhood for hours but struck out at every turn. The people we spoke with who had been to confession were horrified to learn what happened, but none of them had seen anything out of place. One young man said he had been to see Father McLaughlin near the end of the day, but he hadn't seen anything wrong, and from what he remembered, he recognized most of the people in line.

Near seven o'clock, Ribs and I called it a day and headed out. On the way home, we talked about what it could be. "It has to be connected to the drugs," Ribs said. "I can't see any other reason."

I switched lanes and slowed down a little. "I'll buy the drug connection with the first one—Pablo—because it was obvious. He was found with drugs and a lot of cash on him. What I don't get is how it spilled over to Langer and McLaughlin."

"Langer was a witness," Ribs said. "He told us that much, remember?"

"I know he told us, but I don't see him blabbing it around the neighborhood, so how did the *killer* know he was a witness? Who told him?"

Ribs nodded repeatedly. "Cuz, I think you may have hit on

something. We know it wasn't Father Burns. Hell, we had a difficult time getting anything out of him. And I don't see Langer or his wife telling anyone about it. If that's the case, that only leaves—"

"A cop," I said. "If Burns turned in the data like he said he did, and if we didn't get it—like we should have—then where did it go?"

"I can't believe that would happen," Ribs said.

"We've seen worse. Need I remind you of the problem a few years ago involving another drug cartel. We had two bad cops. Hell, it got your partner killed. Fortunately, at the time, I wasn't your partner."

Ribs nodded yet again. "You're right, cuz. As much as I don't like admitting it, the logic *is* pointing in that direction."

"But even if we go that far, that still leaves a missing piece to the puzzle. What did McLaughlin have to do with it? If it had been Burns, I'd say the pieces fit because that's who Langer talked to. But McLaughlin?"

"I hate these difficult cases," Ribs said. "I'll have to go home and mull this over."

"You mean, you and a bottle of wine?"

"Exactly. You know what they say, *'in vino veritas.'* For those of us who aren't educated, that means, 'in wine lies truth.'"

I laughed. "And those of us who *are* educated know that saying has nothing to do with what you're talking about. So stop trying to make excuses for drinking wine."

"Looks like I'm going to have to solve another case by myself," Ribs said. "Just drop me off at the house and rest well knowing that your partner is home working his ass off."

Chapter Eleven

WHERE'S THE CONNECTION?

Harris looked as if he were busy, sitting at his desk rifling through files. I walked in and sat across from him. "Harris, you worked the Galleria area a long time, didn't you?"

He looked up. "Hell, yeah. Probably ten years. Maybe more."

"Did you ever get any bad vibes about Arlen Langer or any of the priests at St. Michael's?"

Harris laughed. "Gino, you're going to have to dig a lot deeper than that. I was pretty tight with most of the residents around there, and nobody had a bad word to say about anyone at St. Michael's. And as far as Langer goes, not only was he viewed the same way, that idolatry extended to I-10 and even inside the Loop. The guy was forever spreading money around and doing good deeds. And he was one hell of a fundraiser for the church. He and Father Burns raised more money for the church in ten years than half a dozen priests did in the thirty years before that."

"I've got to find something," I said.

Harris moved his chair closer to the end of the table. "What? No leads?"

"Not a damn one, and not for lack of trying. Now we've got Langer dead and one of the priests from St. Michael's too."

"No shit," Harris said. "Who? I didn't hear that."

"McLaughlin. Got two in the head while he heard confessions. What a damn miserable way to go too. Spend hours listening to all the shit people did, then someone sends you off with two bullets."

"That's a shitty way of looking at it, Gino, but you're right. Pretty damn miserable." Harris stood and picked up his files. "Gino, I gotta go, but I'll put out some feelers. We still don't have anything on the drug dealer in the pickup we found, but if I hear anything, I'll call."

"Okay, Harris. Thanks."

Ribs walked in a moment later carrying two cups of coffee. "Damn, Ribs, forget all I said about you, you're an okay guy."

"But will you still think so when I tell you that *both* of these coffees are for me?"

"You son of a bitch," I said. "I should have known. You're trying to wash all that wine from your system, aren't you?"

"Reserve your judgment until *after* you hear what I have to say."

I closed my eyes, though I should have plugged my ears. "Shoot, Ribs. I'm kind of listening."

"What do you say to the possibility that Langer was into drug dealing or distribution? That would explain his connection to Pablo."

"Instead of just laughing, or even worse, crying, I'm going to attempt to reason with you like any other rational person."

"I would hope so," Ribs said.

"First, you were there when we interviewed Langer's wife. Did you get any vibes that didn't seem right? If I recall, I even won money from you regarding that."

"No, I didn't get any vibes, but that doesn't mean a damn thing. And look at some of the facts."

"I'm listening."

"She said her family was in law enforcement in Dallas and San Antonio. Hell, San Antonio has more Mexicans than Mexico City."

"Ribs."

"All right. Maybe not more than Mexico City, but it has a hell of a lot. And no matter how you slice it, that means someone there has connections to the drug trade in Mexico."

"What the hell does any of that have to do with Langer?"

"His wife," Ribs said. "She's connected to law enforcement, and they definitely know the drug people in the city. Hell, half the force is probably on the payroll of some cartel leader."

I stood. "Partner, don't ever call me cynical again. Now, I'm going to get my own coffee—since my partner didn't bring me any—and then we'll *sanely* work on this case to see if we can come up with something. Besides, there isn't now, nor was there ever, a connection between Langer and Pablo. Where the hell did you come up with that anyway?" I tossed a pencil at Ribs as I left to get coffee. "Stupid shit," I said.

☙

I returned with a coffee for myself and sat back down. "Ready?" I asked.

Ribs laid a few papers on the desk and spread them out.

"Just for grins, I'll go along with you for a minute. If we assume Langer was clean, that points to him being killed because he was a witness. But McLaughlin wasn't a witness, which throws a wrench into the mix. We then have to ask why McLaughlin was killed."

"Then what's your thought process regarding that? Was McLaughlin involved with the drugs? Was he an innocent bystander who happened to be hearing confession when someone walked in and shot him?"

Ribs shrugged. "I haven't figured that out yet. I don't think he was involved with drugs, but if he wasn't a witness, I don't see why he'd have been killed. He sure as hell wasn't an innocent bystander."

"The bottom line is, you don't know," I said.

"The bottom line is, I can at least see why Langer was killed—assuming he's not involved—because he was a witness. However, I can't find a reason for killing the priest unless he was involved because he *wasn't* a witness."

"Unless it was a mistake," I said.

Ribs shook his head. "I don't see whoever did this committing that kind of mistake. People don't kill people by mistake. They're more careful than that."

"Are you saying murderers don't make mistakes, Ribs?"

"No, but I have more faith in murderers who do direct hits. Guys who do drive-by shootings make mistakes. People who order or do select hits on people usually don't. I think whoever killed Langer did it for a specific reason, and it had nothing to do with him witnessing a crime."

"Where does that leave the priest? And why did they kill McLaughlin and not Burns?"

"I haven't put that together yet, cuz. Give me some time and a few more bottles of wine, and I will."

I laughed. "Time's something we don't have. You heard Coop. She's gonna be all over our asses on both these cases."

"I know. I know."

"You realize what you're saying, Ribs? You're saying Langer was involved with drugs, and if Langer was involved, the priest was too."

Ribs cleaned off the table and wiped it down. "I guess we need to look at both cases some more. No matter which way it leads, Coop will keep us honest about it, so we better get moving."

"We can agree on that, Ribs. And I'm betting we'll discover Langer was no more than a witness; in fact, I'd be less surprised to find out Burns was involved. I think Langer and his wife were both clean."

"Have faith, cuz. Things aren't always as they seem, and they're certainly not as dark as what you imagine when it comes to the church."

"There's not much left for us to do, Ribs—aside from the normal investigative procedure, and that means starting with Langer's books. Mrs. Langer offered us access, so let's take advantage of it."

"I'll call her and get it set up," Ribs said. "I'll get our best financial experts on it."

"The other thing we need to do is follow up on why the witness information never got passed on from the tip-line people."

"There is that," Ribs said. "I say we put Fat Charlie on it. Julie's busy as hell, but Charlie always has time."

"Let's stop by and tell him the good news," I said. "The sooner we find something out, the better off we'll be."

"You know Charlie's not as good as Julie," Ribs said.

"I know, but he's a hell of a lot better than us, so I'll take what he finds."

~

We stopped by Charlie's desk and provided the details. "What we need," Ribs said, "is a thorough, and I mean thorough, look at all the tips that came in."

"What?" Charlie asked. "All of them?"

"That's right, Charlie. All of them. We're looking for any tip that came in mentioning a gray car, especially if the tip included a license plate number."

"And when you find it," I said, "separate it and make note of the date, who called it in if that's listed, and who took the information."

"Get the time it was called in as well," Ribs said. "And the part about who took the information is critical, so don't forget that."

"Well, shoot. Y'all don't want much, do you? There must have been a few hundred tips called in."

"More like a few thousand," Ribs said. "But you're up to it, Charlie. I know I can count on you. Tip told me how sharp you were."

"Tip? Tip said that?"

"Sure did," I said. "Ribs and I worked that last case with him and Connie, and he told us if we ever needed something done, to tag you first."

Charlie smiled ear-to-ear. "Well, I'll be," he said, then walked over to where the files were. "I'll get this done for you right away, Gino."

Chapter Twelve

IT WAS A RENTAL

R ibs answered the phone after looking at the caller ID. It was Father Burns. "Father, good to hear from you. How are you?"

"No better than expected, Detective, but I did have some information for you."

"I'm listening, Father. Any information you have is appreciated."

"I thought a long time about the license plate number I'd given you, and I wanted to make sure it was the right one, so I had the phone carrier check my texts. The number I gave was off. The correct one is PRK 7425. That's the number of the car driven by the people who killed that man. I'd bet they're the same ones who killed Arlen as well, and possibly even Father Tom. But the rest of the information should be correct. It was a gray car, though it may have been a four-door."

"Father, this will be a big help. We're greatly appreciative. Thanks."

Ribs hung up from the priest and rushed over. He couldn't wait to tell me what the good Father had said.

"I'm glad he told us, Ribs, but I'm now even more suspicious. Why did it take him this long to figure that out? And I'm pissed off too. Why didn't we think to check with the phone company before this?"

"Pissed off or not, we've now got a lead. Let's get this to Julie so she can run this plate and see who it belongs to. We may finally be on track."

"I'm not excited yet," I said. "We'll see."

Ribs called the plate number into Julie. "I need this as soon as you can get it. Gino and I are on our way there, but we need to know where to go."

"Detective Delgado, if I didn't know you better, I'd be worried about your mental health. How can you be on your way somewhere when you don't know where to go?"

"Don't ask me," Ribs said. "I learned that from Tip."

Julie laughed. "That explains everything, Detective. No need to say more. I'll call back shortly with what you need."

Ribs turned to me and smiled. "That was Sixties Julie. She's gonna run the plate and get back to us. How about stopping for either coffee or a beer?"

I spun my head around and looked at Ribs as if he were nuts. "A beer? Do you know what time it is? You can't drink a beer this time of day."

"Then just get coffee, cuz. I didn't want a beer anyway. It was just a way to get you to stop for coffee."

"It's getting close to me switching partners, Ribs, and I don't care about your blackmail tape."

Julie called moments later as we were leaving the station. "Got a hit. Of course, that's easy when you have a real plate number."

"Screw you," Ribs hollered. "Just tell us where to go."

"I could tell you where to go, Ribs, but the plates lead to a rental service at the airport. Enterprise Rental at the Bush Intercontinental."

"Okay, Julie. Thanks. We're on our way."

Ribs got his coffee, then we drove to the rental place and questioned the clerk at Enterprise, but he swore he had no cars with that plate number. In fact, he said he's never had a car with that plate number.

"How about looking up all Impalas from 2017 on and see if you have any plates that are close. Maybe they were off by a few numbers."

We waited for almost half an hour while the guy ran numbers. Finally, he returned with a printout of cars and plate numbers. "These are all the Impalas we've got from 2016 on, and none of them have plates that come close to the number you gave me."

I called Julie and told her what we'd found out from the rental site. "Hang on," she said. "Let me check again."

I put the phone on speaker and waited. After five minutes, Julie came back on the line. "Gino, I don't know how this happened, but the plate came from the Enterprise site on I–45 North, up by The Woodlands. I'm sorry. I—"

"Don't worry about it, Julie; we're on our way."

As we drove toward The Woodlands, Ribs talked. "Cuz, something about this doesn't seem right. If this was a low-level drug dealer, he wouldn't have rented a car beforehand to kill Pablo and dump the body. And he sure as hell wouldn't have kept the car to kill Langer. It doesn't add up."

"Not only do I agree with that logic, Ribs, but it makes me wonder how he knew he'd need to kill Langer. How did he know he'd have a witness that was a problem?"

"I hate to say this, especially to you," Ribs said, "but the one connection to all the dead men is Father Burns. He supposedly saw the murder of Pablo, or at least part of it; he knew Langer well and talked to him about being a witness. And he had known McLaughlin for years."

I thought about what Ribs said. "You're right about all of that, Ribs. I don't see the motive yet, but I definitely see the connection."

"I'm with you, cuz. I haven't ruled out the possibility of a corrupt cop. Not yet. That may depend on what Charlie turns up. But I'm not discounting Burns either."

"I'm not discounting anyone yet," I said. "Not Mrs. Langer, not his poker buddies, and not even the priest. I don't see how or why any of them would be involved, but I'm not discounting any of them. All I know is, we need to dig deeper until we find something solid."

"Then we'll agree on that, cuz. In the meantime, stop for a refreshment before we get to Enterprise Rental. I think there's a Starbucks close to there."

I shook my head and cursed. "Connie is looking better all the time."

"You mean her ass, cuz? Because if that's what you mean, I'll tell Fabrizio. I know Marissa's a badass, but if it came down to it, I'd go a round or two against her before I would Fabrizio."

Instead of waiting in the drive-through, we went inside and sat. We both got a latte, then took a seat to chat. "Before we go barging into Enterprise, I'd like to have a plan, Ribs, and that includes questions we need to ask the guy who rented the car—assuming he's here, of course."

Ribs acted as if he were giving it thought, then said, "Obviously, we want to know if he remembers the guy. It's doubtful, but we can ask. And we need to get a printout of whatever the guy used for ID. It's more than likely fake, but you never can tell. I've seen worse."

I tapped Ribs on the arm as he wrote. "And don't forget to see if he has video by chance. Again, I doubt it, considering the location. It's not like it's a busy spot or anything."

Ribs lightened up. "If we're lucky, he'll have the car on the lot so we can impound it and process it for DNA."

"If you think we're going to be that lucky, you should go buy a lottery ticket, Ribs. There's not a snowball's chance in hell there will be DNA evidence in that car, and you know it."

Ribs shrugged. "Worth a try," he said.

"The bigger question is why rent a car to do it in the first place? It's not like drug dealers can't put their dirty paws on a junker somewhere. They could have spent less money buying a piece of shit from one of the neighborhoods, then ditching it, or burning it."

Ribs nodded. "I thought about that too, Gino. When something like this goes down, whatever car is used is typically found in a bayou or at the back of a parking lot next to an abandoned warehouse. But *not* in a rental car lot."

"And that's one more reason why I'm leaning toward someone like Langer—or his class—or the priest. They may not have the connections to put their hands on an old junker."

"God, but you're a cynical old shit," Ribs said. "Let's just get our asses to the rental-car facility. Maybe we'll get some real police work done."

I cleared the trash from the table, tossed it into the wastebasket, then headed toward the exit. "You realize most cases are solved by luck or accident," Ribs. "Real police work, as you like to call it, results in a lot of paperwork and not much else."

"Think what you will, cuz. I'll keep doing the work."

I sighed. "And I'll keep solving the cases."

Chapter Thirteen

WHO RENTED THE CAR?

I stopped for coffee as Ribs requested—as Ribs always requested—and then we drove toward the rental-car facility on the freeway.

Ribs turned to me and said, "Julie said the car is registered to Enterprise Leasing on I-45 near The Woodlands. Are we headed in that direction? You know where it is?"

"We're almost there, Ribs. I live nearby, remember?"

"If you don't know, I know exactly where it is. I looked it up on my phone. You exit Woodlands Parkway, then head south on the feeder."

I shook my head. "Just let me know where to go when we get close."

It took about five minutes to get there, at which point, I took the exit to I-45 and headed south. As I drove down the feeder, I pointed to the side of the road and said, "Right there, Ribs. See that small lot."

"Damn, you really do know where you're going," Ribs said, as I pulled into a space near the front door.

I parked the car, then got out. "Keep your fingers crossed, Ribs. This place doesn't look like it has any cameras."

I walked in alongside Ribs, and we approached the man behind the desk. I showed my badge and introduced myself. "I'm Detective Cataldi, and this is Detective Delgado. We're here regarding a homicide, and we think the killer may have rented one of your cars."

"I'll help any way I can," the clerk said. "Which car? You got a plate?"

Ribs handed him the plate number, and the clerk typed it into the computer. "Got it," he said. "Rented by a Mr. Gordon—Jesse Gordon."

"Can you—"

"I'm printing out his information now," the man said. "But I *do* remember him. Mostly because he gave me a hard time."

"In what way?" I asked.

"He had an attitude. Most people will ask you something like 'Hey, you got a light-gray car? Or, I'd like a beige sedan.' Something like that. Not this one. He started right off demanding what he wanted. He looked me square in the eyes and said, 'I want a gray sedan, late model, low mileage, and with a plate number that's not easy to remember.'" The clerk looked at both of us. "I think that's what did it for me. I never had anybody ask me for a plate number that wasn't easy to remember. I almost didn't rent it to him after that, but I didn't have a valid reason to refuse either."

The printer stopped while the clerk talked, and when he finished, Ribs gestured back to it. "Is that done? Is that the printout?"

The clerk looked over his shoulder and nodded. "Yeah, that's it," he said, then he walked back and got the papers.

Afterward, he handed the printout to Ribs. "Here you are: name, address, and license number."

I looked around, then asked, "I don't suppose you have a video of the transaction?"

The man shook his head. "I wish we did, but we don't. I can give you a description, but it won't differ much from the ID on the license. A black-and-white copy is on the printout, but I'm sure you can get a better one from the DMV. At least it will be a color one."

"Thanks," Ribs said. "We're also going to need the car to run some tests."

"I'm afraid I can't do that," the man said. "It's against policy."

I stepped in front of Ribs and took the lead. "I understand, but I'm afraid you have no choice. That vehicle may have been used in a homicide. We strongly suspect it was, and if so, our techs need to process it for DNA and other evidence."

After a pause, the man nodded, reached behind him, and pulled a set of keys from the rack. "Here you go, detectives. It's in the second row from the rear, fifth car from the left."

I nodded. "Okay, thanks. We'll get back to you if we need anything else. And please keep the keys. We'll have the techs pick up the car shortly. Just make sure no one touches it before they get here."

The clerk put the keys in his pocket, and said, "One thing, Detective. ."

"You remember that much detail?" Ribs asked.

"Not usually, but when something doesn't add up, it sticks with you. This one didn't add up; besides, there was something strange about the way the guy acted. I can't place it, but it was different. Suspicious like."

Ribs waved his hand at him. "Thanks, that'll help."

I called the techs and gave them the details. "The man working behind the counter has the keys, and he's expecting you."

On the drive back, Ribs called Julie. "Jules, I need a rundown on a Mr. Jesse Gordon. I'll text you the details when I hang up, but I need the newest picture, address, and all financials. I also want work history. In fact, just give me everything you can find."

Half an hour later, Julie called back. "Ribs, it's Julie."

"That was quick," Ribs said. "Let's hear it."

"You're not going to like what I have to say," Julie said.

"Shoot," Ribs said.

"I was able to get the new color photo, but that's all I was able to get."

"What do you mean?"

"I mean, nothing else is there. The address is fake. There's no credit history. He shows no employment, no tax returns, nothing."

Ribs looked over. "It's like we figured, cuz? We've got a car rented by a guy with a fake ID. One who has no address and no work history. But why? What's it about? Why did Langer text this to Father Burns? And what's so important about it that it got two people killed?"

Ribs redialed. "Jules, get us any crimes in the vicinity of the Sage crime scene that involved a gray or beige sedan."

"You got a model or year?"

"I want *all* gray or beige sedans, but you can prioritize by Chevy if you want."

"See me when you get in. This might take a while."

Ribs disconnected the call, then turned to me. "Julie said it might take a while. You want to grab a bite? I'm starved."

I got in the right lane and exited the freeway. "I know this deli on Spring Cypress that has the best damn cheesesteaks I've had since leaving Philly."

"No shit? What's the name?"

"Vito's. And they've got fantastic subs and great pizza too."

"Guess I'm in, cuz. How far away are we?"

"About fifteen minutes, and then you'll be in heaven."

"Damn, you're getting me hungry. What do you recommend?"

"Only one way to go. Large cheesesteak to eat there, and a large Italian sub to go. Get ketchup, mushrooms, and fried onions on the steak, and get sweet and hot peppers on the sub, along with everything else."

Ribs laughed. "How about you order for me? I'll trust you."

We ate an early lunch, then took the subs with us and headed back to the station. Julie met us at the top of the steps. "About time you got here. I've had your information forever."

"Then I'm sure you're dying to spew out all those facts. Come to my lair and tell me about it."

Julie laughed. "Your lair? What the hell, Ribs? Are you a pervert now?"

I laughed. "He's been a pervert for a long time, Julie. He's just hidden it well, but now the secret's out."

Julie followed us to our office, then proceeded to tell us what she'd found. "I checked all crimes that had been reported within a mile of the Sage address. I was going to cross-check with the car details, but I didn't need to."

"Why's that?" I asked.

"Hours before Langer was hit, a man was murdered, and it wasn't more than a block away."

"What? I didn't hear about that murder."

"I can't help it if you didn't hear about it, but it's in the system. Name's Tico Farandaz. He's got no record, but his sheet says he is suspected of being involved with drug dealing."

"Who's handling the case?" I asked.

"Schmidt and Richardson," Julie said.

Ribs was on the phone before Julie finished. "Schmidt, this is Delgado. We ran into a potential crossover with your murder, and I thought we should compare notes."

"You mean Farandaz?"

"Yeah, it's Farandaz. How many murders have you got, Schmidt?"

"All right, smart ass. Meet me in the coffee room in ten. I'll bring the file."

We met Schmidt in the coffee room, and we brought the file on Langer. "Where's Richardson?" I asked.

"He's out today," Schmidt said. "But I've got the file, and I'm familiar with the details."

Ribs sat at the table and pushed a chair toward Schmidt. "Have a seat and share what you've got," Ribs said.

Schmidt placed his cup of coffee on the table, then sat and opened the file. "Tico Farandaz has nothing on his sheet, but everybody we talked to said he was connected with drugs, and most of them mentioned the Mexicans, a guy named Raul from Monterrey, in particular."

"You have anything yet on what happened to him? Or why?" I asked.

"What we've got so far is one witness who saw a car pull up next to him, rolled down the window, and took two shots at Tico. Afterward, the car raced away. The other witness mirrored the initial report, except they said the guy took three shots. Tico only had two shots in him, so if three were fired, one missed, and we haven't found it yet."

"How about the car?" Ribs asked.

"Both witnesses claim the car was a gray sedan. Neither one of them knew the model or year, and they didn't get a plate."

"What have you heard about why he might have been killed?"

Schmidt shook his head. "Not a damn thing. He was generally liked in the neighborhood despite being a drug dealer. We haven't heard of any rival gangs, and nobody knew of any of his men who were trying to take over." Schmidt took a sip of his coffee. "How about your case? What have you got?"

Ribs spread a few papers on the table. "Arlen Langer. Doesn't have a sheet. Nothing on any suspicious list. No reason to suspect him of anything."

"But . . . ?" Schmidt asked.

"But he was run down by a late-model gray sedan the same day that your guy was murdered, and it was less than a block away."

"Same time?" Schmidt asked.

"No, that's the strange thing," Ribs said. "If it were the same time, I might say Langer witnessed the murder, and your guy killed him to be safe. But Langer was killed hours later—a lot of hours later."

"And there's no other reason you can think of why he was killed?" Schmidt asked.

"None."

"Are you sure it was the same car? I know it would be a God-awful coincidence, but it *could* happen."

Ribs leaned on the table. "We live in the real world, Schmidt. We *try* to live a world where hit-and-runs and murders by the same kind and color car don't happen on the same day as a murder only a block away. Also, we got a plate, but when we looked into it, we found out it was a rental car, and whoever checked it out used a fake license and fake address."

Schmidt nodded. "Sounds like whoever rented the car had less-than-good intentions."

"Like murder," I said.

"I'm thinking the same thing," Schmidt said. "And in light of where and when your guy was killed and considering he had no record or reason to be killed, I'd say he may have been run down to shut him up."

"If your vic was a respected and well-liked member of the community, and if nothing has happened to make you change your mind on that, then I think we've got a conundrum."

"A conundrum? That's a damn big word for an asshole like you," I said.

Schmidt stood to get more coffee. "By the way, how did you get a plate?"

Ribs looked at me, eyebrows raised. When I nodded, Ribs continued. "Our dead guy, Langer, texted the plate to his priest, who happened to be his friend."

"And the priest told you?" Schmidt asked.

"Not quite," I said. "The priest told us about it, but then another priest was killed."

"This guy killed a priest?" Schmidt asked. "What the hell is going on? That's almost as bad as killing a cop."

"I don't know," Ribs said, "but I suggest we keep each

other up-to-date on our investigations; in fact, it might be good to meet once a week or sooner to go over things."

"Agreed," Schmidt said. "I'll inform Richardson when he gets back too."

"Great," Ribs said. "We'll make sure to look into any possible drug angle on our case. I doubt if we'll find anything, but we'll look."

After Schmidt left, I tapped Ribs on the shoulder. "I know it's standard procedure, but to be safe, make sure that forensics checks the paint off that rental car against the hit-and-runs, and also any dents in the grill or fender. We don't want anything to slip by."

"Already put it in as a request, partner. We should hear soon."

"And one more thing, Ribs. Let's make sure Julie and everybody else knows to keep us in the loop about any other murders. I don't like finding out about them by accident or hearing about them on the six o'clock news."

"Got it," Ribs said.

Chapter Fourteen

A NEW SUSPECT IS CLEARED

We were running out of suspects, and truth be told, we were getting desperate. Langer was hard to figure, no matter how hard we tried, and McLaughlin couldn't be framed. He hadn't been dirty since he was a kid and neglected to take a bath.

"We should talk to Chicky," Ribs said. "If anybody's going to know what's going on, it's him."

"I know that, Ribs, and I've stopped by to see him, but he hasn't been around."

"Then we park our asses down at his spots and wait. It's not like the guy's on a world cruise or anything."

I laughed at that. "You're right, Ribs. Let's do it."

We hit several of Chicky's main hangouts but struck out. "I say we park at his main place, the one down on Westheimer," Ribs said. "I can't see him staying away for too long."

"I'll do it, but you're buying the coffee," I said. "And be warned, it might be a lot of it."

~

We weren't sitting in the parking lot more than an hour when the familiar call rang out. "Gi-nŌ," Chicky hollered from the other side.

"Chicky, my man. How's it going? Haven't seen you in a long time."

"Only one reason for that—you haven't been here in a long time."

"You're right about that, Chicky. I've been busy."

"Well, enough of that bullshit. Tell me what you need, 'cause I got it, and you know I got it."

We told Chicky about the murders, and about our confusion on why they were happening, and who might be doing them. After we finished, we headed out and asked him to call, promising a few bills for good information.

"Need to be good bills," Chicky said. "I don't want to see you trying to pass off no Jacksons. I'm talkin' Grants or Franklins."

"You get me what I need, Chicky, and I'll get you what you want," I said. "For the right information, I can easily see a Grant *and* a Franklin."

~

It didn't take long for Chicky to get back to us, and when he did, he had a lot to say.

"Gino, I rolled around the city and kept my ears open, and all that listening made one thing obvious—Houston's got a drug problem, and it's not just usage. Two factions are fighting it out.

"I'm still listening," I said.

"Raul has been dealing the cards here for a long time, but the word is that Ortega is making a move. Nobody will swear to it, but a lot of people are guessing these killings are Ortega's doing."

"Where's Ortega from?"

"Ortega slithers into Texas through El Paso, and Raul comes up from Monterrey. Both of them are deadly, amigo. I mean 'don't give a shit' deadly. They'll kill cops as soon as they will a junkie, so you and Ribs need to watch your asses."

"I hear you, Chicky. Before I go, I've got one more question. If Raul had such a hold on Houston, what changed to make Ortega think he could move in?"

I heard Chicky light a smoke and shuffle from one foot to the other. "From what I hear, Ortega paid big to get a few of Raul's men to push *his* dope instead of Raul's. Pablo was one of them, and he got caught. Once he was caught, it was the end of the story for Pablo."

"Raul did that?"

"Nah, not Raul. I doubt he's even seen Texas in five years. Look for his man, Rodrigo. He's the muscle, and the word is, he's meaner than Raul."

"And the others? The priest and the rich guy?"

Chicky sighed. "Gino, man, you know I don't hear about shit like that. Rich people and padres are out of my league. All I get is street talk. But don't be lettin' that affect the image on them bills."

I smiled. "Chicky, meet me at your place in fifteen, and I'll have a Grant for you. Get me something I can act on, and I'll double that, or more."

I met Chicky in fifteen minutes, his smile visible from across the parking lot. I handed him the money, and he stuffed it into a hidden pocket inside his pants. "Shit, Gino, you know I'll be out talkin' it up now. Won't be long before I find out what's goin' on."

"I'll be waiting," I said. "Gotta go now, Chicky. See ya later."

~

Ribs had been napping in the car while I met Chicky, but when I got back in and drove away from the scene, Ribs turned to me and said, "What Chicky had to say was interesting, but it does nothing to explain why Langer or McLaughlin were killed."

Surprised, I turned to look at him. "You were listening, huh?"

"Of course, I listened. I can't leave you to interpret Chicky's gibberish."

"You're right, Ribs. He sometimes speaks gibberish, and you're also right that what he said doesn't explain about either of them. I guess we're going to have to figure that out on our own."

"Don't worry, cuz, I'll figure it out, and I think you'll be surprised once I do."

I made a turn toward the station, then continued in that direction.

"Where are you going?" Ribs asked.

"I thought we should chat up Harris again with this new information. I'd like to hear what he has to say about it."

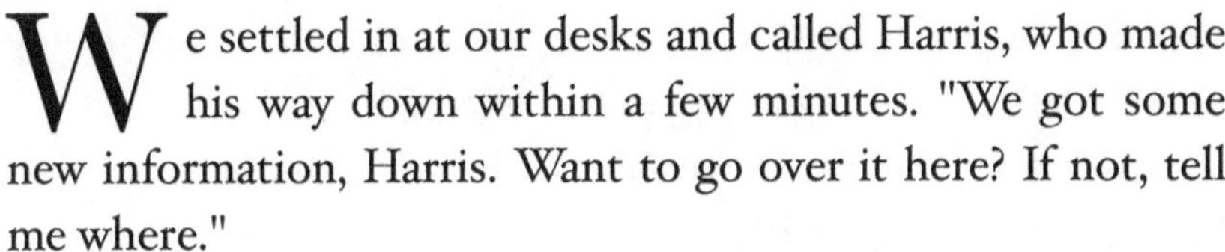

We settled in at our desks and called Harris, who made his way down within a few minutes. "We got some new information, Harris. Want to go over it here? If not, tell me where."

"I'll be back in ten minutes. I need to hit the coffee room and the bathroom, but not in that order."

Harris returned by himself, and he was carrying a handful of files. "Okay, Cataldi, let's see what you have?"

"Langkon still AWOL?" Ribs asked.

"He's gone for another week. Had a funeral to attend. A brother, I think."

We told Harris what we'd learned from Chicky, and he sat back in the chair as if giving it thought. "I haven't heard of Ortega moving into Houston, but it doesn't surprise me that he's trying."

"You've run into Ortega before?" Ribs asked.

Harris nodded. "He's the major player in all of West Texas, and recently he moved further into San Antonio. My contact tells me he owns San Antonio now, so it's not surprising to me if he's making a move into Houston. I haven't heard, but I'd bet Dallas and Austin are targets before Houston. It would make sense distribution-wise to control that I-35 corridor."

"Not to mention that's a hell of a lot of people," Ribs said.

"And not just a hell of a lot, but three of the top ten or eleven cities within a two-hundred-mile stretch. That makes it easier to control."

"If you throw Houston in the mix, it adds a lot of people, but it's still not far away," I said.

"Knowing Raul, though, Houston won't be a walk in the

park. If this really is Ortega, there will be a lot more bodies showing up, and not just here."

Ribs leaned closer to Harris. "Tell me what you know about Dallas. Is Ortega a big player there?"

"Not as big as San Antonio, but he's been in San Antonio for a longer time, so it's to be expected. Give him a year or two, though, he'll be established as if he's been there for decades. I've seen Ortega work; he's smooth. If I were a betting man, my money would be on him."

"How does he normally operate?" Ribs asked. "In other words, does he go all out war, or does he try to work his way from the inside?"

Harris smiled. "Sounds like you're working from his playbook. Ortega isn't like his rivals. He works his way up from the inside by buying off the dealers. He treats them better, and more importantly, gives them more money. That's what earns him loyalty. A dealer will do a lot out of fear, but money commands more respect."

Harris sipped from his coffee cup. "Oh, and he is fond of offering protection too. And he's good at it. Word in El Paso was that there isn't a drug raid that Ortega doesn't know about. Some people have said he even orders a few small raids on himself to keep up appearances."

"So Chicky might be right," I said. "It sounds as if Ortega is buying his way into Houston. Or trying to."

"If he's trying to, he'll do it," Harris said. "I've seen him take El Paso, Lubbock, Amarillo, San Antonio, and half of Dallas. If he's working on Houston now, it's only a matter of time. And like I said, Austin's got to be in his playbook. I'm not up to speed with what's happening there, but it's only logical."

"Good deal, Harris. You've once again been a big help. We'll get back to you if we hear anything new," Ribs said.

"And I'll do the same," Harris said, then he picked up his files and left.

Ribs stared as Harris walked down the hall, and once he was out of earshot, he said, "Are you ready to pay yet, cuz?"

I looked at him with a question painted on my face. "Pay for what?"

"You heard what he said—San Antonio. Ortega's the man who matters in San Antonio, not to mention he's almost there in Dallas."

"What the hell does that have to do with anything?"

"Remember Langer's wife? The one who had family in law enforcement in Dallas and San Antonio. The one with the cute little ass, and the same one I said was involved in these murders somehow."

I almost laughed, but I was too stunned. "Ribs, for Christ's sake, having a family in law enforcement in a city where there are drugs doesn't mean you're guilty of anything. For Christ's sake, every city of any size has drug problems."

"When your husband is killed suspiciously, it means something. As far as I'm concerned, it almost cements it."

I whistled. "All I can say is I'm sure glad you're not a judge."

"If I were a judge, we'd have a lot fewer people on the street," he said.

"And a lot more innocent people in jail," I said. "I'll stick with what we've got."

"You still don't think Mrs. Langer has anything to do with this?"

I shook my head. "I didn't think it before, and I still don't.

And her family being in law enforcement doesn't change my mind one bit."

"Damn, but you're gullible," he said. "It's no wonder Marissa's got her claws into you."

"Her claws? What the hell is that supposed to mean? Should I tell her your feelings?"

"Like hell. If you do, I'll tell Rosalee you called her fat."

"What? I *never* said she was fat."

"You think she'll believe that if I tell her otherwise?" Ribs asked.

Chapter Fifteen

RIBS AND GINO THINK ABOUT SAN ANTONIO

As Ribs and I drove home, he talked incessantly, as usual, but this time it was about work. "How about if she *is* involved?" he asked.

"We've been through this for the last half hour, Ribs. I can't see Mrs. Langer involved with drugs, let alone with the death of her husband. First off, he was too damn rich. I know she was too, but when you're as rich as they were, what's the sense in dealing drugs? At some point, money doesn't matter."

"Rich or not, drugs bring in a *lot* of money," Ribs said.

"I know drugs are more than lucrative, but Langer had a ton of money, and he had no kids or other heirs to his fortune. That means all Mrs. Langer had to do was wait him out, not to mention she could enjoy the good life while she did; besides, like we talked about, she had her own money. She didn't need to rely on him."

"I hear you, cuz, but sometimes it's about more than the money. If it's in the blood, it's hard to get rid of."

I shook my head. "Ribs, some things are in the blood.

Liking eating pasta and liking strong coffee, the ability to eat hot peppers, a craving for fine cheese, and a good bottle of wine, but the desire to deal drugs is not one of them. Trust me."

"I don't know, cuz. I've seen it."

"You've seen it with poor people. Mrs. Langer doesn't qualify as *poor people*. She doesn't qualify now. And she hasn't for a long time."

"I'll cede to your wisdom, partner. For now, I will. But heed my warnings. She's involved with this somehow, both her and her family."

"Prove it to me, and we'll head out to San Antonio. I'll even drive," I said.

"Shit, you're making it too easy for me, bro. Call Harris and Langkon, and I guarantee we'll get the information we need. If not them, call Chicky back. One of them will deliver the dope."

"Deal," I said. "But it's got to be more than what we have now because we don't have enough for probable cause right now."

We called Harris first, and fortunately, Langkon was in as well; he'd come back early from the funeral. That was good because Langkon spent ten years in San Antonio, so he knew the players even better than Harris did; in fact, that's where the funeral was—San Antonio.

We sat down in the coffee room to trade notes and info. Ribs provided the details. "His name was Langer, which, of course, is her married name, but from what our contacts tell us, her maiden name was Boswell, so that's the name her father and brothers would be known under in San Antonio."

"Boswell, shit, I know them," Langkon said. "I worked the north side with Sean Boswell. He was a character."

"A character in what way?" I asked.

"A real cowboy," Langkon said. "I think he shot four people while I was there."

"Good shootings?" I asked. "Justified?"

"I don't know if they were truly justified," Langkon said, "but they were written up that way. No one was surprised about that though 'cause Sean's father was a captain with long-standing, and he pulled a lot of juice with the politicians."

"Any of the Boswells in Narcotics?" Ribs asked.

Langkon nodded. "The captain had a brother who was a lieutenant in Narcotics, and two of his sons worked for him. If I remember, they did a pretty good job. Cleaned out the Western faction of the cartel and prevented Raul from getting a foothold. The only one he didn't do too good with was Ortega's men, but they were a tough bunch."

"You talking about the group from Ciudad Juarez?" Ribs asked.

Langkon nodded. "They're the ones. Mean sons of bitches."

"Why is it he had such a difficult time with them?" I asked.

Langkon shook his head. "Can't say for sure, but from what I heard, they kept getting the best of them. Always one step ahead. And I'll tell you another thing, they didn't worry about who they shot. They'd kill a uniform as soon as anyone else."

"Ever hear talk of the Boswells being dirty? I mean, if they couldn't control the drugs, maybe it was because they didn't want to."

Langkon shook his head. "Never heard any talk, and I don't know if I'd buy it if I did. As far as I could tell, they did their honest best. Hell, one of the younger boys got shot while trying to take them down. He didn't die, but it did push him off the force with a disability."

"What did the Boswells do afterward?" I asked.

"Did what anyone would expect," Langkon said. "They doubled down on their efforts to get rid of the scum, but it didn't work. Don't get me wrong, it wasn't all in vain; they managed to put a stop to the massive drug trade for a while, but it was only a while, and it was a short while."

"How did Ortega bring the drugs in?" Ribs asked.

"This is hearsay, so take it with a grain of salt, but I heard they would schedule a day to move drugs into the city from Ciudad Juarez, but they didn't do it with a truck. They used several cars and sent them all out from El Paso at once, and then they'd have them enter the city at different spots so if one car was stopped, the others were likely to get through. The profits are so damn big with drugs, they could afford risks like that."

"And nobody picked up on that?" Ribs asked. "If you heard, others must have too."

Langkon nodded. "I'm sure others *did* hear, but even if they did, what could they do about it? You know how many cars come into San Antonio every day or night? And you know how many roads they could use to come in on?"

"I imagine it's a hell of a lot," Ribs said.

"Damn straight it's a hell of a lot, and there's no way to stop and search all of them. But that's the way those drug people work. They just wear you down, knowing you don't have the resources to stop them. That's one of the ways they get the drugs across the border too. They try everything. They smuggle it in in cars, trucks, animals, tunnels, planes, boats . . . You name it, they've tried it. I've got a brother-in-law with the DEA. He said it gets to the point where there isn't enough manpower to stop it all, so while some drugs get picked up, a lot more sneaks in."

"Let's get back to the Boswells," I said. "How much influence do they wield in San Antonio law enforcement and how much in politics, if any?"

Harris laughed. "I can answer that one, Gino. As far as San Antonio law enforcement goes, let's just say a lot. If a person wants to get promoted, they're gonna need the blessing of the Boswells. In politics, not so much, but I'm guessing that's still up for grabs."

Langkon stood and looked as if he was leaving. "Forget about influence in San Antonio law enforcement for a minute, and take a gander at where else they carry a big stick. They've got half the top police jobs sewed up in Dallas, Amarillo, and Lubbock as well. And from what I hear, they're moving up the ladder in El Paso."

Ribs looked at me, then back to Langkon. "And you don't think that's a bit strange? That they'd be in all those cities?"

"I didn't say it wasn't strange, Delgado. I just answered what you asked, and you never asked about them."

Langkon looked to Harris, and said, "If you're staying, let me know, because I've got to go. And before long, we both need to be joining the others on that canvass."

Harris gathered up a few folders, tossed his trash in the basket, and joined Langkon. "I may as well go now. I think Delgado sucked all the information out of me anyway."

Ribs laughed and slapped him on the shoulder as he passed. "Don't worry, Harris, I'll be pestering you again soon."

When they had left, Ribs looked my way. "Well, cuz? You ready to don your cowboy hat and boots?"

"I'm still not sure we'd do any good going out there. What are we going to turn up that some concentrated poking around won't?"

Ribs continued staring until I laughed. "All right, for Christ's sake. I'm guessing there's a damn restaurant you are dying to eat at or something."

"Come on, Gino. That's not the *only* reason. But now that you mention it, there is this place on the River Walk . . ."

"I knew it," I said. "I knew this had to be about more than work. You're as predictable as a two-dollar whore, you know that?"

"You're showing your age, cuz. Or your stupidity. Two-dollar whores haven't been around for a long time."

"Maybe I'm showing my purity," I said.

Ribs shook his head as he stood. "Nah, don't buy it. Age and stupidity are my guesses."

WHO WANTS TO VISIT THE ALAMO?

Houston, Texas

I picked Ribs up in the morning, and then we drove downtown to the office. We weren't even settled in for the day's work when he started.

"Gino, I think we hit on something with the San Antonio connection."

"Hit on what? We didn't discover a damn thing," I said. "And we went over this already. I thought we agreed we could do more good by simply digging in deeper here."

"I don't think so," Ribs said. "Weren't you listening to what Harris and Langkon had to say? They pointed fingers at the Boswells. They did as much as name them drug dealers."

I got up and walked toward the snack room, and unfortunately, Ribs followed. "Ribs, you heard a different conversation than I did. Harris and Langkon may have cast some disparaging remarks about a few of the Boswells—even them as a family if you want to stretch it—but it was far from naming them drug dealers or implicating they were connected in any way."

Ribs got a bag of chips from the vending machine and sat across the table. "I say we pay a visit to the Alamo and check things out while we're there."

"Ribs, I've been to the Alamo. I don't need to go there again, nor do I *want* to go there again; besides, it would cost us vacation days because sure as shit stinks, Coop will *not* approve a trip to San Antonio. Not based on the evidence we have—which is nothing."

"All right, I'll make a deal with you. If I convince Coop to approve a trip, will you go?"

"There's not a snowball's chance in hell of doing that, but sure, if you can do it, I'm game. But I still don't want to visit the Alamo. It's nothing but an old church with a wall around it and a big tree in the courtyard."

Ribs blessed himself quickly. "That's sacrilegious, Gino. Where is your pride?"

"I wasn't born here," I said.

"That's not how it works in Texas," Ribs said. "But that's fine. Stay put while I work my charms on the sweet captain. You'll have religion by the time we get there."

I laughed. "There are two things wrong with the first part of that statement, Ribs. You *have no* charms, and the captain hasn't been sweet since she was sixteen."

"We'll see," Ribs said, and took off down the hall.

Ribs slowed his pace as he got close to Coop's office. "Hey, Cindy, is Captain Cooper in?"

Cindy smiled. "Captain Cooper, huh? You must want something."

"Is she in?" Ribs asked.

Cindy leaned close to the intercom and spoke in a soft voice. "Captain, Delgado's here, and he'd like to see you."

"What's he want, Cindy? Do you know?"

"No, ma'am, I don't know what he wants, but he may as well be carrying flowers."

Cindy sat up straight and gestured to the office. "Go on in, Ribs. She's expecting you."

Ribs walked into Coop's office and took the seat closest to her desk. "Good morning, Coop. How are you?"

"No need for pleasantries, Delgado. Just tell me what you need."

Ribs placed his elbows on his knees and leaned forward. "I'll get right to it, Captain. Gino thinks we should go to San Antonio for further investigation on this case, and after listening to him ramble on, I agree with him."

"If Gino thinks so, why didn't he come here to present his case?"

Ribs shook his head. "I owed him a favor, so I said I'd do it for him."

Coop laughed. "In other words, you're lying out your ass, and he doesn't think you should go? Is that about it?"

Ribs sat up straight. "That's close, Coop, but you know what a damn hardhead he can be."

Coop leaned back in her chair. "Tell me what you've got, and why you think you need to go."

Ribs pulled out his notepad and flipped through a few pages. "First off, know this is not simply speculation. We've done our homework on this."

"In other words, you talked to Harris, or maybe Langkon, and something they said coincided with an idea that was stuck in your craw, so now you want to spend *my* money to take a vacation and scratch that itch. Is that it?"

"Coop, I don't know. You've tossed a lot of sayings into one little sentence. All I want is to solve this case."

"And what you *need* to do is show me how it is that going to San Antonio will help you do that?"

Ribs got newfound enthusiasm, and his voice reflected it. "Coop, remember we told you Langer's wife had a family in law enforcement in San Antonio and Dallas both. Well, it turns out, they have had a lot of run-ins with the Ortega cartel, although some people question if the run-ins were real or staged."

Ribs waited until he saw Coop was about to ask more questions. "The way I see it," Ribs said, "is if Gino and I go talk to them, we'll either get the runaround—which says one thing—or we'll get cooperation, which will help our cause. Either way, we get something that advances the case."

"And where did you think you'd stay if you did go? And how long would you be?"

Ribs got even more excited. "We could find someplace

cheap, I'm sure. And I'm betting we won't need more than a couple of days."

"In other words, just enough for you to get the meal you're craving, then get back home?"

Ribs shot up straight. "Captain? I'm appalled."

"No, you're not," Coop said, then she leaned over and spoke into the intercom. "Cindy, get Ribs and Gino set up on an expense report for San Antonio. Make it for the Marriott on the Riverwalk and make it for a maximum of a week. And put a damn limit on the meals too."

Ribs cocked his head and looked in awe. "Coop, the Riverwalk? And a week? What's gotten into you?"

"I'm guessing the way to play this might be to hint that you are two cops from Houston there to help ease Ortega's entry into Houston. If the cops are dirty, you might get a nibble. If not, you'll know too. But if you're to be believed, a cheap motel on I-10 won't convince anyone. And unless I miss my guess, two days won't cut it either. So take your time, enjoy yourself, and make some damn headway on this case. We need it solved."

Ribs almost jumped from the chair. Once standing, he snapped a salute and left the office.

"Mission accomplished," Cindy said as he walked out the door.

He smiled at her. "I can't believe it, but you're right, Cindy. Have a great day."

～

Gino sat in his reclining chair with his feet propped on the desk. "How'd it go, cuz?"

Ribs looked dejected. He plopped into his chair and

sulked. "I'll tell you how it went. I went in there and politely asked for two days—two damn days—and a rat trap of a motel, and what the hell does she do?"

"I'll tell you what she did, she probably shit in your hat—if you had a hat, that is."

Ribs smiled. "Not quite. She okayed a week at the Marriott Riverwalk," he said, then leaned back with his arms folded.

Gino brought his chair up in a hurry. "What? Are you shitting me?"

"Pick me up early, cuz. I want to get a good start on the case. The only thing I'm pissed off about is that we didn't place a bet on this."

"I'm surprised you didn't get her to approve taking the family."

Ribs scrunched his eyebrows. "Damn, Gino, I didn't think of that."

Chapter Seventeen

RAUL CALLS A MEETING

Monterrey, Mexico

Raul's villa sat high in the mountains outside Monterrey, and the view from his patio was magnificent. He sat at a table while he waited for the others to show.

Once everyone arrived, he began. "I'm certain that all of you have learned why I called this meeting. At the last meeting, we spoke about the failure to infiltrate specific markets in Texas, and I was guaranteed better performance in the future.

Raul stopped and glared at each attendee. "Well, this *is* the future, and so far all I'm seeing is more trouble." He pointed to Rodrigo, sitting at the first table. "You, Rodrigo, not only guaranteed me better results in Houston, but you said you would make progress in Dallas as well."

Raul pointed to a short, stocky man seated at the third table. "And you, Felipe, were given the southwestern region, including El Paso, in return for your guarantee of at least ten percent market penetration."

Felipe nodded. "I know that, sir, but El Paso has proven to be more of a challenge than a gift. Ortega's men have an iron grip on the city, and they *own* Juarez as well as the smuggling into the city. It makes it difficult to move products."

"Texas is a big state, Felipe. I'm sure you can find a way to get product into El Paso, and once it's there, moving it should be no problem. El Paso has grown into a big city."

"But Ortega's men—"

"Are just men, Felipe. No different than your men. They get hot and cold. They grow hungry. And I have it on good authority that bullets kill them."

Felipe bowed his head. "Yes, sir, Raul."

"I expect to see a minimum of fifteen percent market share in two months. If you haven't achieved that, there will be no sense in attending the meeting; in fact, there will no sense in remaining in Mexico. Or the United States. Or the western hemisphere."

Felipe gulped. "It will be done, sir."

Raul continued glaring, then turned to Rodrigo again. "And while I'm on the subject of bullets killing people, I see that bullets have become a little too popular in Houston. I admire your aggressiveness, Rodrigo, but what I want is for my people to remain *invisible*. How many times do I have to tell all of you that business must be conducted *quietly?* Quietly means no bodies, or at least, none who are not junkies or drug dealers. *Quietly* means no killings that incite the newspapers to place our business on the front page, and most of all, *quietly* means nothing that will pressure the police to pursue our operations, which they are doing now with a vengeance."

Rodrigo spoke in his defense, but he managed to keep his

tone respectful. "Raul, I feel I need to stand up for my men, but at the same time, accept responsibility. My men caught Pablo selling drugs for Ortega, so they followed my orders and killed him. If anyone is to blame for that, it's me."

Raul smiled. "Rodrigo, it's not Pablo's death I worry over, not even the careless way it was handled. What bothers me—bothers me greatly—is the other two deaths. I've said it many times, and this will be the last time before repercussions occur. We do not kill rich people, we do not kill members of the cloth, and we *absolutely do not* kill cops." Raul kept his voice raised. "Does everyone understand these rules?"

After all in attendance acknowledged it, Raul continued. "I want everyone to go back to their business and do what needs to be done. But do it *quietly*."

As the men left, Raul took Rodrigo by the arm. "Stay and talk awhile. Enjoy some coffee with me."

Rodrigo smiled and sat down next to Raul. "I would be happy to."

Raul turned to a nearby servant, and said, "Armando, two espressos, please."

Rodrigo waited for Armando to leave, then asked. "You wanted to talk to me, Raul?"

"Was it Jorge who took care of Pablo?"

Rodrigo nodded. "It was, but as I said, it was on my standing orders."

"And whose orders did he follow when he killed the priest and the socialite?"

Rodrigo hesitated.

"Well?"

"He acted on his own, Raul, but he did it in good faith. He felt he was doing the right thing for all of us."

Raul patted the back of Rodrigo's hand. "I understand,

and I'm sure he *did* feel that way, but unfortunately he made an error in judgment. I think the rest of the organization needs to see that Jorge was mistaken in how he handled things."

"Do you mean . . .?"

Raul smiled. "You *know* what I mean, Rodrigo."

The servant set two espresso cups on the table and filled them to the brim. "Anything else, señor?"

"Nothing, Armando. And remember your English, please." Raul took a sip of espresso and sighed. "I so much love a good cup, don't you, Rodrigo?"

Rodrigo sipped his and leaned back. "I do, Raul. I definitely do."

After a short pause, Rodrigo spoke again. "You didn't say much about Dallas. How do you want to proceed there?"

"Dallas is important, as you know, but it is more important to establish firm control in Houston. It is best to plug a leak while it's small, Rodrigo. Don't you think?"

"Indeed, I do, Raul. And plug it we will. We'll keep Ortega to San Antonio and El Paso, then we'll take Dallas and the others away one by one."

Raul smiled. "That's just the kind of enthusiasm I like to hear, Rodrigo. Finish your espresso, then have a safe trip back to Houston."

Rodrigo gulped the last swig of espresso and wiped his mouth. "And this business with Jorge. Are you sure that's what you want?"

Raul nodded. "I'm positive, my friend. Lessons must be learned. If others see people getting away with things, it might encourage them to try, and we can't have that. Do as I asked, and we will put an end to these troubles."

Rodrigo placed the napkin on the table and stood. "It will be done before we meet again," he said.

"I have no doubt," Raul said. "*Ve con Dios.*"

"I thought we only spoke English," Rodrigo said.

"We do, but when speaking of God, and when making love, only the native tongue should be used."

Chapter Eighteen

RODRIGO ORDERS A HIT

Houston, Texas

Rodrigo arrived back in town, but he handled all transportation himself. No one knew he was back. For that matter, no one knew he'd been gone. He liked it better that way. He dialed the number where only one person would answer.

Mangua answered the phone. "*Olla*," he said, in a slight Mexican accent.

Rodrigo's anger rose at once. "Don't make me come down there and teach you English. You won't like my instructions."

"I'm sorry, sir. My apologies."

Rodrigo regained his composure. "All right. Now listen because I'll only say it once."

"I'm listening."

"I want Jorge and Ranza taken care of. And I want it done *quietly*."

"Jorge and Ranza?"

"Do I have to repeat myself?" Rodrigo asked. "I know I spoke plainly."

"Why?"

"Should I add another name to the list? Should it be Jorge, Ranza, and Mangua?"

"No. Just tell me where, when, and how," Mangua said.

"The *where* is a quiet place. The *when* is a quiet time. And the *how* is quietly," Rodrigo said. "I hope you understand."

"I understand you want these done *quietly*."

"Then you understand well," Rodrigo said.

"One final thing," Mangua said. "How do I know this is Rodrigo?"

"You know because if I were anyone else, I would kill all three of you myself. And if you don't follow orders, I still may."

"Consider it done, then."

"How long?" Rodrigo asked.

"Within two days," Managua said.

"If it's three, you'll be keeping them company," Rodrigo said.

Jorge picked up the ringing phone. "Hello. Who the hell is this?"

"It's Mangua. *¿Cómo éstas?*"

"If Rodrigo hears you using Spanish like that, you'll end up dead or at least crippled."

Mangua laughed. "I know, but this English is such an ugly language."

"I agree, Mangua, but we need to make sacrifices. Now tell me what the call is about."

"I hate to say, Jorge, but Raul has asked me to talk to Nuncha, and he wants it done soon."

"Nuncha? Why? What did he do?"

"Jorge, I don't ask. You know that; besides, do you think I'd get an answer if I did ask? More than likely, I'd get the same thing as Nuncha."

"Shit, I liked Nuncha," Jorge said. "I can't imagine what he's done."

"I heard everyone liked him," Mangua said. "But I don't like to think about that. Just tell me where I can find him. Give me a location or a phone number. You don't need to be there."

"No," Jorge said. "I brought him into this, so I'll be there when he goes out. When do you want him? I'll bring him to you."

"You're not going to go crazy on me, are you, Jorge?"

Jorge laughed. "Not on you, Mangua. Just give me a place and time."

"How about tomorrow at lunch, down on Navigation?"

"Noon?"

"Noon it is, Jorge. See you at Ninfa's at noon." Mangua almost hung up, then he thought of something. "Jorge, you might want to bring some muscle with you. I doubt we'll need it, but just in case."

"Will do," Jorge said. "I'll bring Ranza."

Mangua sat in his car in front of Ninfa's, and as he waited, he listened to the radio, a Latino station broadcasting from San Antonio. As he listened to an old Johnny Rodriguez tune, Jorge pulled into the parking lot.

He pulled into the first available parking space and sat. Mangua pulled away from the curb and parked a few spots farther down. He called to Jorge as he got out. "Jorge, how the hell are you?"

Jorge opened the door and raced across the parking lot, greeted him, and hugged. "Good to see you, Mangua. It's been a long time."

"Too long," Mangua said, then greeted Ranza and Nuncha, who had ridden with Jorge. "I hope everyone's hungry," Mangua said. "I know I am."

"I guarantee there won't be any food left for anyone else," Ranza said. "Not if I can help it."

The four men ate a hearty meal of mostly fajitas, then chatted for another half an hour. When it appeared as if the waitress may boot them out, Mangua paid the bill, and they left.

Jorge drove up to I–10 and got on the ramp heading east.

"Where are you going?" Nuncha asked.

"I thought we'd take a ride," Jorge said, then glanced at Ranza and nodded. "Besides, Mangua asked me to do something for him by the end of the week. I may as well get it done now—unless you have someplace to be, Nuncha. If you do, this can wait."

"No, I'm fine," Nuncha said. "As long as I'm back by five."

"We'll be done long before five," Ranza said, then he took out a gun and shot Nuncha in the head. Blood splattered all over the back seat and even got on Ranza.

Jorge continued driving as if nothing had happened. After a mile or so, he turned toward Ranza. "Did you arrange for the other car to be where I said?"

"It's there, Jorge. Right under the bridge."

Jorge exited the freeway on the last exit before entering Louisiana. He made a U-turn under the overpass and parked the car on the side of the road. Not fifty yards away sat the car Ranza had arranged to be there.

They got out of the car, made sure the other one started, then backed up and set the one they had driven on fire before leaving.

It took an hour and a half for Jorge to get home. When he and Ranza walked in the door, they found Mangua waiting on the sofa facing them. He held a gun pointed in their direction.

"Where is Nuncha?"

"We got rid of him," Ranza said, "But don't worry, no one will find him for a while. Or should I say, it will take a while for them to identify him?"

"I didn't tell you to get rid of Nuncha," Mangua said.

Jorge kept his hands raised but sat in a chair. "It sounded as if you wanted it done, so we thought we'd do it for you."

"Who did the killing?" Mangua asked.

"I did," Ranza said. "It was clean."

Mangua shot Jorge twice in the chest, then pointed the gun at Ranza. "I'll let you sit for a moment and think about dying before I shoot you."

Ranza panicked. "But we thought you wanted him taken out."

"You shouldn't think, Ranza. It's not good for you." Mangua looked at the time on his phone, then he looked up at Ranza. "Time's up," he said, and pulled the trigger two times.

When he finished, he stepped carefully around the mess on the floor, opened the door, and left.

On his way back to his house, he dialed Rodrigo. "It's done, just like you asked. Nothing obvious, but if someone investigates, they will think Ortega did it."

"Good, Mangua. I like people who follow directions. Thank you."

"Call me when you need something else," Mangua said.

"I will. And the money will be deposited into your account in Monterrey by tomorrow. There will even be a bonus for such quick delivery."

"My thanks, once again, Rodrigo, although it isn't necessary. I did my job; that's all."

"Mangua, it's getting to be more difficult to find a person capable of performing satisfactorily, let alone superbly. When someone exceeds expectations, I like to reward them."

"I appreciate it, Rodrigo. Until next time."

Mangua disconnected the call, set all the traps and alerts, then got into the spare car and drove to his other home—the one no one knew about. It's not that he didn't trust Rodrigo, but long ago, Mangua had learned it was better not to trust anyone.

Chapter Nineteen

A NEW METHOD OF SMUGGLING

Juarez, Mexico

Ortega relaxed on his balcony while his advisors spoke. "You asked for new ideas, señor, and I think these men have some. They are worth listening to."

After the man spoke for a few minutes, Ortega dismissed him. "We've tried animals before. We've even tried humans, but the packages kept breaking, and that resulted in people dying, which resulted in a lot of pressure from the authorities. We need something new."

Mateo stepped up. "But this should work well, señor. The plastic for the packages is much improved. We have tested it, and it doesn't break, at least, not as much as before. And the cattle have been going over the border for a long time. They've been bred in this part of Mexico for hundreds of years, and they've been shipped to the US for almost as long."

Ortega sipped his tea as he listened. "Tell me again how it will work."

Mateo sat on the edge of his seat. "We have two doctors in Juarez. One of them owns an animal hospital, and it has a good reputation, so it should not draw the attention of the police. The doctors will operate on the bulls or cows, and they will insert drugs covered with the new plastic bags into the cows."

"Inserted where?"

"In the intestines. And like I said, it is a new plastic compound that we are ensured won't break."

Ortega stared at Mateo. "What about when the cows have to vacate themselves? What happens then? We'll have border agents staring at packages of heroin covered in shit. The next thing we know, they're coming after us."

Mateo smiled. "We've thought of that, señor. The bowels will be emptied before the drugs are inserted, then the cows will be given only water to drink. Nothing to eat. With nothing to eat, they should be fine until they cross the border, and the drugs are removed."

"But won't the agents suspect something when they don't see anything?"

"The cows will be mixed with many others that have nothing inserted, so there will be no way of telling that a few cows are not emptying their bowels. Don't worry, señor. There will be plenty of shit," Mateo said.

Ortega nodded. "Tell me what happens after they get over the border?"

Mateo smiled. "This should be the smoothest part. After crossing, the cows are then taken immediately to Dr. Phen's facility north of El Paso. He is set up to remove everything safely. After that, the cows are placed in a small pasture to heal, and the drugs are given to our men in Texas for distribution. Once we get them into Texas, it should be foolproof."

"I've heard of many things that were considered foolproof, Mateo. We'll see how this goes."

Mateo smiled. "The best part, señor, is that if it goes as expected, you will have the upper hand. You will be able to charge the other cartels a big fee for smuggling in their drugs."

"Or we could leave them operating on their own," Ortega said. "It remains to be seen which would be better."

Ortega insisted on several more trial runs before he okayed a real operation. Once he okayed it, the men were ready.

The first shipment went through the initial process two days later, and despite the trial runs, Ortega insisted that it only be eighty cows and with only a handful of them carrying drugs. Still, that amounted to about one hundred million dollars worth of product—if it all got through successfully."

"If this works as we think," Mateo said, "We can prevent all the losses from seizures."

"We'll do no such thing," Ortega said. "If we discontinue the current operations, the agents will know we've found another way to smuggle drugs in, and they'll start looking for how we're doing it. If they focus on searching for new ways, it won't take long for them to find out."

"So what do we do?" Mateo asked.

"We let them continue finding what they have normally found, and in the meantime, we slowly use the new process more and more."

Mateo nodded. "It will be done right away. You won't be disappointed, señor."

"I'm sure that I won't," Ortega said. "See that it is so."

Dr. Santiago finished the insertion process and placed the cows in a facility to rest before shipping them across the border. He issued instructions for the care and feeding, including the orders for water only. No food. Before long, they were mixed with the other cows and put in line to be shipped.

El Paso, Texas

The cows passed border security with ease, then made their way to Dr. Phen's facility north of El Paso, where they underwent a minor operation to remove the bags of heroin, all of which passed through safely—no busted packages. When removed, Phen handed the heroin to Ortega's men, who then took it to Ramon for distribution to Dallas, Austin, and San Antonio.

Ramon gathered around the three men who were to distribute the drugs. "Your cars are being adapted as we speak. Each of them has been fitted with three small compartments underneath the vehicle. From the underside, the compartments appear as a part of the car, but when the car is put on a lift and raised, a small opening on the side is revealed, which is how the drugs will be accessed." Ramon handed each of them a slip of paper, then said, "When you reach your destinations, you will go to these addresses."

"And what are we to do when we get there?"

"There are people at these addresses who will remove your cargo and turn it over to you. It should all go smoothly."

"What else?" one of the men asked.

"All of you are to take I-10 east, but then make your way around to the east of the cities of Dallas, Austin, and San Antonio. You are to enter the cities from the east side only. It can be the northeast if you want, but not the south or west."

"Understood," they all said.

Ramon paced while he spoke. "Furthermore, you will keep to the speed limit and obey all laws. If you are caught speeding, you will die. If you run a traffic signal, you will die. If anything happens to prevent the successful delivery of these drugs, you will die." Ramon looked at each of them. "Is this understood?"

All the men acknowledged what he said.

"Then let's not waste any time," Ramon said. "Dallas leaves first, followed in half an hour by Austin, then half an hour after that by San Antonio. Good luck."

San Antonio, Texas

Ten to fifteen hours later, the men pulled into the three cities and went to the repair shops, where the drugs were removed from the cars. It worked seamlessly, as Ramon predicted, and when the operations were completed, the men took the drugs to the stash houses that had been previously set up, then made plans to restock the supply chain. It wouldn't be long before tens of millions of dollars flowed back to the coffers of Ortega's operations.

Lanza wiped his mouth, then ordered espresso with his dessert—the Hotel Emma had some of the best espresso. Roberto walked over and sat, but he waited until he was alone with Lanza to speak. "Everything went well with the delivery. It's all done."

"And you felt there was a need to report this, Roberto?"

"I, uh, I just thought you'd want to know," Roberto said.

The waiter brought the espresso with Lanza's dessert and set them on the table before him. He looked at Roberto. "Señor, you would like something?"

Roberto looked to Lanza, then shook his head. "No thank you, Señor. I'm fine."

Lanza sipped his espresso. "I don't need to know when things go right, Roberto. Only when they go wrong. I expect things to go right. Things are *supposed* to go right."

Roberto stood. "Si, señor. I will not bother you again," he said, then made his way out of the restaurant.

Once Roberto had left Lanza alone, he pulled out his phone and dialed. "*Capitan*, this is your amigo. I just wanted to let you know there may be increased activity for the next week or so."

"That's no problem."

"I know it's no problem, but I called out of courtesy. It is the thing business associates do."

"And I appreciate it, Señor Lanza. Thank you."

Lanza hung up and went back to his dessert and espresso.

The captain disconnected his cell phone, then immediately picked up the office line and dialed his lieutenant. "Wesley, expect more activity on the west side for the next week or two but pay it no mind. Just let it run the course."

"Yes, sir, Captain. Will do," Wesley said.

"Keep the pressure on the south side of town, though. Nothing's changed there."

Chapter Twenty

WELCOME TO SAN ANTONIO

San Antonio, Texas

It usually took about four hours to drive to San Antonio, and we were halfway there by eight o'clock—right on schedule.

"You ought to stop for breakfast at the next exit," Ribs said.

"Why? Because the sign said 'World's Worst Breakfast' or because you've eaten here before?"

"Cuz, you need to get out more. If a restaurant advertises itself as the world's worst, or having the worst of something, you can usually bet it's damn good."

"If you say so," I said. "I'm hungry, so I guess we'll get some."

We parked the car, went inside, and each of us ordered a big meal, along with a continual supply of fresh coffee. And surprisingly, it *was* fresh.

And as Ribs surmised, the breakfast was excellent, not to

mention, they served huge portions. I stuffed so much, I doubted if I'd have to eat before dinner.

"Now that was a meal," Ribs said as he almost lay down in the car's front seat.

"You're going to be useless as a backseat driver," I said, "Or for that matter, as a conversationalist, so you might as well go to sleep. I'll wake you when we get there."

Ribs bundled up a jacket, stuffed it between the seat and the window, then leaned his head on it to rest. "Don't get in a wreck while I'm napping. I'll never forgive you."

We checked into the hotel about eleven, then walked down to get some coffee while we planned the day.

"Where you want to start?" I asked. "You think we should go straight at 'em? Or you think we should chat up a few uniforms first?"

"You know what I think already, but it might be difficult to get the uniforms to talk."

"That's the difference between me and you," I said. "I prepared properly."

"I'm listening," Ribs said.

"I called Tip last night and asked if he knew anyone in San Antonio."

Ribs slapped the table. "Shit, I should have thought of that."

"Yes, you should have," I said. "Anyway, he gave me two names—Charlie Burk and Dan Nickles. He said they've both been here almost twenty years, and neither one has any connection with the Boswells. In fact, he said they had a few pissing matches with them when they were moving up."

"Damn, that's what we need. Good ol' Tip. How the hell does he know everybody?"

I laughed. "When I called him and asked him, he said, 'Of course, I know someone in San Antonio. If it's south of the Red River and North of the Rio Grande, I know 'em."

"I know Tip's full of shit, but he's only half lying. That son of a bitch knows more people than you can imagine. And the thing is, they all seem to owe him favors."

"Ain't that the truth? I worked a case with him, and every time we needed a lead, he knew somebody that got us one."

"Then I guess we know where to head," Ribs said. "We need to find Charlie Burk or Dan Nickles, and we need to find out what they know about the Boswells."

"More specifically, what they know about the Boswells as it relates to Ortega."

"Let me worry about what questions to ask, partner; otherwise, you'll screw things up. And since you're driving, I'll provide directions. Head toward the west side of town, and I'll point you to Burk's precinct."

For a big city, San Antonio was easy to navigate, and there wasn't much traffic. We made it through town in less than twenty minutes, then we walked into the station and showed our badges. Despite being from out of town, the badges carried enough weight to earn us an audience.

We walked into Burk's office, once again showing our badges. He scowled. "Okay, so we've got a couple of detectives from Houston. What's that supposed to mean?"

Ribs stepped up with an attitude. "Tip Denton said you were an asshole, but I reserved judgment—until now."

"Tip? That old cowboy son of a bitch. Why didn't you tell me he sent you?"

Ribs smiled. "I thought I'd play it safe. You never know how an introduction from Tip might play out."

Burk laughed his ass off. "Ain't that the truth, an introduction from that lying son of a bitch is just as likely to earn you a punch in the face as it is a handshake. But as far as we're concerned, it's a handshake. Tip's a good guy."

"He said the same about you, Burk, along with a few other things. But I'm not here to trade lies, I need some information on the Boswells."

Burk looked around, then grabbed my elbow. "If that's what you need, maybe we should go for a walk," he said.

We went outside with Burk, and he opened up once we did. "Those Boswell sons of bitches are as crooked as a rattlesnake's tail."

"How so?" I asked.

"They came to San Antonio when they were just a couple of brothers in the police force. Before long, they were both moving up the ladder, and by coincidence, the drugs were moving into town—every part of town, but especially where the Boswells had influence."

"You're saying they were dirty?" Ribs asked, never one to be subtle.

"I can't swear to it, but every time a case was brought against one of Ortega's men, something happened to make it disappear. Maybe the evidence was lost, or the Miranda rights weren't administered properly, or a search warrant was obtained illegally. It didn't matter what—it was always something. But it was always something with Ortega's men only, not the other cartels."

"That's it? That's all you got?" I asked.

"If you want more coincidence, try this. As the Ortega's rose in influence and control of the city's drugs, the Boswells rose in power in the department. Before long, they held two captain positions and quite a few lieutenant spots, not to mention the choice Narcotics jobs."

"But I heard one of the Boswells was shot while doing his job," Ribs said.

"And you heard right," Burk said. "Hey, every family has to have a good soul, right? Not all snakes bite."

"You're saying they gave up one of their own for the sake of propriety?"

Burk looked at Gino with an unbelieving stare. "You think that's the first time a family's given up their own blood? History is full of such examples."

"That's some cold shit," Ribs said.

"Cold or not, that's what happened," Burk said. "I'll go to my grave knowing that."

"And he was injured enough to earn disability?" I asked.

Burk shook his head. "Not really. He was shot. No doubt about that. But his wounds healed within a few weeks according to the inside dope from the hospital. His family, however, sung a different tune. They said he was disabled and had to retire. I heard he got a sweetheart deal and moved to a lake house with his wife and kids. Afterward, the Boswells went on a rampage against the drug dealers—all but the Ortegas."

"Nobody ever noticed?" I asked.

"They noticed," Burk added, "but the ones that inquired about it were demoted or shoved out to the suburbs. If they were politicians, they weren't re-elected. The Boswells had become the power in town, and everyone knew it."

"Power or not, didn't the paper question it, or the judges?" I asked.

Burk laughed. "I'm happy that you've lived in a city where corruption hasn't eaten its way to the top. Money buys almost everything—papers, politics, judges, and cops. And it doesn't take long to happen." Burk stopped to light up a smoke. "Here's hoping it doesn't happen in Houston," he said. "Or that you don't notice it happening."

"You mean all this is going on and nobody does anything about it?" Ribs asked.

Burk nodded. "Nobody *can* do anything about it."

"How about the judges or the mayor?"

"I've already told you, they're bought and paid for. There are plenty of good beat cops, but the brass is owned by Ortega."

"How about the FBI?" I asked.

Burk laughed. "The FBI relies on their influence, in other words, getting locals to help or do the grunt work for them. If they come in—and they have—the locals spill the beans to the drug dealers, then all plans are lost. Nothing gets done."

"How about the DEA?" Ribs asked. "They operate on their own."

Burk nodded. "They do. But they focus on preventing drugs from coming across the border. The problem is that by the time Ortega gets to San Antonio, he has already gotten his drugs across the border. His challenge is getting them from El Paso to San Antonio or Dallas, and then getting them distributed."

"So you're saying we're screwed," Ribs said.

"As long as the Boswells are in power, yes, you're screwed."

"How do we get them out of power?" I asked.

"Short of killing them, I have no idea. Some of my associates and I have even considered that drastic option."

"I didn't hear that," I said.

"I don't care if you heard or not," Burk said. "I mentioned that it's something we *considered*. I didn't say we tried it or plan to try it."

"Who's the top guy for Ortega in the city?"

"That's easy," Burk said. "It's Lanza. And he's easy to find. He stays in the best hotel in town—the Hotel Emma—and he always occupies the best suite."

"Maybe we should pay a visit to Lanza," Ribs said.

I shook my head. "No way, Ribs. If we go as cops, it will put him on edge, and if we try as anything else, it will put him on edge. Either way, we risk putting him on edge."

I looked at Burk. "So if Lanza is in town, it's likely got something to do with the Boswells. If we keep an eye on both of them, we should be safe."

Burk nodded. "I'd buy into that. In fact, if that's your plan, my partner and I will help you. We'll each pair up with one of you at night to keep an eye on these sons of bitches."

I looked to Ribs and smiled. "Sounds like a deal," I said. "How about we stir up some shit with the Boswells first, give them a reason to contact Lanza, then we're bound to hit gold."

Burk nodded. "I like it. I'll get Nickles to go along and we'll meet at around seven. How's that?"

"Seven's good," Ribs said, then handed a card to Burk. "Here's where we're staying."

Burk tossed the card into a trash can. "No sense in keeping trouble," he said. "I can remember the name of a hotel."

Chapter Twenty-One

A MEETING WITH THE BOSWELLS

San Antonio, Texas

We had made up our minds we were going to lure the Boswells into the open, but we didn't have a solid plan to do it.

"I say we go right at them, not in an accusatory way, but pretending we're asking for help."

"Explain," I said.

Ribs gathered his thoughts, then told me of his plan. After hearing it, I agreed, so we decided to set things in motion.

Shortly after lunch, we walked into the downtown precinct where Captain Boswell was. "Here to see the captain," I said, after displaying our badges.

"Houston Homicide? What the hell are you doing out here?"

"I believe we'll reserve that information for when we speak to Captain Boswell," Ribs said, and he made sure his tone reflected his attitude.

"Just asking," the desk sergeant said, then he buzzed Boswell on the intercom. "Sir, I've got a couple of Houston Homicide cops asking to see you."

"Show them up, please."

The desk sergeant looked as if he wasn't happy with Boswell's decision, but he begrudgingly asked someone to take us to see Boswell.

We entered the captain's office and were greeted by not one, but two beautiful young women who offered us everything but sex, and I'm not so sure that wasn't implied in one way or another.

One of the young women came back and handed us coffee. Her skirt was so tight, I thought it would split when she bent over.

"My name's Savannah, sugar. Captain Boswell won't be a minute, but if he's any longer, you holler, and I'll see if we can't find something more interesting to do."

We waited almost fifteen minutes, after which Savannah showed us back to see Captain Boswell. He stood when we entered and then shook hands. "Ernie Boswell," he said. "What can I do for the HPD?"

We sat in two comfortable chairs in front of his desk. "Captain, we came out here on a case we're working in Houston."

"And that case brings you here?" he asked. "In what way?"

"In a roundabout way, it does bring us here," Ribs said. "It started with a dead drug dealer. That led to a witness being killed, and then a priest. When we investigated, we found evidence that indicated it may have something to do with the Ortega cartel, which we know has major operations in San Antonio. We suspect he may be making a move into Houston."

Boswell sat straighter in his chair. "Assuming it is Ortega, and I wouldn't be surprised if it was, what do you expect to find in San Antonio? I'd think you would be better off looking in Juarez."

"I hear what you're saying," Ribs said, "but if Ortega is involved—even if he's behind this and operating from Juarez—I think he'd run it through San Antonio. At least, that's what we've heard. That's why we came here—to either verify it or find out we're wrong."

Boswell nodded. "You could be right, Detective. I'll have my men keep open ears for anything changing on the street."

"We were hoping for more than that," I said.

"In what way," the captain asked.

"I was hoping you'd let us tag along with a few of your people in Narcotics. I'd like to talk to some of Ortega's people myself. At the least, I'd like to listen in while your men talk to them."

Boswell seemed to think a moment, then he shook his head. "I don't think that's something I can do, Detective. It would be placing my men in more danger than they are already in, and I can't ask them to do that."

"You *could* let them decide," Ribs said. "If your men are anything like the ones I've worked Narcotics with in Houston, I'd bet they'd be happy to go along with it. The undercovers I know, usually do anything to bring a dealer down."

"You may be right, Detective, but it wouldn't be right for

me to ask that of my men. They may foolishly agree to your request, hoping to curry favor with me and assuming it would reflect well on their record. Even worse, it may cause them to act recklessly. I can't allow that to happen. I'm sorry, Detective."

"What *can* you do, Captain? I hate to think we came all this way for nothing, and I can't believe there's *nothing* you can do."

"I can go this far. I'll tell my men that if any officer busts someone suspected of being associated with Ortega's operations, I'll allow you to sit in on the interviews, and I'll even allow you to participate in them." Boswell stood then, an indication that the meeting was over.

Ribs and I took the hint, thanked Boswell for his help, then exited the building. "What do you think, Ribs? Is he dirty or not?"

Ribs sneered. "As Tip would say, he's so damn dirty, you can't wash the stink out of him."

"And for one of the few times, I'd agree with Tip," I said.

"What do we do now? Due to the beneficence of our magnanimous captain, we have several days remaining at a nice hotel which sits in a great city and has an almost endless supply of nice restaurants. And last, but not least, it's all on the department's budget."

I shook my head and laughed. "Ribs, some people think about more than nice hotels and good food. I'm more concerned with finding a killer."

"That's your problem, cuz. You need to get your priorities straight."

"I think we should contact Burk again, or Nickles, and see if they can help out."

"First, we need to set the bait," Ribs said. "You think enough time has passed since we left?"

"I'd say so. Let's do it," I said.

We turned around and went back inside, where Savannah greeted us with a smile and her familiar southern drawl.

"Good Lord, look who came back to see us. Hello, detectives." She cocked her hip to the side and said, "Come back for more of my good coffee? Or somethin' else?"

I smiled so that Ribs didn't have to speak because I'm sure he may have stumbled over his tongue. "We forgot to mention a few things to the captain," I said.

We re-entered Boswell's office, and he stood to greet us, though he did appear surprised. "Detectives, what can I do for you now?"

"We forgot to mention one thing," Ribs said. "Our information mentioned that Ortega had one of his top men either in San Antonio now, or coming here. A man named Lanza. You know him?"

Boswell shook his head. "I can't say that I do, but it's been a long time since I've been on the streets, Detective."

"I realize that," I said, "but I assumed you may have seen his name on the reports your men turned in. We heard he'd been a major player for quite a while."

"If he's been a player for that long, I'm sure my men have track of his activities, so his name must have slipped my memory. Write it down, though, and I'll make sure they check it out."

I didn't risk smiling at Ribs, but inside, I beamed. *The trap is set.*

~

We walked back to the car, feeling good about the situation. "You think he'll bite?" Ribs asked.

"I have no doubt. Did you see his look when I mentioned Lanza's name? I thought he was going to pick up the phone and call Lanza right then."

"I don't care if he calls him," I said. "We've got no way of monitoring that. But I'm hoping he issues orders for someone to pay Lanza a visit."

"All right, cuz. I'll connect with Nickles. He and I will take the Boswells. That leaves you and Burk to watch Ortega's men. Between the two of us, we should get him."

"But what are we getting him for? Lanza doesn't have a warrant on him. He hasn't broken any laws. What are we supposed to do with him?"

"All we can do is watch him," Ribs said. "If he breaks any laws, we can nail him, but if not, we have to wait a little longer. One thing's for sure. If Lanza works for Ortega—and we know he does—he'll be breaking laws before long. And if it's not him breaking the laws, his other men surely will."

We got in position: Ribs and Nickles in the hotel waiting to spot Boswell or his men, and us on a cold, damp street on San Antonio's south side. Sometime near eight o'clock, I got a call.

"Gino, I think we're screwed. Nobody has shown up here at all, unless you want to mention a couple of young women, one of whom could have passed for Savannah."

"Ribs, get her off your mind, or I'll tell Rosalee. If I do that, you really *will* be screwed. We've had no action down here either, and Burk said it's unusual for *nothing* to happen. I'm beginning to wonder if just maybe Lanza and his men were warned."

"I'm past wondering about it. I'm pretty damn sure of it. We need to do something more drastic, and we need to do it soon. We only have a few days left."

My phone alerted me to an incoming call. "Gotta grab this call, Ribs. I'll get back with you."

I pressed the button to accept the call, simultaneously disconnecting my call with Ribs. "Hello?"

"Gino, where are you?"

"Coop? You know where I am—in San Antonio."

"Shit, I forgot for a moment. All right, listen up. You and Delgado need to come back. We've got two more bodies, maybe three."

"Who?"

"Two men who Narcotics said are Raul's men, meaning they are Rodrigo's men. A man named Jorge, and one named Ranza. They were found dead in their apartment, shot with small-caliber bullets, and nothing was taken from the apartment—*nothing*. They even had dope in their pocket."

"And the third body?"

"I can't swear that it's related, but it looks like it. We found a car set on fire near the border with Louisiana. The medical examiner identified the body as Latino, and he's confirmed he's been shot, but we don't yet have a firm connection."

"Chances are good, there will be a connection, Coop. I'd bet on it."

"Unfortunately, I would too, which is why I'm calling the two of you back. I need you on this."

"All right. I'll get Ribs and we'll head back. He won't be too happy about it though."

"Cataldi, I quit worrying over what Delgado is and isn't happy about a *long* time ago."

"You got it, Coop. We'll head home tonight, but we drove, remember, so it will take a few hours."

"See if you can get here before the results of the medical examiner's team come in. Having three more bodies is going to send the chief over the edge."

Chapter Twenty-Two

GINO AND RIBS INVESTIGATE

Monterrey, Mexico

Raul's minions crowded around a few tables on the patio of his Monterrey villa. "What do you think he wants this time?" Felipe asked. "We just had a meeting last week."

Tico and Umberto entered late and hurriedly took seats at a table near the back. Raul scanned the room, doing a count of who was and wasn't there. "Now that I see everyone is finally here, we can begin. I know it hasn't been long, but I called a special meeting—specifically to ream out Rodrigo."

A collective gasp filled the air, but Rodrigo showed no reaction, even as Raul began speaking.

"Rodrigo, not only have you showed no progress in Dallas, but my operations in Houston continue to lose both money and men. The latest reports tell me that Jorge and his man, Ranza, have been found dead."

Rodrigo gaped at Raul but didn't say a thing. Half an hour

later, when all other business was done and everyone had left, Rodrigo approached Raul. "Raul, I mean no disrespect, but I followed your orders regarding Jorge and Ranza."

Raul stared at him, then sat down, indicating Rodrigo should too. "I gave no orders to kill them. I said to make an example."

"Yes, you did. And when I asked, 'Do you mean?' you said, 'You *know* what I mean, Rodrigo.'"

Raul shook his head. "Rodrigo, someday you will have to learn that things need to be clarified. You should have asked me specifically what I meant. But it's over with now. Get back to Houston and set things right. And make sure I hear no more about any of these killings. Murder is bad for business."

Rodrigo got up and turned to go. "Yes, sir. I'll make sure it happens."

Houston, Texas

We broke the Houston city line about five in the morning. "What's your call, Ribs? Should we go home and nap some? Go to the office and try to nap? Or grab a couple of hotel rooms and really nap?"

"It's a unanimous vote for the hotel rooms," Ribs said. "I say we hit the Four Seasons."

"What the hell do you mean by 'unanimous'? I may have chosen to see Marissa."

"I decided for you, cuz. I guessed you would opt for the hotel rooms, so I saved you the trouble of voting. Besides, if you hadn't chosen the hotel rooms, I'd have shot you, which means, either way, it would have been unanimous."

We checked into adjacent rooms and caught a few hours of much-needed sleep. At nine o'clock, a knock on the door woke me, and I got up and let Ribs in.

"Come on, sleepy. Coop's gonna have our ass if we don't hurry. I'm surprised your phone hadn't rung yet."

"If we don't hurry, it will. Count on it," I said. "We need to make time for breakfast, though. I'm starved."

"I've got a table held for us," Ribs said. "I knew you'd be hungry."

"Is that because you and Nickles feasted at the Hotel Emma last night while Burk and I stuffed on potato chips and peanut butter crackers?"

Ribs laughed. "I might have made my assumption based on that, yes. But quit complaining and follow me to the restaurant so we can eat."

We were waiting for the food when I decided to call Coop. She answered right away.

"Cataldi, where are you? I thought you were coming back."

"We're on our way, Coop. Not far now. I'm guessing another hour. No more." Someone tapped me on the shoulder, and when I turned to see who it was, there stood Coop.

"About an hour, huh, Cataldi? Since when does it take an

hour to get from the Four Seasons to our station, which sits only a few miles from here?"

"Captain, I—"

"Captain, nothing. I expect to see you *in* my office no less than fifteen minutes from now. That's *in* my office. Your ass *in* a chair facing me. Is that understood?"

I gulped. "Yes, Captain. We'll be there. Don't worry."

"I'm *not* worried, but you should be."

We arrived at Coop's office with three minutes to spare, and Cindy showed us in. "Captain, about this morning . . ."

She continued reading a report while talking. "What about it? You want to know how I knew where you were?"

"Actually, sir, I do."

"Ask your partner. He called me fifteen minutes before you did."

I reached for Ribs, ready to wrap my hands around his throat. "You son of a bitch. You son of a bitch. You didn't even tell me."

"Gino, I suggest you settle down, compose yourself, then get your ass to the crime scene and solve it. With the one found under the bridge, this makes six bodies. And that's not counting the two bodies you didn't catch. Either way you look at it, it's far too many for the chief to tolerate."

Ribs and I both stood and saluted. "We're on it, Coop. You'll have a preliminary report tonight."

"I'm sure I will. Stop at Cindy's desk on your way out and get the details, then stop at Julie's desk to see if she has any updates. I had her running financials and phone logs for both men. We'll compare that with the third body once we get an ID from the medical examiner."

"You want us to call when we get there?" I asked.

"Cataldi, I have no desire to monitor your whereabouts. Just do what you promised and deliver me a report by tonight. Now get the hell out of here."

R ibs and I pulled up to the apartments and went inside. There was a uniform guarding a door marked with crime-scene tape, and he looked bored as hell. I didn't blame him. It was a boring, thankless job.

Ribs flashed his badge. "Delgado and Cataldi," he said. "Here about the bodies."

The officer stepped aside and let us through.

We entered the apartment, but there were no bodies, just white-chalk drawings where the bodies had been found. I turned around and looked at where they lay compared to the entrance. "Looks like they were barely home before it happened," I said.

Ribs pointed to the sofa, which sat five or six feet in front. "And I'd bet whoever did this had been sitting right there, waiting for them to get home."

I called the medical examiner's office and got hold of Jeanne. "You got anything on the two bodies from yesterday?" I asked.

"We've got some preliminaries, but not much."

"How about an ID on the guy found under the freeway?"

"Nothing there. As far as the first two, small caliber, two shots each, and the crime scene shows the shots came from about six feet away."

"How about time-of-death?" Ribs asked.

"I estimated it happened between four and six, but that could be off by an hour or so either way. And if you're curious, no signs of drug use, or at least no drug use via injection. Early toxicology results show them both to be clean as well."

"That's four or six p.m., right?" Ribs asked.

"Exactly," Jeanne said. "What's interesting is what we found in the victim's pockets."

"Can you text it over to us?" I asked.

"It'll be there in a few minutes," Jeanne said.

Ribs and I searched the apartment room by room, doing our best to be meticulous. We emptied each drawer, looked underneath each one, and checked the shower drain and the toilet holding tank. Ribs even checked the electric sockets and the light bulbs.

We searched thoroughly under the sink, and in all the appliances including the oven and fridge. After hours of looking, we admitted to ourselves that there may be nothing there. "I'd bet they had drug dogs through here already," Ribs said.

"Probably," I said, "But it never hurts to double-check. I've seen the dogs miss something before."

Before we left for the day, we received a text from Jeanne.

Items found on the bodies of Jorge Rinaldo, and Ranza Xuten:

Jorge:

Beretta pistol, M9A1.

Two grams of Mexican Brown (heroin) and three bags of it. Each package was marked with a wolf's head.

Six hundred forty-seven dollars.
Keys to his apartment (verified) and to several cars.
Cell phone (iPhone) and a burner phone as well.

~

R*anza:*
Beretta pistol, M15.
One gram of Mexican Brown (heroin) and two bags of it. Each package was marked with a wolf's head.
Three hundred sixteen dollars.
Keys to a vehicle as yet unidentified.
One burner phone.

~

Ribs looked at the report over my shoulder, and when he finished, he whistled. "That's a lot of money for someone to leave on a body," he said.

"It wasn't any junkie," I said. "Not if they left that much in money and drugs."

"None of this adds up," Ribs said. "If these two were killed for money, whoever did it would have taken the money and the drugs, plus the guns—which would bring in a lot of cash on the street."

"I've been waiting for you to comment on the drugs," I said.

"If you mean the fact that the drugs found on the bodies belonged to Ortega and not Raul, then you were right to wonder. It fits, since we suspected as much after Pablo got killed, more than likely for the same reason."

"If, and I emphasize *if,* we prove, or at least conclude, that these murders are tied to a problem between Ortega and Raul, we're going to bring holy hell down on both of them. And we'll find a way to put pressure on San Antonio too. So much pressure that if Boswell doesn't respond, he'll be showing his hand." I looked at Ribs. "You *do* remember how this started, don't you?"

"Of course, I remember," Ribs said, "But I also want to know who the hell *you* know who can exert that kind of pressure?"

"Nobody. But maybe Tip does," I said.

"Before we call the president or something, let's make sure it's all real. Did Jeanne compare the dope with what we found on Pablo?" Ribs asked.

"I don't know," I said. "But we'll ask her to do the tests. In fact, we'll ask her right now."

I called Jeanne and explained our problem. "We need the drugs you found compared against the drugs turned in on the first murder, the one on Sage Street—Pablo . . . something was his name."

"I can have that for you tomorrow," Jeanne said. "I'll call you."

"It looks as if we'll have to wait until tomorrow," I said.

"Bull," Ribs said. "Let's proceed as if we have confirmation. We'll deliver our report to Coop, and we'll ask her if she has any ideas."

"I don't know if we should mention it to Coop until it's verified, and I definitely don't think we should mention San Antonio. She's strict about that kind of shit."

Ribs grabbed me by the arm and led me toward the door. "Let's go, cuz. If you get me back early, I'll write the report."

As we got into the car, Ribs pulled out his phone and dialed. "Jeanne, I forgot to ask, but will you please send photos of both men as well. Gino and I haven't even seen them."

"Do you need body number three?"

"From what Coop said, it was unrecognizable, so it's not as important. You can send it, but it's not critical."

~

We handed our initial report to Coop, and she asked us to stay while she read it. "So you think this was the same killer as the one who did Pablo and probably Langer and the priest?"

"I think it was, Captain. And for all the reasons in the report," I said. "But keep in mind, this is only the initial report. We have a lot more digging to do."

"This stinks to all hell," Ribs said, "But if it holds up as being the same person, it makes solving it easier. All we need to do is catch one person."

As I waited for Coop to digest the information, I said, "I almost forgot, Captain, but Jeanne is running a comparison of the dope found on Pablo against the new dope. I'm betting it matches. If it does, we have an excellent lead in San Antonio and may be able to finally wrap this up."

Coop removed her glasses and set them on the desk. "Gino, whenever you and Delgado start thinking like this, it seldom works out, and I usually end up unhappy."

"And you're right to think that," I said. "Ribs is like the man behind the curtain in the Wizard of Oz. You should pay no attention to him."

"He's wrong, Captain. The man behind the curtain is the one with the best plan. Once we show you the connection to a man named Lanza in San Antonio, all we need to do is put pressure on the police there to help us nail him."

"Why would they need pressure?" Coop asked.

"Because we believe they are in Lanza's employ—at least in San Antonio. We think they work for him now, and have for a long time. We're not as sure about Dallas, but I wouldn't doubt it."

"And what would you do if you could get this pressure?" Coop asked.

"Forget about it, Captain. We'd need a lot of stroke, and it would have to be enough to really threaten these assholes. They're not the type to buckle under at the first raised voice."

Coop smiled. "Sit back gentlemen, I think I have an idea."

Ribs turned to me and smiled. "I think we're going back to San Antonio, amigo."

I sighed and looked at the captain. "Coop, if any part of your plan *doesn't* involve me partnering with this idiot cousin of mine, let's go with that one."

WHO IS JORGE?

I hadn't even had my coffee when the phone buzzed. I didn't recognize the caller ID, which made me consider not answering it, but I did anyway. "Cataldi."

"Detective, this is Jeanne from the medical examiner's office."

"Forgive my possibly grumpy-sounding voice, Jeanne, but I just woke up."

"That's all right, Ben has us working overtime here to catch up to all the bodies being dropped. Anyway, I wanted to tell you that the dope from that apartment was a dead match for the dope from the first murder—Pablo, I think his name was."

"Dead match? No doubt?"

I could almost see her reaction. She was sure. "No doubt at all."

"Okay, thanks, Jeanne. I appreciate it."

"Hang on a minute," Jeanne said. "That's not all. We

caught a lucky break and matched fingerprints to one of the victims."

I perked up when I heard that, but I was also confused. "I thought we had IDs on both the bodies?"

"We thought so too. We had Ranza Xuten as one of them, but prints matched someone named Ranza Gonzales, and he came here from Monterrey four years ago. We got a hit on his prints because he had a brief, part-time job with a security company when he first got to Houston, and they printed him."

"Then where did the Ranza Xuten come from?"

"When we initially processed the bodies, we went with the ID they had on them. Ranza Xuten matched his. But the prints tell us it's not so."

"How about the other guy—Jorge?"

"He checked out. I think we're safe to say he is who he is."

"Okay, Jeanne. Thanks again."

Marissa walked into the kitchen wearing a smile. "Good morning. How goes my hard-working detective this morning?"

I leaned over and kissed her. "Damn, you're beautiful when you smile."

She filled the teapot with water and placed it on the range to heat. "You know what that tells me? That you should do all that's possible to make me smile at all times."

I pulled her to me and held her tightly. "That goes both ways, you know. And I happen to know one thing that will surely put a smile on my face." I kissed the nape of her neck. "And did I mention we've got plenty of time?"

Marissa turned and kissed me slowly. "But we don't have time. I already called Connie and told her I'd pick her up in thirty minutes. We're going shopping today."

"Son of a bitch," I said. "Well, at least pick up something sexy to wear to bed."

The teapot whistled, indicating the water was heated. "Don't worry about that, Gino. You won't be disappointed."

~

An alert sounded on my phone, announcing that an email had arrived. I opened it to see it contained the photos of the bodies from Jeanne.

"Anything exciting?" Marissa asked as she finished dressing.

"Not unless you're into looking at dead bodies," I said. "If you're into that, have I got a treat for you."

"Go to hell, Gino. But have a nice day while you're at it. I'm leaving to pick up Connie."

"Know that I'll be cursing you while I spend my day with Ribs."

Marissa kissed me on the cheek, then headed for the back door. "Tell Ribs I said hi."

~

I drank a second cup of coffee while waiting for Ribs. I was just about to call him when he pulled up.

I locked the door and walked to his car. "About time you got here. I've been waiting far too long."

"You're full of shit, cuz. I just passed Marissa on her way

out, and if she is leaving now, either you two just finished coffee, or you just finished something else."

I shook my head. "Damn, but you're a pervert. No wonder you have six kids."

Ribs started to say something, but I stopped him. "Before you get going, take a look at the photos Jeanne sent."

We sat in the driveway, the car in idle, while Ribs looked at the photos. "You know either of these, Gino?"

"I can't say that I do. Certainly don't know them enough to put a name to them," I said.

"We don't need a name," Ribs said. "But one of them sure looks like a match, or a possible match, for the description of the man the clerk at the rental agency gave us."

I pulled the phone from him and took a closer look at the photos. I was still staring when Ribs spoke up again.

"Remember, the clerk said the man's license showed him bald or with a shaved head, but the clerk also said he was already growing it back in when he was there? Remember, he said he had to look closely to make sure it was him?"

"I don't recall it all that well, but if you think it's possible, let's send a photo up to see if he can confirm or deny it."

∽

Ribs got the number from Julie, and he emailed the clerk a photo array which included several autopsy photos for equal comparison. We got an email back within minutes.

∽

That's him. No doubt about it.

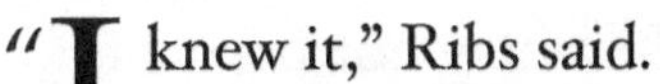

"I knew it," Ribs said.

"Okay, now what the hell do we do with it," I said.

"We need to canvass their neighborhood to see who they were, and why they were killed. If we can determine that, it may go a long way toward solving these crimes."

"I don't know if I buy all that, Ribs, but I'm willing to give it a shot. I'll get the addresses from Julie while you drive."

I got the home addresses from Julie while Ribs made his way toward Navigation Boulevard. "I had a feeling that apartment wasn't where they lived," I said. "It didn't look right. It didn't have that 'lived in' feel to it."

"Not to mention, they didn't have the right food," Ribs said. "It looked like they were living off takeout menus from what we found."

"Well, the good thing about going to Navigation is you can eat at Ninfa's if nothing pans out."

Ribs smiled. "You got that right, cuz. But don't worry, I'm sure we'll find something on one of them—either Ranza or George."

I grinned. then chuckled, then burst out laughing. The kind of laugh you couldn't stop. The kind that made your sides hurt.

"What the hell are you laughing about?" Ribs asked.

"I'm laughing because it's not pronounced 'George.' It's 'hor-he.'"

I then laughed some more. "Ribs, if you're going to

pretend to be Mexican, at least learn to pronounce the words right."

"Screw you," Ribs said. "Now I'm definitely not paying for lunch."

"Since when were you going to pay for lunch?"

"I'm not sure, but in case I did think about it, you can forget it. It won't happen."

We pulled up to Jorge's house and knocked on the door. A short, overweight woman answered. "Si?"
Ribs showed his badge and introduced us, then he asked if we could talk.

The woman showed us inside, where we sat at a small table in an eating area off the kitchen. Julie had told us notifications had already been made, so the difficult part had been handled, and thank God for that. I *hated* to do notifications.

After two hours of talking, we said goodbye to Jorge's wife, then got in the car and drove to Ranza's house. Ranza had no family, and his neighbors weren't helpful, so we headed back to the station to digest what we'd learned.

Jorge's wife told us he worked for somebody named Rodrigo, and she said she had heard Jorge talking to Ranza about a man in Mexico named Raul. Aside from that, she knew nothing.

From what she described regarding Jorge's work hours and habits, we assumed he worked as some kind of muscle, although his bank accounts didn't reflect the normal pattern of income from that.

"If these were the ones Raul used to take care of Pablo—

maybe even some others—why is he getting rid of them now?" Ribs asked. "And if they did something wrong, I sure as hell can't see it. They've had us chasing our dicks with nothing to show for it."

"Unless Raul or Rodrigo were tying up loose ends," I said.

"That's going to extremes, even for the cartels," Ribs said.

"Whether it's extreme or not makes no difference," I said. "Until you show me otherwise, I'm going with that as an explanation."

"If that's what we're going with, it means Rodrigo is the man we're after."

"Save the rest of your logic for Coop. We're going to need to fill her in when we get back."

"She's waiting," Cindy said as we came down the hall. Ribs walked in first, and we both took seats across from Coop's desk.

"Spit it out, gentlemen," she said.

"He's got the answers," I said, and gestured to Ribs.

Ribs took a deep breath and leaned forward. "Captain, the way we figure it, is Rodrigo, who must have been taking orders from Raul, had Jorge and Ranza (the two recently deceased) kill Pablo and probably Langer and McLaughlin. Unless I'm mistaken, they also killed the others on Fondren and Westheimer."

"And how did you arrive at this conclusion?" Coop asked.

"We sent photos of the dead men to the clerk at the rental agency, and he identified Ranza as the one who rented the gray Impala. If we assume from the ID that they were the ones who killed Pablo and then Langer, and by association, McLaughlin, it must have been on Rodrigo's orders."

"Or Raul's," I said.

"So why were they killed?" Coop asked.

Ribs looked at me, then back to Coop. "We don't have an answer for that yet; in fact, we have no idea."

"I suggested they may have done it to tie up loose ends, but that feels weak," I said.

"I agree it feels weak," Coop said, "So you need to find me something better. One thing is certain. The body count is growing, and the chief isn't happy."

"What the hell, Captain? We can't do anything about the body count," Ribs said.

Coop stared without blinking. "You can't do anything. You're a damn Homicide cop. If you don't solve the crimes, who will?"

"I didn't mean it like that, Captain. I meant—"

"I don't give a shit how you meant it. The fact that it came out of your mouth was bad enough. Now, get the hell out there and solve these murders before I have to assign them to someone competent."

"Don't worry, Captain," I said. "We'll get it done."

"I know you'll get it done eventually," Coop said. "But I need it done *now*."

"Fine," Ribs said. "Tell the chief to give us the resources, and we'll get it done, but if we do this by ourselves, it's going to take time. Like everything else."

Coop stood and glared. "Don't try to bullshit me, Delgado. I've given you everything you've asked for so far, even going to the extremes of providing first-class accommodations in San Antonio, not to mention expense vouchers that lieutenants don't get. So I don't want to hear any excuses about you not getting resources. Now, get the hell out there and find whoever is behind this. If you need something—ask. But no matter what, get the job done."

Ribs stood and snapped a salute. "Yes, sir, Captain."

Chapter Twenty-Four

FATHER BURNS HAS AN ACCIDENT

Houston, Texas

Rodrigo went to a location where he could speak privately, and then he dialed the phone. It was answered immediately.

"Mangua."

"Mangua, it's Rodrigo. I need something done. It has to be done soon, and it has to be done meticulously. And, of course, it has to be done *quietly*."

"Who do you want killed? And how do you want them killed?"

"No one. I want no one killed, but I do want someone, shall we say . . . roughed up."

"In that case, tell me who the target is and how bad you want them roughed up."

"The target is easy. He's a priest at St. Michael's on Sage Street. As to how bad I want him roughed up, nothing deadly, but enough to convince him of his wrongdoings."

A long pause followed, then Mangua spoke. "Rodrigo, you know I have done everything you've ever asked, but I've never done harm to men of the cloth."

"This is no ordinary man of the cloth. He has seen things he shouldn't have, and he knows things that are dangerous to know."

"But he is still a man of the cloth, no?"

Rodrigo worded what he said next carefully. "Yes, Mangua, he is a man of the cloth, but he doesn't deserve the normal respect a man of the cloth commands; besides, I'm afraid he will speak to the police about what he knows. He may have already spoken to them."

"He may not earn the normal respect, or any amount of respect, but I still don't hurt men of the cloth. Blame it on my mother or blame it on the nuns who taught me, but I don't do it. I don't hurt men of the cloth."

Rodrigo paced as he talked. "Mangua, suppose I told you that this man of the cloth is not like a typical man of the cloth."

"In what way?"

"He worked for Ortega, though he pretended to work for Raul. I think you know in our business that kind of loyalty, or should I say disloyalty, is not allowed. Usually it is punishable by death, but an exception is being made because of who he is."

Mangua laughed cynically. "Rodrigo, you and I have done a lot of business, but I find it difficult to believe a priest has been working for either Raul or Ortega."

"You should know by now that money drives everything, even the church."

"You're not lying? This man deserves a beating?"

"I was raised by nuns, Mangua. They taught me everything

I know. When I tell you this man deserves a beating, you can trust me. But you must follow instructions.”

“I'll think about it. Tell me the details.”

Mangua and two of his men sat in a late-model Ford at the side of the street. They had waited for almost two hours, and still the target hadn't shown himself.

“Do you think he'll come, Mangua?” Little Chappo asked.

“Why don't we just go get him?” Delano asked.

Mangua turned to look at them and scowled. “I'm beginning to think I brought the wrong men. One is impatient, and one is insolent. I tolerate neither.”

“I'm sorry,” Chappo said, and that sentiment was echoed by Delano.

“Good, now keep your eyes open and your mouths shut. If you do that, we will get along much better. And remember the orders. We are to rough up the priest, bruise him, maybe even break a bone or two, but nothing permanent, and definitely no death.”

“Understood,” Chappo said, and it was echoed by Delano.

Before long, a priest walked out of St. Michael's church. He walked toward the street, then across it.

A half a block down the street, a late-model Ford started up and sped in the priest's direction. When the car got close, it came to an abrupt halt, then the back doors flew open, and two men jumped out. One of them grabbed hold of the priest and pummeled him, starting at the head. The second man joined him, kicking the priest in the stomach and the head.

The priest fell to the ground, covering his head as he did, and all the while fighting back by kicking the men every chance he had.

After a moment, Mangua stepped out of the car and hollered, "Hurry up. We need to go."

The men kicked the priest a few more times, then dragged him into the street in front of the car. After that, they jumped in the back seat. "Let's go," Chappo yelled. "Hurry."

Mangua hit the gas, gunning the car, but the priest rolled to his left at the last moment, and the car rolled over top of him, barely avoiding crushing him.

As Mangua sped down the street, Delano looked out the back window. "Jesus Christ, you ran him over. You killed a priest."

Mangua knew that having a reputation for doing such a thing may be beneficial, but he didn't know if he wanted it. Besides, his reputation was good enough already. "I didn't kill a priest. Understand? I did nothing of the sort."

Sienna Mattis opened her door and walked to St. Michael's. She needed to say a few prayers for her sick uncle. As she neared the church, something moved in the street, close to the curb.

She ran toward it, thinking it was a dog, but as she got closer, it became clear it was a person. She knelt beside the person, then gasped. "Father Burns. Oh, my God, what happened?"

Blood covered his face, and he had a difficult time speaking or moving. "I . . . hospital." He held out a phone for her to use.

Sienna grabbed the phone and dialed 9-1-1. She stayed beside Father Burns until an ambulance arrived. By the time they took him away, a small crowd had gathered. She asked one of them if she could use his phone, then reported the incident to the police.

Two cop cars arrived at the scene within minutes. Sienna approached them, then told them what happened.

"I didn't see anything, but I found him in the street when I was on my way to church."

"And you didn't see any people or cars leaving the scene?" one of the cops asked.

She shook her head. "Nothing. I might not have seen Father Burns if he hadn't moved."

Two more cops got out of the other patrol car and walked around. One of them knelt by the curb where Sienna indicated she found Father Burns.

"He was right here? No one moved him?"

"I was afraid to touch him, he looked so bad," Sienna said. "I think the ambulance techs took a picture though. I saw the flash from the camera."

The first cop on the scene looked to the pair of newly arrived officers. "How about you two visit him at the hospital and see if he's able to tell you anything. While you do that, we'll stay here and canvass the neighborhood."

"Will do," the officer said.

"And don't worry about the paperwork on the front side; we'll handle that. You just turn in your report from the time you get to the hospital."

Captain Cooper sipped from a cup of coffee as she walked down the hall toward her office. She turned the corner and saw someone standing by Cindy's desk.

Despite her curiosity, she continued at her normal pace until she stood next to the man. "Good morning," Coop said. "May I help you?"

"You may or may not recognize me, Captain, but I'm your

new mayor, Sonny Tubbs." He reached out to shake hands. "Let's go into your office and chat."

Coop suspected this was not going to be a pleasant visit, but she led Mayor Tubbs into the office and took a seat. "How may I help you, Mayor?"

"I just read a report about a priest who had been brutally beaten and left to die in the street. A priest beaten—in *my* city. What the hell is going on?"

Coop nodded. "I just heard about that on my way in, Mayor. I'm not up to speed on what happened or the status on it, but I promise, I'll find out."

Tubbs sat back and thought before he spoke. "Captain, I understand that large cities have problems as they grow even larger. I understand there are drug problems and many other problems, and as a result of those issues, I understand there will be murders. But let me make this *very* clear. I can tolerate a certain number of junkies being killed. I can put up with drug dealers dying. But I *will not* abide the killing of police or men of God."

"Sir, I understand completely. I'll get my best men on it."

"Are these the same men who are looking into the other priest's murder?"

Coop hesitated, but then nodded. "It is, Mayor. They're good detectives, and we think they're on the right track."

The mayor stood and leaned on Coop's desk. "Then I suggest you get them whoever they need as back up—as much as they need—and you find out who the hell did this, and you hang the son of a bitch."

"Yes, sir," Coop said. "I'll get it done right away."

My phone rang, and I picked it up. "Cataldi."

"Cataldi, this is the captain. I don't care if you're in the middle of having sex. I need your ass down here now. And don't worry about calling Delgado. I'll get hold of him when I hang up."

"I can leave right away, Captain, but tell me what happened?"

"We've got another priest hurt. This one's not dead—not yet, but he's in the hospital, and from what I heard, he's bad."

"Shit. Who is it?"

"A priest named Burns from St. Michael's. Isn't he the one you spoke to?"

"He is, Coop. Son of a bitch. Okay. I'm on my way."

I grabbed my keys, kissed Marissa goodbye, and raced for the door. "Gotta go. They got another priest," I said. "He's not dead, but he *is* in the hospital."

"Call me when you know something," she said. "I'll be with Connie, but I have my phone."

WHO ORDERED THIS?

Houston, Texas

Ribs and I waited in Coop's office, drinking the coffee Cindy had gotten us and wondering where Coop was.

"She's normally in before this," Ribs said.

"Hell, she's the one who called," I said.

We sat around a few more minutes, and just as we finished our coffee, Coop walked through the door. She carried a mug of hot tea and wore a sour face.

"I'll bet you're surprised you beat me in, aren't you?"

"We are," Ribs said, "and we demand an explanation."

Coop laughed. "Screw you, Delgado. Now sit back and listen."

"We're listening, Captain, despite what you see from my partner. Now tell us what you've got," I said.

Coop leaned forward and looked at both of us. "I told you I had a plan, and I've now cemented that plan."

"Care to share?" Ribs asked.

Coop nodded. "The sharing part is easy. The execution is what will determine if we're successful."

"We won't know what to do if you don't tell us about it, so let's hear it," I said.

"You won't like this, but you're going to have to live with it," Coop said. "I went to Cybil for help, and she pulled through with a plan."

"You're right that I'm not happy about it coming from Cybil, but let's hear it anyway."

Coop stood and walked to our side of her desk. She sat facing us. "No matter what you may think of Cybil, she has connections. The fact is, since Rusty died, her connections have gotten stronger."

"We're in, Coop. We'll go with what we've got. All we want is to see that whoever is responsible for these murders is punished."

Coop smiled. "Then sit back and listen up. Cybil is damn good friends with the mayor of San Antonio and the governor of Texas. Between the two of them, we can exert enough pressure on the Boswells to make sure they either bust the drug dealers responsible or show that they are complicit. The bottom line is, if the Boswells come through, we get the dealers, and if they don't, we get the Boswells. It's a win-win situation."

"And what about here?" Ribs asked.

"You and Gino have it covered, don't you? If not, you better get your shit together."

"We've got our shit together," I said. "Just tell us what you think we need to do to move this forward."

"What we've got to do is simple. We've got to put pressure on the dealers, and we've got a priest who *had to* have seen something; they beat him nearly to death. You don't get beaten that badly and not see anything."

I looked at Coop while squinting. "So you're saying to lean on the priest?"

"What I'm saying is he knows something, and I want you to find out what it is. If you have to lean on him to get it, do so. Our investigation here was close to a dead-end; now we've got a new thread to start anew. I'll get things kicked off in San Antonio while you two get your asses to the hospital and talk to that priest. And don't leave without getting something we can act on."

San Antonio

The mayor of San Antonio walked into Captain Boswell's office with no advance notice. Boswell's secretary didn't even have time to warn him.

"Boswell," he said, "We need to talk."

Boswell stood, smiled, and extended his hand in greeting. "Mayor, what can I do for you?"

"There's a lot you can do for me," the mayor said, "but what I need is for you to follow orders, and that means do *exactly* as I say. Nothing more and nothing less."

"And I'm sure you're going to tell me what those orders are," Boswell said. "I'm all ears."

"I'll tell you in no uncertain terms," the mayor said. "You're going to send a half-dozen men to the Hotel Emma, stake out Lanza's room, and arrest him as soon as he shows his face. And don't try telling me that he wasn't there. We've already confirmed he is staying at the hotel."

The mayor pointed a finger at Boswell. "And don't tell me you don't know Lanza because I know you do. Furthermore, you will assign *every* officer you have to all known drug corners and then arrest every drug dealer you see. *No one* is to be released. I want every one of them in a cell until I say differently. Me and no one else. Is *that* understood?"

The phone rang, and Boswell picked it up. "Captain Boswell."

"Boswell, this is the governor. Put the phone on speaker."

Boswell put it on speaker and sat back.

"Mayor, can you hear me?"

"I can, sir."

"All right, Boswell, listen closely. I am ordering you to do exactly as the mayor instructs, and I want it done tonight. If Lanza or his men appear to have been warned, you'll be fired and will likely go to jail; in fact, if anything goes wrong, you will go to jail. Is that clear?"

Boswell gulped. "Yes, sir. I understand."

"Good, then get moving, and know that we'll both be watching."

The mayor walked out of the office, and when he was gone, Boswell picked up the phone to dial. He punched in the first few numbers of Hotel Emma, then paused and hung up. It would be his career if he did that."

Boswell leaned back and gave it thought, then he dialed his lieutenants. "Manko, we need three units at Hotel Emma right away for a stakeout. And we're going to need every available unit for a major sweep of all drug corners. And this is all to be done quietly, Manko. Not a word to anyone."

"But, sir—"

"There are no buts, Manko. Do it."

Boswell hung up and dialed Dorfman and issued the same instructions, then he sat back and waited. He had an urge to warn Lanza, but he knew he couldn't; instead, he used a burner phone he had stored in the top drawer of his desk and called Ortega. "Señor Ortega, this is Boswell."

"*Capitan*, how can I help?"

"I am risking everything, but my superiors are planning to raid Señor Lanza at the hotel, and I believe they're doing it tonight."

"How sure are you of this information?"

"The mayor of San Antonio just left here, and the fucking governor just called. Does that give you an idea of how sure I am?"

"Are you saying it's too late for me to do anything?" Ortega asked.

"It's past too late," Boswell said. "I only called in case you could get some paperwork out. Lanza is long gone. He's going down, and there's nothing you can do to stop it."

"Then I have nothing to worry about," Ortega said. "All

paperwork is sent to me daily and then erased. Lanza is on his own. But tell me, *Capitan*, who is behind this?"

"I'm sure it's a couple of Houston cops named Cataldi and Delgado. They're the ones you want."

"Don't leap to conclusions, *Capitan*. I never said I want them. I simply want to know what made them decide to pressure my operations at this time? And I need to make sure they don't bother my other operations."

"If you plan to stop them, I suggest you get busy. I met these two, and they don't seem like the type that you can scare off. And I'd guess you definitely can't buy them off."

"Thank you, *Capitan*. Now, I must 'get busy,' as you say."

Burk and Nickles waited while the undercover officers slowly gathered around them. "In case anyone has questions, we're here for one reason only. To bust Ortega's operations and chase his ass out of town."

"I thought we busted up his operations a few days ago," a rookie cop said.

"We did," Burk said. "But then it was only a few low-level dealers; besides, even it had been big, he's had an opportunity to re-supply and bring more dope in, so we need to do this all over again." Burk smiled as he stared at each of his men.

"But this time, we're doing it big time. And we're going to keep doing it until the mayor tells us not to. Like I said, we're going to push Ortega out of the city."

"That may be more difficult than expected," Sanchez said. "I've been working Narcotics for ten years, and I can tell you, Ortega has a lot of juice in this town; hell, he has juice in a lot more cities than you'd like to think. I'd be willing to bet he already knows about our plans to raid his operations."

Burk looked at Sanchez, then the others. "It doesn't much matter if Ortega knows we're coming. His top man and his street men are already in trouble. We'll soon have Lanza arrested, and we've got most of the others under surveillance, just waiting for them to screw up. There's no getting out for them. In fact, Sanchez, I want you over the south side now. You're in charge of that operation. If anyone has a problem with it, they're to call me."

"Yes, sir. I'm on my way."

~

Shortly after Sanchez left, Burk got on the radio. "Attention all units at Hotel Emma. All units. It's time to move. Repeat, it's time to move."

~

Burk's undercover men waited for Lanza to exit his room. They tailed him down to the restaurant, and after he ordered, they moved in and cuffed him. Burk clamped the cuffs tightly. "Señor Lanza, you are under arrest. You have the right to remain silent. Anything you . . ."

" . . . say may be used against you. Detective, I know the law. I also know I have the right to a phone call, so take me where I can exercise that right."

Burk handed a phone to Lanza. "You can have your phone call any time you want, sir. But I insist on one of us accompanying you."

Lanza walked ten feet away, then he dialed the phone and

waited. When no one answered, he dialed another number. "Si, señor. Find Señor O. Tell him that Lanza needs to talk. Tell him it's important."

After a moment, the man returned to the line. "Señor O is not available. Do you have a message for him?"

"Yeah, I've got a message for him. Tell him Lanza is in San Antonio and needs help. Tell him he needs to hurry."

Burk drove Lanza downtown and put him in the interview room.

"I need to make another call," Lanza said. "I never connected with the first one."

When the phone call ended, Burk took his phone back, then he let Lanza sit by himself for a couple of hours. Once he felt Lanza had given his situation enough thought, Burk entered the interview room, notepad in hand. "Are you ready to talk now? If not, I can give you more time."

Lanza shrugged. "More time won't solve anything. I'm waiting for someone, so I think I'll continue waiting."

Burk smiled. "Don't wait too long, Lanza; besides, I have a feeling your friend, Ortega, won't be coming. That is who you called, isn't it?"

"I don't know anyone named Ortega, and who I called is none of your business. Your only concern right now is figuring out what you can charge me with. You found no drugs. I know because I didn't have any. You found no money. I know because I had less than a hundred dollars. And I definitely had no guns because I don't use guns." Lanza lit a cigarette and grinned. "As far as I can tell, Detective, you have nothing to charge me with."

"Nothing to charge you with? You've got to be shitting

me? I can charge you with any fucking thing I want. And trust me, whatever I charge you with, I'll make stick. I'm going to make sure you take the full weight of what I bring down on you. And no matter what you believe, Ortega isn't getting you out of this."

Lanza shrugged again. "If he doesn't, he doesn't. There's nothing for you to hold me on. I've done nothing wrong."

"We'll see about that," Burk said, then he turned to the cop with him. "Lock him up. If anyone wants to see him, call me first."

The officer locked up Lanza, then he joined Burk, and they raided every street corner where dealers operated. Before the night was over, almost a dozen had been busted and locked up."

As they processed all the dealers, Burk grabbed a low-level one and took him aside. "What's your name?"

"Nester."

"Nester, you've got two choices. You can do as I ask, or spend ten years in prison."

"I'll do the dime," Nester said.

"Really? You haven't heard what I asked yet, and you're willing to do ten years? You must like dicks up your ass."

Burk waited for an answer, but when none was forthcoming, he continued. "Well? Do you like dicks up your ass? Is that what you want? If it is, I'm sure we can arrange that."

Nester looked over his shoulder, then back at Burk. "All right, just for grins, tell me what you want."

"What I want is easy," Burk said. "Go back to Juarez, or whatever shithole place Ortega is hiding in, and tell him he's done in San Antonio. Tell him Lanza is gone, his operations are finished, and his support from Boswell is over. He can't expect Boswell to help him anymore."

Nester held back a smile. "If that's all you want, I can do it, but I must tell you, this isn't over by any means. Lanza will be out in days, if not sooner, and his men won't be held for much longer. As to Boswell, he'll have your ass before dinner time tomorrow."

"Just do what I asked, Nester. If you do, you've got a free pass. If you don't, you'll be going to that place where the dicks roam free. Understand?"

Nester lowered his head. "I understand. And rest assured that Ortega will get your message."

Burk nodded to the guards at the door. "Let him go and escort him to the airport. See that he gets on a flight to somewhere in Mexico."

Chapter Twenty-Six

QUESTIONS FOR A PRIEST

As we drove to the hospital, Ribs talked nonstop. Not that his incessant talking was unusual, but he seemed anxious as hell. He was like a college grad on their first job interview.

"Ribs, calm down. He's a damn priest; he's not Jesus."

"Where the hell are we going anyway? Where did they take him?"

"He's at Memorial Hermann on Gessner at I–10. It's only a few minutes from here."

We got to the hospital within minutes and were shown in to see Father Burns right away. He lay in a bed with a cast on his right arm, and bandages covered his face and head. He looked to be asleep when we entered.

"Father Burns. Father Burns," I said in a whisper.

When he didn't respond, I walked up and tapped his good arm lightly. "Father Burns, are you able to answer a few questions?" I asked.

Burns opened his eyes and looked at me, then over at Ribs. "Detectives, excuse me," he said as he tried to sit up straighter.

"Don't try to get up, Father," Ribs said. "We can talk while you rest."

He raised his bed a few inches, then settled in to talk. "How can I help?"

"We're trying to find out who did this to you," Ribs said.

I leaned forward and asked, "And we'd like to know *why* they did it? It isn't often someone beats a priest. In fact, I don't think I've ever seen it. I've seen cops beaten, firemen, soldiers, and others, but I haven't seen a priest beaten."

"I'll do what I can to help," Father Burns said as he tried to sit up straighter.

"I came out of the rectory and was walking to a parishioner's house, a young woman with several young children."

"And why were you going there?" I asked.

"She likes to go to Confession every week, but sometimes she doesn't have anyone to watch the children. She has three of them below the age of four."

She called the rectory and asked if I would be near her house, and if so, if I would be able to stop by and hear her Confession.

"I hadn't planned on being over there, but it wasn't far, so I told her I'd be by that evening. That's where I was going when it happened."

"What *did* happen?" Ribs asked.

"As I said, I was on my way from the rectory, and, no

sooner had I stepped into the street, a car sped up from the south. I stopped walking to let it go past, but it screeched to a halt, then two men got out and beat me."

"Did you get a look at the men? Or the car?"

Father Burns shook his head. "It was already dark, so identifying the men proved difficult, and as I already mentioned, I'm not good with cars."

"Did you get the color of the car? Anything?"

He shook his head again. "It was too dark to tell the color," he said, and reached for a cup of water on the table near him.

I handed it to him and then replaced it when he finished. "But just thinking on the color tells me something," he said. "If it was too dark to distinguish a color, it must have been a dark color. I would think that even at night, a light shade would be easy to tell."

Ribs nodded. "You're right about that, Father. Anything else?"

"Now that I'm telling the tale, some specifics are coming to light. It was a four-door car. I know because I remember the back doors opening, and the men getting out."

"How many men were there?" I asked.

"Two," he said. "One got out of each side."

"So there were at least three men altogether," Ribs said. "Someone had to be driving."

Burns grew more animated as he nodded vigorously. "You're right, Detective. I hadn't thought of that. I don't recall three men, but there had to be that many or more since two got out of the back."

"What else?" I asked.

"The men rushed over, and I remember thinking, 'What

do these men want?' just before the first punch landed. After that, I felt one blow after another until I fell to the ground."

Father Burns reached for his water again and sipped from the straw. "Once I hit the ground, they kicked me repeatedly. All I remember is covering my face, or trying to, then they kicked my stomach and back."

"Did you get an idea of how tall the men were? Or did you notice their hair color? Were they white, black, or Latino?"

Father Burns shook his head again. "I didn't see anything. When I hit the ground, I closed my eyes and covered my face. All I remember is the pain. I wanted to cry, but I recall thinking of how much Jesus must have hurt when His tormentors did all those things to Him, and that provided strength."

"How long did it last?" I asked.

"It seemed as if it had been hours, but I'm sure it was only minutes, if that. Even though my eyes were closed, I recall them dragging me toward the center of the street and leaving me. They got back in the car, and I heard the engine start, then the headlights came on, and I saw the car moving toward me."

"You mean they were coming straight at you?" I asked.

Father Burns nodded. "I remember specifically thinking, 'They're going to run me over.' I managed to roll to my left, and it was enough so that I fit into the space between the wheels."

"Then what?" Ribs asked.

"After they left, I was able to continue rolling until I got close to the curb. I couldn't stand, but I lay there praying for God to send help. And He answered. Not much time passed before some kind lady came by and gave aid."

"And that's it?" I asked.

"Until I woke up here," Father Burns said. "I don't even recall the ambulance ride."

"If that's all you recall about the beating, Father, let's see if we can focus on the reasons why it may have happened."

Ribs stepped closer to the hospital bed. Originally, he stayed far away, almost as if he was afraid to go closer. "Father, before we move on, I have a question."

"Go on," he said.

"What made them stop beating you and drag you into the street? No cars came, or at least none stopped. And it doesn't seem as if anyone walked by. Surely they'd have stopped to help."

"I don't know why, Detective. I hadn't given it any thought until you asked. Perhaps they wanted to get it over with and run me over. I don't know. I'm just thankful they stopped when they did. I don't know if I could have taken much more of a beating."

"Why do you think they beat you? Have you done anything that may have offended anyone?"

Father Burns shook his head again. "I've done nothing. I haven't witnessed any crime, not since the one you spoke to me about, and I haven't heard any confession from anyone who has done any wrongdoings of significance." Father Burns smiled. "I can tell you that much without breaking the sanctity of confession."

"You *must* have done something," Ribs said. "You may not have recognized them, but they had to have recognized you, and that means they were beating you for a reason."

"And not just beating you," I said. "If they tried to run over you with the car, it was an attempt to kill you. So, whatever you did to piss them off couldn't have been a trivial matter."

"Detective, you can ask as many times as you want and in as many ways as you want, but it won't change my answer. I have *no* idea why someone would want to do this to me. And I definitely can't imagine who would want to do it."

"Father, I know we've gone over this before, but I believe it has to be connected to the murder you witnessed," I said.

"I realize that logic would indicate that," Father Burns said, "but I don't see why. I did whatever damage I could to those people when I turned in my evidence, but that was a while ago."

"Did you tell anyone you called in evidence?" Ribs asked. "Because if you didn't tell anyone, I can't see how the killers knew. The tip line is anonymous. Your name and number should have never been associated with the crime."

Father Burns lifted his head up. "I never gave out my name, and I specifically recall blocking the caller ID before I called, so they wouldn't have had my name or number."

"That makes it more puzzling," I said.

"Despite that," Father Burns said, "it has to be connected some way. After all, Arlen and Father Tom were both killed, and we can all be tied to witnessing the murder in one way or another."

"But how would anyone know that?" Ribs asked. "If you didn't tell anyone, how did the killers find out?"

Burns shook his head. "It will go down as a mystery. I can't imagine Father Tom or Arlen saying a word to anyone, so I don't know."

"All right, Father, we're going to figure this out, but for now, we need to get going so we can investigate further."

Father Burns tried making the sign of the cross, but it didn't come off well. "Go with God, my sons."

~

As we walked out of the hospital, I turned to Ribs and said, "What do you think, partner? Did he shoot straight with us?"

Ribs smiled. "I know you will discount what I say, but yes, I thought he shot straight. In fact, what he said about Langer or McLaughlin not saying a word to anyone got me thinking. Langer definitely told his wife, who you may recall, is a part of the family of cops in San Antonio who seem to be knee-deep in shit with the drug cartels. If that's not motive, nothing is."

I nodded. "It is, and it isn't, Ribs. Remember, it was Ortega's drugs that were found on Pablo, then again on Harris's case, and finally on Jorge and Ranza. If these people were selling drugs for Ortega, why would he kill them?"

Ribs opened the door, bringing us into the lobby. "I was already wondering something similar," he said. "We found Pablo with Ortega's drugs, but we also found Ortega's drugs on Jorge and Ranza, the men who we're pretty sure killed him, which all leads me to ask what the hell is going on?"

"Exactly," I said. "I can see Jorge killing Langer *and* the priest if he thought they'd be witnesses, but somebody killed Jorge. If we assume Jorge killed Pablo, then the question is *who* killed Jorge and *why*. I mean, I know Jorge and Ranza were just street muscle, but I doubt a vengeful father or a junkie killed them. This was a pro, and that means the orders had to come from high up."

"The only scenario I can think of is that Raul had Jorge kill Pablo, Langer, and McLaughlin, then he found out that

Jorge was selling Ortega's drugs as well, so he had him killed." Ribs shrugged. "I know it sounds crazy, but it's all I can think of."

As we walked across the parking lot, I clicked the remote to unlock the car doors. "It's all we've got for now, Ribs, so let's see what else we can find out."

Chapter Twenty-Seven

THE NEWS IS UPSETTING

Dallas, Texas

The governor had issued orders similar to those in San Antonio for Dallas as well as Austin. Shortly after dusk, police from the local units, the state police, and even the DEA swarmed all known drug corners and any suspected stash houses simultaneously, not giving time for a warning of any kind. By the end of the night, almost three dozen high-end arrests had been made, and more than twelve kilos of heroin had been seized in Dallas alone, and all of it was marked with Ortega's El Lobo label.

Austin, Texas

The results of the sweep in Austin mirrored that of Dallas. Dozens of arrests and more than a few kilos seized. No matter how much money the cartels had, this was going to hurt. It was a major pinch on the drugs, for sure, but arresting that many men also had to hurt the operations. If Ortega hoped to retain a good reputation, he would have to pay for legal defense—which didn't come cheap—as well as spend a lot of money taking care of his employee's families.

Ciudad Juarez, Mexico

Nester got off the plane in Juarez and took a car to see Ortega. "Detective Burk sent me to see you. He said Lanza was going down and so was Boswell. He also threatened your operations in the city."

"And how did you get out?" Ortega asked.

"He sent me as a messenger," Nester said. "It was do this or go to prison for ten years."

Ortega drew a gun and shot Nester in the head. "You should have taken the ten years," he said.

San Antonio

Boswell drove home, heading west on State Highway 16, then left on Ranch Parkway. As he sat at the first traffic signal, a man opened the passenger door and got in. He pointed a gun at Boswell. "Keep driving," he said.

Boswell glanced over at him, then moved ahead when the light turned green. "I didn't say anything about his operations. I never even mentioned his name."

"You didn't know about it beforehand?"

Boswell shook his head. "I didn't know a thing. Not until the mayor came to my office, then the governor called. Somebody with a lot of juice did this. A *lot* of juice."

"You know they'll find problems with your books once they start looking."

"I'm clean there," Boswell said. "I've had two accountants keep them clean."

"Were they good accountants?" the man asked.

"They *are* good accountants," Boswell said. "I have used them for years."

"Pull to the shoulder of the road," the man said. He handed Boswell a small notepad and pen. "Write their names and numbers down."

Boswell pulled to the side, turned in his seat, and stared. "What do you need their names for? I told you they were good."

"We want to make sure they don't talk," the man said.

"There is nothing for them to talk about. They don't know anything."

"And I'm to make sure it stays that way," he said, then he shot Boswell three times. "Just like I am to make sure you say nothing."

He wiped the car clean, then got out and into the car that had pulled up behind them. He got in and nodded to the driver. "Let's move. It's done."

"What now?"

He held up the notepad. "We have two more visits, then we'll be through."

Ciudad Juarez, Mexico

Ortega hung up the phone and called in his top lieutenants. "Where are we with business in Dallas and El Paso?"

Eliondo stepped forward with his head lowered. "Dallas is bad, and so is Austin. The police hit them just like they did San Antonio. But El Paso is good. Nothing happened there.

Things are good." Eliondo said. "Nothing different from before."

Ortega stared at Eliondo and held his gaze for a long time. "Nothing different? Do you mean to tell me that all the money we've spent in that city has been for 'nothing different'?"

"No, it's just that—"

Ortega pointed at Eliondo, then walked over and jabbed his chest. "We have spent millions in bribes. We are spending tens of thousands per month for apartment rent, and we have bought a half dozen cars. I haven't even mentioned the money spent for smuggling. If you believe I invested all my money so that our market share stays the same, you must be disobeying my orders and sampling your own product."

Eliondo shook his head. "Ortega, you know I don't touch no drugs. I'm as clean as a newborn. And don't worry about increasing product. We're just starting."

Ortega pulled Eliondo close and patted his back as he embraced him. "You shouldn't worry so much, my friend. You have two months to get something done before I kill you. Two *full* months."

Ortega let go of Eliondo and faced the others standing in the rest of the room.

"We have just had major disruptions in San Antonio, Dallas, and Austin, although El Paso is safe as our friend, Eliondo, reminded me. There are a lot of people who are going to pay for these mistakes, but if someone wants to earn a slight reprieve or their role in any of these mishaps, all they need to do is provide me contact information for one of these two Houston cops—Delgado or Cataldi. The more information I get on them, the more favor you will earn."

Hildago stepped up. "Let me make two phone calls, and I'll have that information, Ortega."

Ortega grabbed a phone from a canvas bag sitting on a nearby table, and he handed it to Hidalgo. "Make the call, but the information better be correct. Reprieves can easily turn into punishment."

Hildalgo took the phone and left the room. It took him four calls to get the information he needed, but he returned to the room wearing a smile, not the look of a man who expected punishment of any kind.

"You have what I need?" Ortega asked.

"I do," Hildalgo said. "I've written down the names as well as the number of the station. There is minor familial information as well."

Ortega scowled. "I'm not an animal, Hildalgo. I would never hurt a man's family, and you should know that. I may threaten to do such things, but I would never do it."

Ortega accepted a cook drink from a servant, then after he left, Ortega addressed Hildalgo again. "What are we waiting for? Get them on the phone."

Hildalgo gulped. "Sir, it is too late right now. We may have to wait until tomorrow."

Ortega nodded. "Be sure to be here early. I want you here when I call them."

———————————

A STRATEGY GOING FORWARD

Houston, Texas

Ribs and I strategized all the way to the station. The problem was, we still didn't know where to begin. All we had were a handful of dead bodies and a nearly dead priest.

"What the hell do we do going forward?" Ribs asked. "We've talked to Harris and Langkon. We've even talked to Tip and Connie. If the six of us can't figure it out, we don't stand a chance by ourselves."

Ribs parked close to the entrance, and we went upstairs to our desks. Julie met us at the top of the stairs and handed us a slip of paper. "A man called for you, and he asked that you call him back when you can."

"Who was it?" I asked.

Julie shrugged. "I don't know. He just called and asked for Detective Cataldi. When I told him you weren't in, he gave me his number and asked you to call."

I stuffed the slip of paper into my top pocket and headed toward my desk. "C'mon, Ribs, let's call this guy, and get the mystery of who it is over with."

⁓

R ibs got us coffee, then we closed the door and made the call. It rang three times before anyone answered. "Olla."

"Who is this?" I asked.

After a few seconds of silence, someone said, "Who the hell is this?"

"This is Gino Cataldi. Someone called this number."

"Hold on. I'll get him."

I waited for almost half a minute, then someone picked up the line. "Señor Cataldi. My name is Ortega."

⁓

A t first, he caught me off guard. I certainly wasn't expecting him to call. "Ortega from Juarez?"

"Is there another?"

"Probably none that would be calling me, so tell me what you want, Ortega from Juarez."

"I understand you've been busting my balls in San Antonio and Houston and other cities. I want to know why. Is it money? Is someone not paying off people down the chain? Fill me in so I know. I can't make things right unless I know what I have to do."

"The first thing you have to know, is you can't kill well-respected citizens in my city. And you definitely can't kill priests. Killing a priest is like killing a cop."

"A priest? Someone killed a priest, and you think it was me?"

"Ortega, don't try to fuck with me. Someone killed a priest, and we *know* it was you. All the evidence points to you. We even found drugs packaged with your stamp."

There was a long pause before Ortega spoke again. "Detective, first let me clear the air by saying any attempt to trace this will be futile. The call has been forwarded and misdirected to the point that all your people will get is that I am somewhere in Mexico. And I will tell you as much right now. I would rather you focus your attention on clearing my good name."

"Your good name? Now I know you're shitting me." I said.

"I know you may think what I said is garbage, but I have a reputation to keep. I deal drugs—true. I kill people—true. I do other horrible things—true. I admit to all those faults—but I *do not* harm priests. I have been to church every Sunday since I was six years old—all but two. Once I stayed home with a high fever, and once I was shot by one of El Cinque's men."

I wanted to call him a liar, to say he was full of shit, but what he said rang true. It was evident in his voice. "Why did you call?"

"I called to tell you my men are not responsible for any attack on the church. If I find out any are, I will send you their ears, eyes, and tongue." Ortega laughed. "I would send the whole head, but with shipping rates it gets expensive."

"And your suggestion is what?" I asked.

"I suggest you continue to look into this, but know that I will also look into this. If I find information that leads to Texas, I will have someone contact you. If the information leads to Mexico, I will take care of it myself. And rest assured, my punishment will be more severe."

"Who would do these things and also plant your drugs on the dead bodies?"

"Obviously, someone who is trying to frame me. Someone who wants to bring the pressure of law enforcement on me. I think it points to no one other than Raul and his top enforcer Rodrigo."

"And you expect me to just believe you?"

"No, I don't. But are you a man who can look another in the eye and tell if they're lying?"

"I like to think so."

"Then I invite you to meet me in Juarez. Unfortunately, I cannot come to Texas, but I offer you safe passage to Mexico to meet me. I will answer any question you have about this, and you can judge for yourself."

I thought for a moment, then decided. The fact that he offered to do this convinced me it wasn't him. I believed him. "Ortega, I'm going to pass for now, but I might take you up on it at another time. In the meantime, I'll do what you suggested and focus on finding out who did this. If you think of any leads, make sure to help me clear your name."

"I will, Detective. I most assuredly will. Thank you for your time."

I hung up the phone and looked at Ribs, who shook his head.

"You believe that bullshit?" he asked.

I nodded. "Actually, Ribs, I did. I don't think he'd have called if he was guilty. Besides, he sounded sincere when he spoke about the priests."

"I don't know, Gino. That guy's scum."

"*Scum* I agree with, but Ortega's not stupid. If he killed these people, why would he leave his own drugs to be found?"

"I don't know," Ribs said.

"Nobody was around. His men could have cleaned up the scene and taken the drugs. It was evidence, not to mention a good deal of money."

Ribs nodded. "I guess you're right. If it wasn't Ortega, and if we presume it was a drug dealer, it would logically point to Raul."

"Raul or one of the others," I said. "Though Raul would be the first choice since he has such a strong presence in Houston."

"And we know he's making a move into Dallas. If he disrupts Ortega in San Antonio, Dallas, and Austin, that takes Ortega's focus off Raul, at least momentarily."

"I think we need to find out more from Burns. Right now, he's our only witness. The only one alive, that is."

Ribs nodded. "I agree, but the good Father seemed tapped out on information. What else do you think he can give us?"

"I'm not sure. I think there's a *lot* he's not giving us. I don't know what that is yet, but I know it's something."

Ribs rolled down the window and breathed the fresh air. "I don't know what isn't adding up, but it's something. There's no way the good Father should have been able to get away from two people who were beating him—especially not two people who one of the drug lords use to do hits. These people aren't the kind that a priest, let alone a sedentary one, should be able to get away from."

"I'm with you on both counts, Ribs. I don't think he should have been able to get away from them, but at the same time, he didn't. They dragged him to the middle of the damn street and planned on running him over. I know that technically that constitutes 'getting away,' but at the same time, it's not."

"Cuz, you know I've been a defender of the priests since we started this case, but I can't ignore the obvious. When was the last time you heard of muscle from the cartel failing to do their job? Usually, they do overkill."

"Maybe it's time we looked into Father Burns more. Call Julie and ask her to begin a thorough background check."

"You sure?" Ribs asked. "Some people resent looking into religious types."

I laughed. "Ribs, not many people are like you, and Julie is a trooper. She'd look into the president if we asked her. Hell, if we asked nicely, she'd look into the pope."

Ribs disconnected his phone and put it in his pocket. "She didn't answer. I'll call her in the morning."

"Bullshit," I said. "If we can't sleep. She can't sleep. I know you've got her home number, so call her now and ask her to get started."

"Christ, Gino. She's got kids. She's a single mom. Cut her some slack. We can wait till she gets in, then we'll ask her to get on it."

I sighed. "All right, Ribs. I'll let this one slide, but we need to make sure we get an early start."

"An early start is no problem for me," Ribs said. "The kids get me up early anyway. You're the lazy ass."

RAUL DEMANDS ANSWERS

Monterrey, Mexico

Raul paced back and forth on his patio. "Where the hell is Rodrigo?" he asked. "He was supposed to be here. Has anyone heard from him?"

"I haven't talked to him in more than a week," Felipe said. "And the last time I did, he was having troubles in Houston. A lot of murders, if I remember."

Raul raised his voice. "I know *all about* the murders," he said. "That's one of the reasons I called the meeting. We've lost several dealers, some muscle, and worst of all—a wealthy citizen and a priest. A goddamn priest!"

He paced more without talking, then he faced the group and yelled. "Do you know the pressure that will bring down on us? Killing a priest is worse than killing a cop. We can't tolerate this shit."

Just then, Raul's phone rang. "Hello," he said.

"Raul, it's Rodrigo."

"Rodrigo, where the hell are you? And what's going on in Houston?"

"Raul, I'm in the hospital. I was attacked the other night, and they almost killed me. I checked into the hospital under a different name, but I doubt it will hold up forever. If they check on it, they'll find cracks."

"Who did it?" Raul asked.

"I don't know yet, but I will. And when I find out, I will kill the sons of bitches. That much, I promise you. They won't get away with this. I'll make them regret not having finished the job."

"You have no idea who did it?"

"I have an idea, but it is only that. Nothing that's proof."

"Then tell me your idea, and we'll look into it also," Raul said.

"I'm pretty sure it was Ortega, but I can't swear to it."

"What makes you think it was Ortega?" Raul asked.

"When I was lying on the ground, one of the men swung a bat at my head. I'm sure he thought it was the killing blow, and it probably would have been, except I rolled to the side at the last minute, and the bat struck the sidewalk before hitting my head. But just as the man swung, he said, 'This is for Pablo' and that told me it was probably Ortega. Remember, Pablo carried Ortega's drugs."

"Goddamn," Raul said. "Ortega will pay for this. All right, Rodrigo. Take time to heal. I will seek retribution for what was done, and rest assured, it will be a just and equal punishment."

"Raul, I appreciate it, but give me some time, and I can handle this myself."

"There is no need, my friend. And there should be no

time. Justice must be served quickly. Ortega will pay many times over for his breach of the rules."

"Then I am indebted to you, Raul. You have my thanks."

Raul disconnected the phone line, then turned to the rest of the group. "For all of you who didn't grasp what was being said, that was Rodrigo on the phone. Someone tried to kill him, and we believe it was Ortega. What that means is that all neutrality with Ortega is off. It is no longer a matter of allowing each other to function. If you run across any of his men, kill them. If any of his men approach you about jointly working a territory, kill them. And if any of them ask for a truce, kill them. From this day forward, there is no peace."

"Is this just for Houston?" Felipe asked.

"It is for everywhere," Raul said. "Dallas, San Antonio, and Austin as well as Houston. This is war."

"You realize that will mean war in Mexico also," Roberto said.

Raul nodded. "I realize. It will mean war in Monterrey, in Laredo, and in Juarez. It will mean war among families and friends, and it will mean a lot of bloodshed. So be it. Ortega is the one who started it. Let him be the one who feels the first bullet."

Juarez, Mexico

Hildalgo pushed through the door, in a rush to see Ortega. "You look to be in a hurry," Ortega said.

"I just got news from a contact in Houston. Rodrigo has been attacked, and they think it was us."

"Is he dead?" Ortega asked.

"He's not dead, but my contact said he is bad. The problem is that Raul will surely think it was us behind the attack. And we all know what that means."

Ortega nodded. "It will be trouble, and not just in Houston. It will probably be trouble in Mexico as well."

"Not to mention Dallas and Austin," Hildalgo said.

Eliondo stepped forward to speak. "I doubt he'd try anything in San Antonio, but he definitely will in Dallas and Austin, especially if he heard of our recent troubles there. We're at risk, Ortega. We need to prepare. I think we should strike first."

Ortega thought for a moment, then turned to Hildalgo. "What is your advice, my friend?"

"We have a solid hold on San Antonio. I think we should give orders to maintain positions and have all men on alert. I think we also need to send a dozen soldiers to Dallas and Austin each. They will surely need reinforcing. And we should send a small contingent of men to Nuevo Laredo, not Laredo. The stash houses are what need protecting."

"What about El Paso?" Ortega asked.

Hildalgo shook his head. "They wouldn't dare attack us in El Paso. They know how strong we are there. Plus, they know how close it is to Juarez."

"And what do we do with the lesser cities of Corpus Christi, Tyler, Brownsville, and others?"

"We need to let them be; in fact, I would pull men from them to defend the other cities. If Raul goes after them, he'd take them anyway, so there is no sense in losing resources. Whoever we have there would serve us better in the big cities."

Raul nodded. "I agree. Let's do it, and let's do it quickly."

"Eliondo, you take command of Dallas and Austin. Hidalgo, you take everything in the east. I'll assign Nuevo Laredo to someone else."

Monterrey, Mexico

Raul presided over the emergency meeting of all his lieutenants. "You've already been told that war is imminent. Let me give you the details."

He began walking to the house. "Follow me to a room where we may speak privately," he said, and led them to a large presentation room situated on the lower level.

Raul turned on the lights, then displayed a large map of Texas on the whiteboard at the front of the room.

He used a pointer and tapped the portion of the map that represented Houston. "This, of course, is our primary interest. No one will be permitted to make headway into Houston. In short, that means as many additional soldiers as we need will be diverted to protecting our territories in and around

Houston. We'll send men from Monterrey and from other parts of East Texas to accomplish this."

He then pointed to Tyler, Corpus Christi, and Brownsville. "These locations will remain as they are. I doubt Ortega will spend resources to try to take over such small locations, which means our men should be able to hold them."

"What about Dallas and Austin?" Felipe asked.

Raul paced from one end of the room to the other, all the while remaining silent. When he stopped, he turned to face everyone. "Dallas is the target. We won't waste a single man in Austin."

Felipe appeared startled. "Why not? Austin is a big market, and it's nowhere near under Ortega's control."

Raul nodded. "Right on both counts, Felipe, but Dallas is a bigger market, and it is not as close to Ortega's base in San Antonio. From San Antonio, he could shuffle men back and forth in no time, but it wouldn't be as easy in Dallas."

Raul looked around the room, then said, "If nobody has more questions, we're done. Let's get it moving."

Chapter Thirty

WE NEED SOME INFORMATION

Houston, Texas

Ribs and I thought we were getting in early enough to get there before Julie, but we were wrong. When we reached the top of the stairs and looked to the right, she was already hard at work.

"Damn, girl," Ribs hollered. "Don't you go home at night?"

She laughed. "I do, Ribs, but I also work during the day, and I start in the *morning*, not at lunchtime."

"I told you not to mess with her, Ribs. She's too sharp for you, but then again . . ."

"Screw you, cuz," he said.

"So what can I do for you?" Julie asked. "I know if you're in this early and being this pleasant, that you want something."

"And you'd be right," I said. "Julie, we need to check out the calls from a person's phone to the tip-line. In fact, it might be better to check out all his calls."

"And who is the person?" Julie asked.

"Some guy who told us he made a call to the tip-line. We just want to make sure he actually did it."

"Once again, I'll ask. Who is the person?"

I gulped. "Father Robert Burns. I believe he is with—"

"St. Michael's?" Julie asked. "The priest who was beaten? The one still in the hospital?"

"By God, I think you're right, Julie. I believe that's the one."

Julie shook her head. "Not that I'm telling you anything you don't already know, but I doubt if you'll get a warrant on a priest's phone, especially this priest."

Ribs looked doubtful. "You don't think so?"

"Detective Delgado, I know you've tried to get warrants on the phones of fellow cops, and you know how difficult that is. Now, imagine that level of difficulty times ten. Judges don't like to mess with the religious side of things. I don't believe you'd get a warrant no matter what you said."

"It would be much easier to get a warrant on a cop's phone," I said. "There would surely be more probable cause. I can't see any probable cause for Father Burns. Remember volunteering to be a witness and getting beaten don't qualify."

Julie wagged her finger at me. "We may not need a warrant," she said.

I stopped and looked at Julie. "I'm all ears."

"If you get me some help, we could go through all the calls made to the tip line that day. From there, we could pick out the call Father Burns made. It won't tell you much, but it will tell you what time he made the call, not to mention, it will verify that he made it, or the call was made from his phone."

Ribs snapped his fingers. He looked excited, like he did when he got a good idea. "And with that, we may be able to get a warrant, claiming that we suspect the call to the tip line may have led to his beating, and we need to see what other calls came from the same phone because it may enable us to track down the killer or to prevent someone else from being attacked."

I patted Ribs on the back. "Cuz, every once in a while—a great while—you get a good idea."

"Julie, in case you didn't understand Gino's glowing compliment, what he means is he would like you to use the brilliant idea that you and I shared, and take a look at the tip-line calls to nail this down. Give me a call when you're done."

"Will do," Julie said. "But I'm still going to need help doing it. I'm sure there were a lot of calls that need to be gone through. And it would help if we could narrow down the time as much as possible."

"That's easy," I said. "Burns said he made the call late in the morning, so check everything prior to one o'clock to be safe."

Julie shook her head. "I don't mind being safe, Gino, but there is no sense in doing extra work. We'll start off checking all the calls between ten and eleven, then eleven and twelve. If we don't find what we need, we'll check between nine and ten, then twelve and one."

"Sounds like a plan," Ribs said. "Go for it, and I'll sign off on whoever you want to help. Just put a requisition on my desk."

Julie nodded. "Thanks, Detective. I'll have it there shortly."

～

By the end of the day, Julie got back to us with her report. "Sorry it took so long, but there were a hell of a lot of calls."

"And . . ." I asked.

"And none of them came from Father Burns," Julie said. "Not if he called from any of the three phones at the rectory, or the church phone, or his cell phone. We checked all of them."

Ribs came to his defense immediately. "You must have missed something. He said he called the tip line."

"We checked, and we double-checked, Ribs. No calls were there."

I was struck by an idea. "Suppose he used a burner," I said. "Then we wouldn't know what number called."

"Why would a priest use a burner?" Ribs asked.

"I'm not his lawyer, and I'm not even saying he needs one at this point, but if he was concerned about retribution because he called in the tip, he might have bought a burner to use."

"How the hell does a priest even know to buy a burner?" Ribs asked.

Julie snickered. "Detective Delgado, he's a priest, not a hermit," she said. "What that means is if he's read the paper, listened to the news, or spoken to anyone under the age of twenty-five, he'd know to use a burner and probably how to go about getting one."

I raised my hands as if to submit to surrender. "Ribs, if you agree that the good padre *might* have used a burner, I'll concede that he may be on the up-and-up, and something else is going on that we don't know about."

Ribs shrugged. "I'm good with that, Gino. Where do you suggest we go from here? We've still got nothing."

"I know, and as much as I don't want to simply because of the shit-storm it may bring, I think we ought to look a little into the priest's past."

"What?" Ribs asked. "Now you want to investigate a priest?"

"Don't think of it as investigating him, Ribs. Think of it as us looking into his background to see if he's experienced previous trouble from being a witness or innocent bystander. If he has, that would explain his use of a burner."

Ribs shook his head. He seemed to be struggling with the decision.

"I'm not saying a priest wouldn't know what a burner is or what it's used for; I'm just saying it's not the usual go-to method for them, but if he's known troubles as a result of testifying, it might explain it. Besides, nobody's going to know." I reached over and patted Julie on the back. "We've got a superstar conducting the research. She'll be done with it before anybody even suspects."

"Not to seem like I know what I'm doing or anything, but it may speed up any investigating we do if you had prints and DNA from Father Burns."

"I realize that, smart ass. That's why Ribs and I are going back to the hospital to see Father Burns."

Ribs and I returned to the hospital, then went back to see Father Burns. We stepped quietly into the room, aware that he may be sleeping. I looked at him and grimaced. He still looked pretty bad, and despite the morphine he was given for pain relief, I knew he had to be hurting just from looking at him. His nose looked broken, and he had multiple lumps and bruises on his face and head. The doctor had told us his ribs were the worst. Seven of them were broken, and his left lung had collapsed, though he said it wasn't serious.

Burns opened his eyes and tried to sit up as we neared the bed. "I'm sorry, my sons, I didn't hear you come in. Please, have a seat."

Ribs leaned close to the priest. "Father, we're working hard on this, an if you're up to it, what we'd like to do is get a tech over here to roll your prints and collect some DNA."

Father Burns shook his head. "No need, Detective. I didn't touch anything. The men just beat me."

Ribs nodded. "I realize it may not seem like it will do any good, Father, but you never can tell what you might have touched. Maybe a part of the car or something."

"There's no need," he said.

"Despite what you may think, Father, prints could help. And DNA even more so. During the course of the beating, no doubt there was some transfer of evidence both ways. In other words, some of their DNA ended up on you, and some of your DNA ended up on them. I'm sure the CSU already collected the evidence from you, but it may help if we get your evidence as well. If that's a problem, I'm sure we can get some from them, but it would be easier to just collect it while we're here."

Father Burns again shook his head.

I laughed. "Don't worry, Father. It won't hurt. It won't even be an inconvenience."

"I don't want it," Burns said.

"Father, it may help us process the crime scene. If we have your vitals, we can rule out the prints and DNA that match yours."

"I said, *no,*" Burns said.

Ribs glanced at me, then asked, "Why wouldn't you want that, Father? We already told you it won't hurt. And it may help us find out who did it."

Burns scooted up a little higher in the bed and smiled. "I'm sorry if it seems as if I'm being uncooperative, detectives, but I doubt if gathering my information would do anything, and I don't feel up to giving it. Perhaps after I'm released, we can revisit this. I'm sure I'll feel more comfortable providing what you need at that time."

"That's fine, Father," I said. "We're sorry to have bothered you again, but I hope you understand. We're just trying to get this solved."

He smiled. "I'm sure you are, and I greatly appreciate it." He made the sign of the cross again, then said, "Go with God, my sons. And good hunting."

We walked out of the room and down the hall. As we walked, Ribs grabbed my arm. "What the hell did we leave for? We didn't get shit yet."

I nodded. I know, but there is more than one way to get it. I walked to the nearby nurse station and asked for the head nurse. When she approached, I showed her my badge. "Ma'am, I know this may seem like a strange request, but would it be possible for you to get us the drinking glass and straw from Father Burns's room? The one that's there now."

She raised her eyebrows and looked at both of us. "From the priest?"

I nodded. "Yes, ma'am. We're trying to find out who did

this to him and having his prints and DNA may help a lot. Father Burns isn't placing a high priority on it though."

She smiled. "Tell me what I need to do."

"Nothing more than remove the tray without touching the glass, then bring it back here. We'll take it from there."

"Easy enough, Detective. I'll have it for you in a few minutes."

We waited less than five minutes, then the nurse returned with the glass, which we deposited into a small box one of the other nurses had given us. "Thanks," I said, then Ribs and I returned to the station.

Chapter Thirty-One

LET'S FIND OUT WHO HE WAS

Houston, Texas

"I'd love to know what the hell that was all about," I said. "I've never seen an innocent man put up such a fight about giving their prints and DNA."

"Some people just don't like it," Ribs said. "They feel it's an invasion of privacy or something."

"That's bullshit," I said. "And you know it is. If it had been anybody but a priest tell us that, you'd agree."

Ribs laughed. "You could be right, Gino. But you know what I'm saying is real. A lot of people really do think that way."

"I know that, Ribs, but all I'm saying is ninety percent of them are guilty as sin of something. It may not be the crime you're investigating, but they're guilty of something."

"Let's focus," Ribs said.

"Focus on what?" I asked.

"On the *why,* as in *why* wouldn't he give us his prints."

"Don't forget his DNA," I said. "He knew it was to help us find the people who did this to him, and he wouldn't give us either."

Ribs nodded. "I agree that's not the norm for an innocent man, but I'm not prepared to say there's a problem. Not yet."

Ribs shrugged. "Who knows? Maybe he's scared we'd do some good. Maybe he's afraid we'll find the guys, and some of their associates will take revenge."

"Ribs, I might buy that if this were someone else, but I can't see it with Father Burns. He's the person who reported Pablo's murder, and he did that to protect Langer, remember?"

"Of course, I remember," Ribs said. "But that's just my point. Look at it from his viewpoint. He was a witness once and his friend, Langer, got killed. Then he got brutally attacked, possibly for his continued assistance. Maybe he's leery of helping the police. I think a lot of people would be."

"I hear what you're saying, Ribs, but I still don't buy it. I think Father Burns would risk anything to bring the wrong people to justice, especially people dealing drugs."

"It's all right to think that, cuz, but how do we prove it?"

"The way we prove anything else. We take the prints and DNA we got from the nurse, and we run them through the databases, and then we have Julie check out every part of his life. It's what we'd do with anyone else."

"Let's put it in motion," Ribs said. "The sooner we get this over with, the sooner we can find the real culprit."

We gave the prints and the DNA to Julie and asked her to run with it. "I want everything we can get on him," I said. "Give the prints to Eric down in the lab and ask him to run a complete profile. Just remember, it's going to take a few days to get the DNA results."

After a few days, DNA results came back. Ribs caught up to Gino on his way back from seeing Julie. "Cuz, we got the results."

"And?"

"And nothing," Ribs said. "No list of his prints or DNA anywhere, but don't get excited. That doesn't mean anything. Julie found history, but not what we expected."

"Don't keep me guessing, Ribs."

"We didn't strike out. Like I said, Julie found history, and guess where?"

"I'm tired of your games, Ribs. What did she find?"

"Guess where Burns was before he came to Houston."

I shrugged. "No idea, and I'm not up to guessing."

"San Antonio," Ribs said.

"Son of a bitch," I said. "That's where Mrs. Langer's family is in law enforcement."

"And where Ortega is running wild," Ribs said.

"Forget about Ortega running wild. Get Julie on the phone and tell her we need to meet."

"What for?" Ribs asked. "We have her report."

"Bullshit," I said. "I want all of the report. Not the highlights. Get her on the phone and see if she can meet us somewhere or if we need to go to her house."

Julie met us at a nearby coffee shop on Highway 290. Fortunately, the babysitter was still at her house when we called.

"All right, detectives, tell me what you need quickly because she can't stay all night with the kids. As it is, it's costing me extra."

"Don't worry about the extra," I said. "I'll cover that if the department doesn't."

"As to what we want," Ribs said. "We saw the report

stating Burns came here from San Antonio, but we need to know the details."

"Is this legal?" Julie asked. "I've never researched a priest before."

"Don't worry about that," Ribs said. "Just tell us what you've got."

Julie looked at Ribs, then back to Gino. "I'm more than worried," she said. "I've seen the stunts you two have pulled. And they've usually been without the captain's approval."

"Julie, I understand your concern, and it's true that neither the captain nor the chief know we're doing this, but rest assured it's all legal. We obtained the prints and DNA from a drinking glass in the hospital, which is a perfectly legal means to do so."

"All right," Julie said. "I'll trust you on this, but I better not get into trouble."

"You won't," I said. "And thanks."

For two days, Ribs and I followed leads and did interviews on the cases we had. Nothing new came up, not even any new leads to follow.

The next day, Julie tracked us down just as we were about to leave the station. "I've got some of what you need," she said, and handed a folder filled with papers to me.

"This looks like a lot of information," I said. "All of this is deals with Burns?"

"All of it deals with Burns," Julie said. "Or it deals with the person we know as Father Burns."

"What the hell does that mean?" Ribs asked.

"Read the report, Detective. I believe you'll find it interesting." Julie smiled. "In fact, I *know* you'll find it interesting."

Ribs grabbed the folder from me and headed toward his

desk. "Let's go, cuz. It sounds as if we have a lot of reading to do, and I know how slow you are."

"I agree with you about me being a slow reader, and since that's the case, I suggest you read the report while I listen." I laughed. "But I *will* listen attentively."

Ribs rolled a chair close to his desk, leaned back, and rested his feet on the chair's seat. "Once upon a time—"

"Just get to the report, asshole," I said.

He scanned the first few paragraphs, then went back and summed it up. "Looks like he came to Houston from San Antonio, as Julie said. He was assigned to St. Catherine's parish for two years before his transfer here."

"Any reason cited for the transfer?" I asked.

"If you mean, was he accused of something, you know the church doesn't list that shit. They don't allow accusations to go public if they can help it."

I reached for the file so I could read it myself. After a few minutes, I said, "Julie shows no reason why he left San Antonio, and St. Catherine's lists no reasons why he quit either. All they show in the file is him moving to Houston. They don't even show which parish he was assigned to."

"Do they show where he was prior to St. Catherine's?" Ribs asked. He took the file back and flipped through the papers, reading them as he did. "I see one notation about St. Joseph's on the western side of the city."

"Isn't that a heavily populated Latino section?" I asked.

Ribs laughed. "Cuz, this is San Antonio. *All* parts of the city are heavily populated by Latinos."

"Let's hear about what he did while stationed at these churches. Did he do anything good, bad, indifferent?"

Ribs read for a few more minutes, then said, "St. Catherine's lists him as being great with the youth, not to mention good with couples who needed counseling. Oh, and also they list him as a great fundraiser."

"And how about St. Joseph's?" I asked.

"Looks similar," Ribs said. "Worked with troubled teens, counseled kids who were in need of tutoring, and he was in charge of the semi-annual carnival which raised money for the church, and apparently it was a lot of money."

I got up and walked around the table. "What bothers me, Ribs, is why would either of the churches let Burns go if he was so good with kids—not an easy thing—and aside from that, he was good at fundraising, which is definitely not an easy thing, especially in lower-income neighborhoods."

Ribs nodded. "I agree, Gino, so I'll echo your question— why would either one of them get rid of him? I can't imagine they would, and yet, they did."

"We need to find out why?" I said. "Both of those actions were not logical decisions, and we need to know why."

Ribs and I agreed once again. "We also need to find out where he was prior to St. Joseph's," Ribs said. "Julie's research doesn't list it."

"We'll ask Julie to dig deeper, but I also think we need to ask Burk and Nickles to check up on it. They've been around San Antonio a long time, long enough for them to know something or else know someone who does."

Ribs nodded. "I'll call Julie; you call Burk. Let's get this done."

Chapter Thirty-Two

WHERE DID BURNS COME FROM?

Houston, Texas

While Ribs called Julie, I reached out to Detective Burk in San Antonio. I'd have rather gone there myself, but I knew we'd face a lot of heat from Coop about it.

"Cataldi," Burk said, "What's up? I assume you need our expertise again or you wouldn't be calling."

"You're right about that, Burk. How did the bust on Ortega go? You do any good?"

"Hell, yeah, we did good. Didn't your captain tell you? We sent a report and a big thanks. We got Lanza, about a dozen mid-level dealers, and we got several leads that might turn up some of Ortega's men. Overall, it was a fruitful operation."

"Does that mean I've got one in the bank?" I asked.

"Shit," Burk said. "As far as Nickles and I are concerned, you and your partner have a couple. Just name it."

"All right, good. I'm going to fax you the file on a guy we're looking into. I'll fax his picture as well, but when he was in San Antonio, he was ten to twenty years younger."

"What did the guy do? Drugs?"

"No. Nothing like that. At least, nothing we know about. He's a priest, and he—"

"A priest? A goddamn priest? Cataldi, this is San Antonio. It may be the most Catholic city in America. Hell, we've got seventy percent of the population Latino. If we go poking around asking about a priest, we might get hanged, or worse."

"I hear you, Burk, and I'm not asking you to blacken his name, but take a look at the file. He only spent a few years at each church and then was assigned elsewhere, ending up in Houston. We can't even find out where he was before St. Joseph's. Anything you can find out might help."

"What's it about? Why are you looking at him?" Burk asked.

"He was a witness in a drug killing, then one of his fellow priests was killed, then he was beaten near to death."

"Holy shit."

"Yeah, but the odd thing is, he doesn't seem to be cooperating. For a man who was beaten so badly, he remembers next to nothing. And to top it off, he is more than reluctant to provide his prints or DNA."

"It would help if we had that," Burk said.

"They're in the file. We got them the old-fashioned way."

"All right, you can count on us getting it done. Might take a few days, but we'll get it."

"Thanks, Burk. I appreciate it."

San Antonio, Texas

Burk and Nickles entered St. Catherine's church and knelt in the back pew. After the mass ended, they walked up the aisle and around to the side door where they found Father John.

"Father John, how good to see you," Nickles said.

Father John hugged Nickles, then Burk. "And you, my sons. What can I do for law enforcement today?"

"It's an odd request today, Father," Burk said, and he handed the folder containing the information. "Friends of ours in Houston have several murder investigations that have ties, though they are tenuous ones, to Father Burns, who used to be at this parish. The worst part is Father Burns has been badly beaten, almost killed, and they're trying to find out if anything in his past may have contributed to this."

Nickles pointed to the picture of Burns. "This is him as he is now. When he was here, it would have been ten years prior to that."

Father John nodded. "No need for explanation, detectives. I remember Father Burns well. He was a friend of mine, and as far as I know, a friend to almost everyone."

"Tell us about him," Burk said.

Father John seemed to think. "He was always calm and patient, and that wasn't easy considering what he did."

"Which was what?" Nickles asked.

"He did a lot of work with the kids, mostly the troubled ones, the ones on drugs. He also got involved with counseling couples who had marriage troubles, and he was exceptionally patient and effective there."

"Is that it?" Burk asked.

"His strongest suit may have been his fundraising. He was outstanding at bringing in money for the church; in fact, the church even lent him out to another diocese to help them raise money. That's why I was so surprised to see him go. At first, I thought he just wanted to go to Houston, but then I heard he was asked to leave."

Burk looked surprised. "Asked to leave? Why?"

"I'm not sure," Father John said.

Nickles tapped his shoulder. "Father, I know you may not be sure, but you must have some idea."

Father John shook his head. "I don't know if I can say."

Burk leaned toward him. "Father, we're not asking this for a gossip mill. Father Burns is obviously in danger from someone. He was almost killed, for God's sake."

Father John struggled with a decision, then he finally nodded. "All right. If I tell you this, know that it is rumor only, not an official report."

"We're just trying to help, Father. We don't want him killed."

"I heard several parishioners talk about Father Burns's counseling of couples, and they said he may have gotten a little too close to the women he counseled."

Nickles took notes while Father John talked. "Are you saying he was having affairs with married women?"

"I'm not saying that he was, but I can't say that he wasn't."

"Is that what got him reassigned to Houston?" Burk asked.

"Again, I couldn't swear to it, but the rumors indicate it was."

"And is that what happened at St. Joseph's also? Is that why they asked him to leave?" Nickles asked.

Father John didn't answer, but he nodded.

"How about before St. Joseph's? Do you know where he was then?" Burk asked.

"I don't know, and Father Burns never talked about it to me. I heard from a parishioner that he may have come from Holy Rosary, but I'm not certain. And if it was Holy Rosary, it might be difficult to find answers. All of the staff from back then have gone, though you may be able to find some long-time churchgoers who are still there."

"Are you talking about Holy Rosary down by St. Mary's right on Camino Santa Maria?" Burk asked.

Father John nodded again. "That's the one. And you could be in luck because a lot of the original parishioners remained in the area."

"Okay, Father, thanks so much. You may have helped Father Burns with his troubles."

"I hope so," he said. "And say hello to him if you see him. Tell him I'll be praying for him."

Burk and Nickles left St. Catherine's and walked to the car. "Should we bother going to St. Joseph's, or skip right to Holy Rosary?" Burk asked.

Nickles opened his car door and slid in. "I say Holy Rosary. I think we know what we'll find at St. Joseph's."

"HR it is," Burk said. "Polish up your silver tongue because these people are a tight-lipped bunch."

"HR?" Nickles asked.

"Yeah, HR—Holy Rosary," Burk said.

Nickles stood and grabbed his keys. "Let's get going then. We've got a lot to do."

As Burk got into the car, he asked Nickles, "You got the picture?"

Nickles patted his jacket pocket. "Right here," he said. "I'm hoping we don't need it, but I've got it in case we do."

We got to Holy Rosary and questioned all the staff: priests, admins, and even a few nuns. None of them remembered Father Burns, or at least, they didn't admit to it, though one of the admins gave us the name of a parishioner who might know.

Burk wrote the address in his notepad, then we got into the car and left. "Those damn priests are as tight-lipped as the Mafia."

"Maybe worse," Nickles said. "At least we have a possibility. Let's see what Señor Reynosa has to say."

A man who looked to be in his seventies answered the door. "Si?"

Nickles showed his badge. "Just here for a few questions, sir. Have you got a minute?"

"Si," he said, and stepped aside, allowing us entry. He sat at a table and invited us to join him. "My name is Miguel," he said. "How can I help you?"

"We're here to ask if you remember Father Burns when he was at the church. It would have been about fifteen years ago."

Miguel shook his head. "I don't recall him but give me a minute, and I might."

Nickles pulled the picture from his pocket and showed it to Miguel. "Here is a picture of him. See if that jars your memory."

Miguel stared at the photo for more than a minute. "I recognize Father Sebastian, but no one else," he said.

Confused, Burk looked at the picture with Miguel. "Which one is Father Sebastian?"

Miguel jabbed his finger at the picture. "Right there," he said. "The one on the right."

"That's Father Burns," Burk said.

Miguel shook his head. "I know I'm old, and I don't see worth a shit, but that's Father Sebastian. No doubt about it."

Nickles got up and stood behind us, staring at the picture. "That's supposed to be Father Burns."

Miguel sipped his lemon water. "I don't know who told you that, but unless he is the twin of Father Sebastian, somebody told you wrong."

"All right," Burk said, "let's assume you're right. Tell us what you know about the man you know as Father Sebastian."

"He's a piece of shit. I know that," Miguel said.

"Pretty harsh, isn't it?" Nickles asked.

"Not if you knew him." Miguel got up and moved to the living room. "More comfortable in here," he said.

Nickles and Burk joined Miguel in the living room, both taking a seat on the sofa. "You said he was a piece of shit," Burk said. "Care to explain that?"

Miguel leaned back. "I didn't say it lightly. When Father Sebastian came here, everyone loved him. He worked great with the kids, he quickly organized carnivals and other money-raising events, and he worked great with married people who were having trouble; in fact, he worked too good with them."

"What do you mean by that?" Burk asked.

"I mean, he ended up seeing the women on the side. One of those women was my granddaughter, and it ended up ruining her marriage. After that happened, the good padre was fortunate to get out of San Antonio alive because her husband went gunning for him."

Miguel laughed. "I never much cared for Carlos, but after he did that, he earned my respect."

"Is that when he left the parish?" Nickles asked.

"It is, but after he left, many more reports came out about his running around with the married women. If he's going under a different name now, it doesn't surprise me because some of those husbands might still be looking for him."

"You can't believe they'd be vengeful after all this time?" Burk asked.

"Detective, if you're asking that, I'm guessing you don't understand the Mexican culture. About the worst thing you can do is dishonor a man's wife or daughter. It's not an act that is soon forgiven, if ever."

"Anything else you can tell us?" Nickles asked.

"No, you now know almost everything I do."

"Almost?" Burk asked.

Miguel nodded. "My granddaughter's husband—ex-husband—was still looking for Padre Sebastian three years ago, which is the last time I spoke with him. If I was a gambling man, I'd bet he's still searching, and I wouldn't want to bet on what he'd do if he found the padre. He was an ill-tempered youth to begin with, and when this happened, it turned him a lot worse."

Nickles put his notepad away and stood. "Señor Reynosa, we appreciate your time and your cooperation." He handed a card to Miguel. "If you think of anything else—anything—call us. And if you need help with a problem of any kind, call us as well."

As Burk and Nickles drove away from Reynosa's house, Burk turned to Nickles. "You think we should go to St. Joseph's now?"

Nickles nodded. "Absolutely," he said.

Burk and Nickles talked to two of the priests at St. Joseph's, but all they got was more of the same: good with kids, good with couples, and good with fundraising. After a lot of pressure, and not getting anything more solid, they left.

Houston, Texas

We got the report from Burk and Nickles just before going home. It wasn't something we expected. "Son of a bitch," Ribs said. "This puts a new light on things."

"Not just a new light, but it opens up the suspect list a lot. Hell, if we consider the reports from St. Catherine's, St. Joseph's, and Holy Rosary, we've got more than a handful of people who may want him dead."

Ribs scoffed. "Cuz, if he ran around with that many women in San Antonio, he's in more danger than the FBI's most wanted man."

I nodded, knowing what Ribs said was true. I'd been married to a lady of Mexican descent for many years. I knew how they thought. "Than I suggest we take this information to your house or mine and go over it all again. Thinks are not adding up and adding new suspects to the list isn't helping."

"Let's make it your house," Ribs said. "My kids never keep quiet."

"My house it is," I said. "I'll call Marissa. Why don't you plan on being there by seven."

Chapter Thirty-Three

WHY HIDE AS A PRIEST?

Ribs got to the house just before seven, and he arrived carrying two six-packs of beer. "You plan on doing a lot of thinking or a lot of drinking?" I asked.

"I hope it's both," Ribs said. "Besides, all of these beers aren't for me. You can have one."

"No shit? How magnanimous of you. In that case, I'll let you have a raviolo, just one, not a plate of ravioli."

"That's pretty cold, cuz. After all I do for you."

I put the beer in the fridge. "Ribs, you haven't done shit for me. As for your beer offering, I don't want any. I'll drink wine with Marissa."

"Suit yourself," Ribs said. "Now let's get down to business."

I pulled out the report we got from Burk and set it on the table. Marissa walked past and placed the cheese on top of the folder. "If you two think you're taking over this table, think again. We're eating here, and it's happening shortly. So move your asses to the dining room."

Ribs jumped up and saluted. "Yes, ma'am," he said.

We settled in at the dining room table within minutes and were hard at work within another few minutes. "Look at this," Ribs said. "The guy is nothing if not predictable."

"What makes you say that?" I asked.

"Take a look at what Burk and Nickles wrote. St. Catherine's, St. Joseph's both listed him as being good with kids. From what the parishioner from Holy Rosary said, he displayed the same talents there."

"Ribs, that's one thing. One thing doesn't make a person predictable," I said.

"But look at the rest. They said he was also good with fundraising at all three churches, and as we now know, good at counseling married couples having difficulty."

"And let's not ignore the fact he happened to be seeing the wife on the side."

Ribs stopped reading the report and looked up at me. "Suppose he never stopped what he was doing?"

"What are you saying?" I asked.

"I mean, suppose he came to Houston to hide out or escape San Antonio, but he never quit running around?"

"We don't have any reports of activity like that. No complaints of any kind."

"I know this will sound crazy," Ribs said. "But suppose he got tangled up with the wife of a drug dealer. Or more likely, the wife of a rich donor to the church, a very rich donor."

"You mean Langer?" I asked.

"If you think about it, it all fits. Langer is a young, attractive woman with time on her hands, not to mention her family is from San Antonio."

"It's not like he needs a woman from San Antonio to mess around with," I said.

"I'm sure he doesn't," Ribs said, "but despite that, San Antonio fits the puzzle. He was there a lot of years. He worked in the Latino districts. And he worked with troubled youths and couples. And let's not forget her family is tied to the drug cartel."

Marissa poured a glass of wine for me and set it on the table, which I immediately picked up and took a sip. "You may be missing the obvious, Ribs. I know you always want to make things more complicated than they are, but some things are what they seem like—simple."

"Meaning?" Ribs asked.

"Meaning, he may have come to Houston from San Antonio and just continued his ways. And those activities might have brought him into contact with the wrong person."

"You don't expect me to buy that, do you?"

"As much as you expected me to buy your line of bull."

"All right, let's start over. We'll assume nothing and look at it logically," Ribs said.

I nodded. "Good idea, Ribs. Let's take a look at all the things each parish has in common. Or should I say, what he had in common at each parish?"

"All right," Ribs said. "Let's look."

I laughed. "Okay, you read through the files while I take a leak, then we'll discuss it."

"You're an ass," Ribs said, "But don't worry, I'll do it."

Ribs shuffled through the papers inside the folder and read through them. He finished before I got back and sat down.

"Damn, you're a fast reader," I said.

"And you're a slow pisser," he said. "I could have read *War and Peace* while you were gone."

"All right, enough of your bull, let's take a look at what we've got," I said.

Ribs already had a list started:

St. Catherine's said:

- He was good with kids, especially troubled ones.
- He was good with troubled marriages.
- He was good at raising money.

St. Joseph's said:

- He was good with troubled kids.
- He was good with troubled marriages.
- He was good at raising money.

And the parishioner at Holy Rosary said:

- He was good with kids.
- He was good with troubled marriages, though his methods were dubious at best.
- He was good at raising money.

I looked at Ribs to make sure he'd finished, then asked, "And St. Michael's?"

"We both know what St. Michael's said. They said everyone liked him, and he was good at raising money. Although when pushed, he'd have given the credit to Langer."

I nodded while recalling all we'd heard about Father Burns. "No one mentioned any problems with him seeing women parishioners, did they?"

Ribs shook his head. "None that I recall."

"Time for dinner," Marissa yelled from the kitchen.

We both walked to the kitchen and sat across from each other, with Marissa between us. As we continued to discuss the case, Marissa occasionally asked questions.

"Maybe he gave up his lifestyle," Ribs said. "People have conquered worse habits."

"I doubt it," Marissa said. "It's more likely that he took his habit somewhere else—a different parish, or the same parish but using a different means to attract women."

"I don't know," I said. "I think guys like that are predictable."

"If you want something predictable, look for the things that show up *every* time, not just most times."

"What's that supposed to mean?" Ribs asked. "His running around showed up in all three assignments."

"But not Houston," Marissa said. "Don't you find it odd that he ran around in all three locations in San Antonio, but when he got to Houston, he stopped?"

Ribs shrugged. "I don't find it so odd. It might be like you said, that he moved his game to another area or changed his method."

"I know I said that, but I didn't really believe it, and now that I give it more thought, I believe it even less."

"Then what?" I asked. "What's he up to, and why?"

Marissa shook her head. "I don't know, Gino. Not yet."

"Maybe he's in hiding. He *did* change his name, according to the guy Burk talked to, he did. He said Burns was known as Father Sebastian at Holy Rosary, and Burk and Nickles both said their guy seemed positive about it."

"You may be right about that, cuz, but we have to figure out what Burns did and why he did it?" Ribs said.

"I'm pretty sure he was involved in the murders, but how and why are the questions."

Ribs said, "Let's assume he witnessed the first murder—"

"We *know* he witnessed the murder," I said, "But if he's connected with the drugs, why would he tell the cops? If you recall, he sent the plates to us and gave us a description of the car."

"But if someone is going to hide out and assume another person's identity, why become a priest?" Ribs asked.

"Are you shitting me?" I asked. "There's not much better than a priest. A cop might be better, but a cop would also be a lot riskier. A guy could go ten years hiding as a priest and have no one question him or look into his background. Hiding out as a cop, you could do a perfect job, with no mistakes, and a partner or another cop could get in trouble, which would get a reporter looking into your background."

"I'm in agreement on that part," Ribs said. "But I also wonder if there isn't another reason. Let's think about it, cuz. What else can a priest do? How could they help the drug pushers?"

"Other than easing the relationships with the local community, I don't know. And from what I saw, Father Burns didn't condone drug use, nor did he ease off on the dealers. He seemed to take a tough stance on everything."

"I hear you on that, Gino, but for that matter, Langer did as well. From what everyone said about him, he always helped people out. He even donated pretty generously each year to the policemen's fund to fight drugs."

I shook my head and took two sips of wine. "So we're back to Saint Robert again?"

"I didn't say that, asshole, but in light of some real evidence, we don't have much to go on."

"We need to look through all the interviews, Burk and Nickles did. I guarantee that somebody said something that carries weight."

"Be my guest," Ribs said. "I've already been through them twice, and I haven't found a damn thing."

We went through the files two more times, but nothing spurred an idea. Finally, after drinking half the wine and all the beer, I suggested we call it a night. Ribs got up to leave, but by the way he stumbled to the door, I knew he shouldn't be driving home.

I grabbed hold of his arm. "Ribs, you can let Marissa drive you home, or you can stay the night, but I can't let you drive in this condition."

He looked as if he may put up a fight, but then he handed me his keys and said, "I'll stay here. Just call Rosalee and tell her you got me drunk."

"So, it's blame it on me night, huh?"

He nodded. "It'll go easier that way."

In the morning, Ribs called Rosalee and apologized profusely. I made sure to listen closely so I could razz him about it later. We ate a quick breakfast, just fruit, bagels, and coffee, then headed out to the office. "You're driving," I told Ribs. "You can have your keys back."

"Screw you, cuz. I've seen you drunk before."

We got in the car and entered the ramp for I-45 going south. "I thought a lot about this last night—*after* my partner had passed out—and I kept arriving at the same conclusion."

"And what, pray tell, is your conclusion?"

"That *something* is wrong with this guy."

"And how did you arrive at that?" Ribs asked.

"Come on, Ribs. Look at what we've got. Burk and Nickles tracked him through San Antonio, then he just disappeared. Not to mention he first changed his name from Father Sebastian to Father Burns."

"Hold on, cuz. We don't know that yet."

"We don't? Then what happened to the records? The church didn't have any. The police didn't have any. And no government agency had any. He didn't just magically appear as a priest. He had to come from somewhere," I said.

"And I'm sure he did," Ribs said. "We just have to find out where."

"I'll tell you where," I said. "I'm guessing he came from Ortega's cartel or Raul's, but one of them for sure. Furthermore, I'd bet a hundred bucks he had more than a little to do with these murders—all of them. I'm guessing he was a crooked priest in Monterrey or Juarez, and one of the cartel bosses corrupted him and got him to work for them."

Ribs laughed. "What do you suggest we do, cuz? He's still in the hospital, and I don't think the chief would appreciate us hounding a recently mugged priest—the chief being Catholic and all."

I thought about what Ribs said, then made up my mind. "I say we hound the son of a bitch anyway. Hell, it's only a job."

"I know it's only a job to you, but you've got a grown kid and a rich as shit wife-to-be. On the other hand, I've got seven kids at home and a dirt-poor wife. I think I have more to lose."

"Don't worry. I'll take the blame. Just head to the hospital."

Chapter Thirty-Four

ANOTHER SHOT AT THE PRIEST

Houston, Texas

We got to the hospital early and went straight to his room. He was awake and sitting up when we entered. "Father Burns, good to see you looking so well," Ribs said.

A smile lit his face. "And good to see you as well, Detective. Or should I say detectives?"

Father Burns scooted up a few more inches on the bed. "What can I do for you?"

"I hope you can help us out on the investigation," I said. "Actually on both investigations."

"I'm happy to try. What do you need?"

"First off, we'd like to cover the night you were assaulted again."

"I believe I told you all I could remember, but ask anything you like."

"Good, let's start with you telling us what happened, and be as specific as possible."

Father Burns sipped from his cup of water, then began talking. "I came out of the rectory and was walking to a parishioner's house—a young woman with several young children."

Ribs snapped his fingers. "Oh, yeah, now I remember you telling us. You were going to hear her confession, right?"

Burns smiled. "Yes, that's right, Detective. You have a good memory."

"I've been blessed with that, Father. But tell me about the attack itself. How did the men grab you? What did they do? And most importantly, how did you get away?"

"I was on my way from the rectory, and no sooner had I stepped into the street, a car sped up from the south. I stopped walking to let it go past, but it screeched to a halt, then two men got out and beat me."

"Did they say anything?" I asked. "Or do you have any idea why they targeted you?"

"That's a good question, Detective. I remember thinking 'What do these men want?' just before the first punch landed. After that, I felt one blow after another until I fell to the ground."

"Then what?" I asked.

"I recall them dragging me toward the center of the street and leaving me. They got back in the car, and I heard the engine start. Then the headlights came on, and I saw the car moving toward me."

"And you have no idea who might do such a thing?" I asked.

He shook his head. "I can't imagine, Detective. I've done nothing to harm anyone or even anger anyone."

Ribs stepped closer and lowered his voice. "How about in San Antonio? Did you do anything there to piss people off?"

Father Burns scrunched his brows. "I don't understand. Of course not. I was in San Antonio for five or six years."

"Five or six?" I asked. "Or was it more like ten to fifteen?"

Burns seemed to get nervous under the pressure, but I have to admit, he kept his cool. "No, Detective. It was five or six. Several years each at St. Catherine's and St. Joseph's."

"And don't forget Holy Rosary," Ribs said.

Burns got a blank look on his face. "Holy Rosary? I was never assigned there."

"Not as Father Burns, you weren't. I know that. But what about as Father Sebastian?"

Father Burns laughed, and surprisingly, it seemed real. "No wonder you're confused, Detective. Father Sebastian was a cousin of mine, and everyone said he looked just like me. We were often confused, even by close associates."

"Oh, that explains it," I said. "Where is Father Sebastian now?"

"The last I heard, he went back to Mexico," Father Burns said. "I believe his mother was sick."

"What part of Mexico?" Ribs asked. "I've got relatives there."

Father Burns shook his head. "I have no idea. I think it was one of those hilltop towns west of Monterrey, but I can't be sure. And before you ask, no, I don't have his number."

"Have you given any more thought to who would want to kill Mr. Langer or Father McLaughlin?"

"Not a clue," he said, "But if I think of anyone, I'll call."

"How about Langer and McLaughlin?" Ribs asked. "Why do you think they were killed, and you were only beaten up?"

"I have no idea of the motives driving these people. Arlen

had witnessed the murder of that drug dealer on the street. And Father McLaughlin had overheard me calling the information in to your tip line. He also witnessed me talking to both of you." Burns shook his head. "Why either one of those actions would make them targets, and not me, is beyond comprehension. I would think it would be the other way around."

Ribs nodded. "I agree, Father; in fact, I'm finding it difficult to grasp how anyone even knew about Arlen Langer since he only told you what he witnessed. You didn't say anything on the tip line, did you?"

"Not a word. If you remember, it's why I called in the first place—because I was afraid something might happen to Arlen. As far as I know, he and I were the only ones who knew he witnessed the killing, although, I guess he may have told Rita. And as I mentioned, Father McLaughlin overheard."

"All right," I said. "I guess that does it for now. I hope you recover quickly, Father. And let us know of anything you think of."

"I will, Detective, and by all means, if you have any of the parishioners from Holy Rosary on hand, bring them by. I'm sure that once they see me in person, they'll recognize that while Father Sebastian and I looked alike, we are definitely different people."

"Okay, Father, thanks," I said.

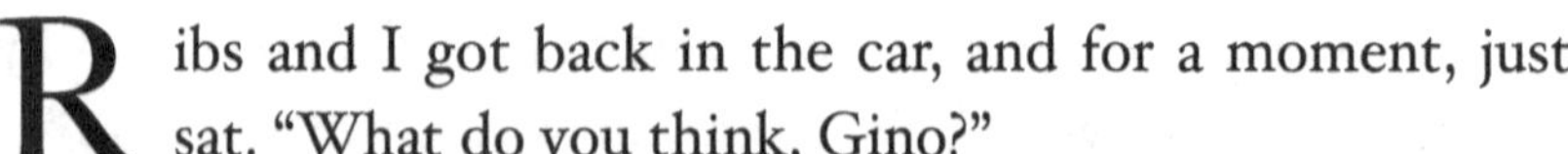

Ribs and I got back in the car, and for a moment, just sat. "What do you think, Gino?"

"I think he's lying out his ass, but he's doing a damn good job of it. He tells just enough truth to make it ring true, and when you combine that with the fact that he's a priest, it makes it difficult to dispute what he says."

"What else can we look into?" Ribs asked. "We have enough bodies to find killers for, so it shouldn't be a problem."

"Let's hit the Hispanic neighborhoods and see what we can stir up," I said. "Who knows, we may get a lead on Jorge and Ranza. And if we get that, I'm certain it will lead us to Pablo and the rest of them."

"Sounds good," Ribs said. "We're close to Spring Branch, so let's start there. Afterward, we'll head to Northside."

~

We spent all day talking to people in the Latino neighborhoods, but we got nothing. Either nobody knew anything or they weren't willing to talk. I figured it was the latter. We had a tough time finding anyone who even claimed to *know* Jorge or Ranza, let alone who might wish them harm.

Ribs drove the speed limit on the freeway, then made a turn onto Beltway 8 and headed north. "I think it's time we called it a day," he said. "I'm tired of speaking Spanish."

"Ribs, don't give me that shit. I did half the talking, but I agree it's time to go home. I'm beat."

"Your house or mine?" Ribs asked.

"What?"

"Do you want to continue this at your house or mine? It's a simple question."

I closed my eyes and shook my head. "God, but you're a

pain in the ass," I said. "Make it my house. I'll call Marissa and ask her to fix something to eat."

"Good," Ribs said. "I'll call Rosalee and let her know I won't be home for dinner. There's no sense in me going to my house, then turning around and going to your place."

"Oh, hell no," I said, "not when you can annoy me all night, nonstop." I called Marissa but got no answer. "I can't reach her, Ribs. You may have to go hungry because I'm not sharing any of my supper."

We got to my house by six, and Ribs parked out front. As we walked toward the house, he took a big whiff of air and said, "Gino, I can smell that garlic from here. I think it's going to be a good meal."

"Ribs, if Marissa served garlic on cat shit, you'd swear it was good."

"Only if she put her sauce on top of it. And maybe some cheese."

I opened the front door and walked inside, grinning as I did. "Hey, babe, we're home."

Marissa walked into the living room a moment later. "I presumed the 'we're' meant you and Ribs, but I figured that already when I noticed you'd called. Dinner's on for three."

We ate dinner but didn't discuss the case while Marissa was there. I was sure she was tired of hearing about our investigation. After Ribs and I helped her clear the table, we volunteered to do the dishes.

"Looks like I'm being spoiled tonight, and since that's the case, I'm calling Connie to see if she wants to go out."

"Go on," I said. "We've got plenty to discuss, and it will be boring for you, so you may as well go out with Connie."

Marissa opened another bottle of wine and set it on the dining room table. "I know you'll need this," she said, then walked out the door.

Ribs poured the wine, and we sat down to work things out. "First things first," I said. "I don't believe Father Burns. Do you?"

"Not even a little bit," Ribs said. "The problem is, we can't prove anything. I wish we'd taped the first interview we did with Burns because I'd swear he repeated his statement word-for-word. And not just part of it, but everything we asked."

"And I'd swear right alongside you," I said.

"People don't usually tell a story exactly as they did before," Ribs said.

I nodded. "Not innocent people," I said. "As Tip would say, 'sure as shit stinks,' that guy was lying."

Ribs poured us each a refill, then pointed to Arlen Langer's file. "What do we know about Langer's death? Not shit. We know he was run over and apparently it was intentional. Other than that, we don't know a damn thing."

"Not quite true, Ribs. We know a lot, but it just doesn't fit the other aspects of the case."

"Like what?" Ribs asked.

"Like he was a witness to Pablo's killing, which means he could have been killed because of that. He also had ties to McLaughlin through the church, though nothing ties him and McLaughlin together to the murders. And of course, he was married to Rita Langer, nee Boswell, whose family we know is tied to Ortega, but we have nothing to tie her and no reason to suspect her."

Ribs sighed. "You're right about all of that, Gino. I tried my best to reason it out so we might blame Ortega, but the trouble is, I believed him when he told us about the priest. I don't think he killed McLaughlin *or* had Burns beaten up. And I think he really was pissed off about it happening."

I nodded. "I'm with you all the way on that, Ribs. He sounded sincere."

"If it's not Ortega, maybe it's Raul," Ribs said. "If he found out Pablo and the others were selling Ortega's drugs, that would be plenty of reason for him to kill them."

I nodded, agreeing with Ribs. "And then he killed Langer and McLaughlin to shut them up. And then Burns and Jorge and Ranza. This might all be about controlling the drug territory," I said.

"I don't know," Ribs said. "If it's all about Raul being pissed over the drugs, where does Rodrigo come into play? From what we've heard, he runs things for Raul in Houston, and we haven't heard a peep from him."

"Maybe we should pay him a visit and see if we can poke the bear," I said.

"The trouble with that strategy is no one has seen the bear in a while. From what Ricky told me, Rodrigo has almost disappeared."

"Then we need to contact Ricky and all our CIs and tell them we need eyes on Rodrigo as soon as we can. And we need to know where he goes and what he does."

The front door opened and Marissa walked in, followed by Connie. "What who does?" Marissa asked.

"Just somebody on this case," I said. "Why are you back so early? I didn't expect you until the stores closed."

Connie sat down and laughed. "Gino, the stores *are* closed. You and Ribs must have been talking longer than you thought."

"You know what I think," Marissa said. "I think you two should tell Connie what you've got so far and see if she can help. An extra set of eyes is usually good, and it never hurts."

Chapter Thirty-Five

NOW WHAT?

I sat back against the cushion and sighed. "All right, Gianelli. Listen up while Ribs fills you in. If he misses anything important, I'll let you know."

Ribs told Connie about our cases—all of them—culminating with our suspicions of Father Burns.

"What is it you think he's done?" she asked. "He's a priest, for God's sake."

Ribs hesitated, so I dove in. "We don't know if he's done anything, but something's not right. He's been too close to a lot of murders, and the connections seem to be more than coincidence."

Marissa refilled my glass and asked Connie if she wanted any, but she refused. "I've got to drive home, Marissa, but thanks."

Connie turned back to me. "Gino, sometimes coincidence is just that—coincidence. It happens all the time with a lot of things. I know a lot of cops—including my partner—who are not believers in it, but it's there, and it's real."

"I know that, Connie. But this is different. Consider the name change in San Antonio, where he went by Father Sebastian, then Father Burns."

"You told me he said it was his cousin."

"That's what he *said,* yeah. But his look-alike cousin has now disappeared, and when we asked Burns where he was during the time Sebastian was at Holy Rosary, he said he was on a mission in the Caribbean. Even worse, there's no way to verify it."

Connie seemed to give it thought, then she looked at Ribs and said, "Delgado, you can chime in at any time."

"Connie, as much as I am usually against my cuz when he goes off on his rants against the church, this time I'm not. I agree that something isn't right with Father Burns. I just don't know what that something is."

"I've got an idea," Connie said, "but if we do this, you can never tell anyone. And I mean *anyone.*"

"Sounds ominous," I said, "but I'm game."

"Count me in," Ribs said.

Marissa walked in and sat down next to me. "I presume you're talking about calling your uncle, and if that's it, I have no problem with you doing it or swearing secrecy."

I looked at her quizzically. "Your uncle?"

Marissa patted my leg. "Her uncle is not quite on your side of the law, Gino. You know that."

"I'll do it if you want," Connie said.

"If you think it might help, go for it," Ribs said. "I'm not against taking help from anyone."

Connie pulled out her phone and dialed. A moment later, Uncle Dominic answered. "Pronto, Concetta. To what do I owe such a wonderful surprise?"

"You're not going to like it, Uncle Dominic. I have a friend who needs a favor, a cop friend."

"Nonsense, Concetta. I have a lot of cop friends."

Connie stifled a laugh. "Uncle Dominic, these are not cops who are looking to be on your payroll, and you know that. Will you talk to him?"

"Of course, but tell me who I'll be speaking to."

"His name is Gino Cataldi, and he—"

"Cataldi? I know the Cataldis. They have the best restaurant in Brooklyn. One of my favorites. Is he there now? Put him on the phone."

Connie handed Gino the phone and whispered, "His name is Dominic Mangini."

"Signor Mangini. My name is Gino Cataldi, and as Connie mentioned, my partner and I have a case that is baffling us. We were hoping you might have a suggestion."

"So you want a favor?" Dominic asked.

Gino hesitated, but then said, "Yes, I want a favor, but I'll be happy to pay for it. I have an uncle who owns a very good restaurant in Brooklyn, and I'll make sure that you get a couple of free meals or more, depending on what's owed."

Dominic laughed. "My favors do not come so cheap, Gino. By the way, I have a cousin in Sicily named Gino. He and I grew up together. I always said if I had a son, I would name him Gino. Anyway, I will do this favor as a gift to my beautiful niece, Concetta. Besides, I have a table at Cataldi's already, and you're right, it *is* an excellent restaurant, one of the best I know."

Gino was shocked. "I didn't know they reserved tables," he said.

"They don't," Dominic said, "but they made an exception for me."

Dominic laughed. "But enough of that, tell me what your problem is, and let's see if we can fix it."

For ten or fifteen minutes, Gino explained his situation to Dominic, taking time to answer questions Dominic had as Gino went along. To finish things up, Gino told Dominic of Father Burns being beaten and in the hospital.

"How badly was he beaten? Dominic asked.

"Pretty badly," Gino said. "Several broken ribs, multiple contusions, and one of his lungs collapsed."

"Your Father Burns sounds as if he's a committed man," Dominic said.

"Committed?"

"Yes, committed. A man not so brave would have opted for a minor beating, but it looks like Father Burns made it seem real."

"You think he faked this?" Gino asked.

"You must believe the same thing, Signor Cataldi. If you didn't, you wouldn't have called. If you believe the beating is real, then the priest is real, and what he told you is the way he sees it. If you believe the beating is fake, then the priest is fake, and nothing he told you is real."

"What makes you say that?" Gino asked.

"Because in all my years, I have never heard of a drug cartel who set out to kill a man and left him only beaten. And not even that badly beaten. Broken ribs are painful, but they heal fast. And collapsed lungs are often minor inconveniences. Trust me, Gino, if the cartel wanted him dead, he would have died that night."

"So you think the priest is somehow involved?"

"In my opinion, you either have a dirty priest or a dirty cop. Since the beating seems to have been staged, I'd go with a dirty priest."

Gino thought for a moment. "But why? What is the motive? What does the priest get out of it? Hell, for that matter, what does the cartel get out of it?"

"Gino, you told me the priest received recommendations regarding his fundraising abilities. Doesn't that tell you something?"

Gino thought for a moment. "I know all churches need a lot of money, and I know contributions have been shrinking. I'm guessing any increase he provided was welcome."

Dominic laughed. "You seem to have a good heart, Gino, but I'm afraid fundraising for the churches is not much different than anywhere else."

"Meaning what?"

Dominic didn't say anything for a moment, then he spoke softly and said, "Money laundering."

"Money laundering? The priest?"

Dominic laughed. "Si, Signor Cataldi, the priest—and I'm sure the church was in on it too."

Gino, still doubtful, posed a question. "If Father Burns was in on this doing money laundering, why was he beaten up?"

"Any number of reasons," Dominic said. "When a person works for the cartel, things must be done a certain way. If the priest failed any of the rules, he would have suffered consequences. A beating such as you described would not be unusual."

"But why would a church do such a thing?" Gino asked.

"The same reason everyone does—money," Dominic said. "*Everyone* needs money."

Gino shook his head and furrowed his brow. "Mr. Mangini, are you sure about this? I've never heard of a church doing money laundering."

"Churches are one of the better resources," Dominic said. "No one suspects them, and it's difficult to prove wrongdoing without an insider providing data."

"How does it work?" Gino asked. "I know how it works with strip clubs, and even with bars and restaurants, but how does it work with a damn church?"

Marissa laughed and got up to get more wine. "Both of y'all want some?"

"I do," Ribs said. "It looks like we're going to be here a while."

"I *know* I'll be here," Gino said. "So, yes, I'll take more wine."

Dominic began to speak, but Gino interrupted. "Signor Mangini, may I put this on speaker so my partner can hear. I don't want to miss anything."

"Put Concetta on the phone, please?"

"Yes, Uncle Dominic."

"Do you vouch for everyone in the room?"

"I do, Uncle Dominic, and I already swore them to secrecy."

"Okay, put the phone on speaker."

Connie set the phone on the table and turned on the speaker. "Go ahead, Uncle Dominic."

Dominic began in a quiet, calm voice. "Simply put, money laundering is the process of making dirty money look clean. As I'm sure all of you know, many money-laundering activities are conducted by cash businesses such as strip clubs, restaurants, clubs, and bars. What you may not know is the church is even better."

"How so?" Gino asked.

"Imagine that a criminal who is a member of the church, or who pretends to be, provides a loan to the church for the construction of a church building, or several stained-glass windows, or statues. The church then pays off the loan by giving checks back to the church member over time. In that way, the money is now into the system as clean money, no association with criminal activity."

"It's that simple?" Gino asked.

Dominic laughed. "Of course not. Often, the church will hold bazaars or carnivals to raise money, then they will mix all that cash with the normal church offerings. Many times, during these fundraising events, there will be auctions of various items that may draw significant bids. The winning bids are usually much more than the worth of the item being bid on. The extra money is once again, put into the system as clean money."

"So they've got this down pat?" Gino asked.

"That's not even the beginning," Dominic said. "The biggest operation is when the criminals fund rescue operations or international aid. Often, these will be for projects like rebuilding after a hurricane or flood or constructing new churches or schools. And, not surprisingly, these operations are often conducted in places like the Caribbean where the banks have secrecy policies to keep out prying eyes. Once the money is donated, it is 'cleaned' through the banks, and it is then clean money."

"So how the hell do you catch a church doing that?" Gino asked.

"It's difficult, but the best way is to arrest the person responsible, or to find the second set of books."

"Second set?" Gino asked.

"Exactly. When laundering money like this, there will always be a second set of books. One for the government and one that is real."

"So we have to find the real one."

"If you know who the middle-man is, you're halfway there already. Just find out how to apply pressure."

"Okay, Mr. Mangini, I thank you for your help," Gino said.

"Not yet, Gino," Dominic said. "Can you take the phone off speaker and step outside to talk, or to another room?"

Gino looked at Connie, but he did as Dominic asked, and stepped onto the porch. "Okay, I'm alone."

"Good. You asked me for a favor, and I did you one. I did it for Concetta, but I still want a promise from you."

Gino got nervous. "Go on."

"I know that Connie's partner looks out for her, and I know that Fabrizio does as well, but I feel there can never be enough sets of eyes watching out for my *principessa*. I am asking you and your partner to watch out for her as well."

Gino breathed a sigh of relief. "You have my word on that, Mr. Mangini. We both like Connie, and we respect her."

"Good. It is settled, then."

~

Gino reached for the door handle, then stopped. Instead, he dialed his Uncle Alphonse at Cataldi's restaurant. He knew it was late, but Uncle Al usually worked late.

"Cataldi's."

"Uncle Al. It's your nephew, Gino."

"Gino. What the hell are you calling about? How are you?"

"I'm fine, Uncle Al, but I have a question."

"And I have an answer," Al said.

"I had reason to ask someone for a favor, someone important, and I wanted to know if they can be trusted."

"Someone important, you say. That could be anyone from Jesus Christ to the devil. I need to know who it is before I can give advice."

Gino waited a moment, then said, "Dominic Mangini."

Alphonse lowered his voice. "So, it's the devil."

"That bad?" Gino asked.

"Maybe. Maybe not," Alphonse said. "Did he just ask for a favor returned in the future, or was he specific?"

"He asked for a specific favor."

"And it's one you can live with?" Alphonse asked.

"Easily," Gino said. "It's no problem."

"Then you're good," Alphonse said. "Dominic is a man of his word if nothing else. If he tells you he's going to kill you, you need to make funeral arrangements. But if he tells you he won't, you can plan a wedding."

"Okay, Uncle Al. This has been a big help. Thank you."

"Come see us sometime, Gino. I know you're in Texas, but flights are cheap."

"Will do, Uncle Al. And tell everyone I said hi."

Gino walked back into the house and took a seat. He

turned to Connie and said, "Your Uncle Dominic is a character."

"He's a lot more than a character," Ribs said. "As Tip would say, he's slicker than cat shit on a slippery deck."

Connie buried her face in open palms. "And I thought I was free of Tip-sayings for the night."

Marissa carried in a bottle and poured another glass of wine for Gino and Ribs, emptying the bottle. Then she walked to the kitchen to dispose of it.

"You may as well open up another one," Gino said. "It's going to be a long night."

"You want the Chianti or the pinot noir?" Marissa asked.

"I don't care," Gino said. "As long as it's red."

Chapter Thirty-Six

THE TALKING IS OVER

Ciudad Juarez, Mexico

Eliondo waited until Ortega finished his drink, then he approached. "Señor, we're ready to go."

Ortega sipped on an amaretto drink and stared. "So why are you standing here telling me instead of driving across the border? I don't think you can retake the cities from here, my friend."

"Agreed, sir. We're leaving now." Eliondo snapped a salute and left the room.

Ortega placed his drink on the side of the table and studied the map. He had firm control of San Antonio, and he had a strong position in Austin, especially since it was so close to San Antonio. He also had El Paso, Lubbock, Amarillo, and Nuevo Laredo and all of them with people firmly entrenched. What he needed were Dallas and Houston, the two biggest markets. Dallas was a possibility. He could send reinforcements from the west and from Austin. And if he sent just a few men to Tyler, it would prevent Raul from using his base there to reinforce Dallas. Houston, he considered a lost cause. He might send some men simply to make Raul think he needed to defend it, but he'd make no play for it. Not yet.

He dialed Eliondo, hoping to reach him before he hit the border. "Eliondo, after you completely secure San Antonio, move a dozen men to Austin and do the same there, but work up from the south side. When you have secured Austin, stay put unless you hear differently."

"What about Dallas?" Eliondo asked.

"I'll handle Dallas," Ortega said.

Monterrey, Mexico

"I'm convinced he'll be attacking Houston," Raul said to Felipe. "I want you to take a dozen men from Monterrey and another ten from Corpus and Brownsville. Take them all to reinforce Houston."

Felipe looked concerned. "Raul, I know you want to keep Houston, but should we spread ourselves so thin?"

"What would you have me do, Felipe? We have no shot at San Antonio or Nuevo Laredo. Austin is doubtful. Dallas is up in the air, and the rest of West Texas is in Ortega's grasp. Houston is the only major city we have left."

"We have Corpus, Brownsville, and Tyler," Felipe said.

Raul shook his head. "Yes, and we have Beaumont as well, but all of them combined mean nothing in comparison. If we lose Houston, we lose Texas. If we keep Houston, we can fight another day. But make no mistake, it will be a fight. Ortega isn't giving up easily, and don't forget, he has the San Antonio police department in his pocket."

Felipe looked as if he wanted to speak. "What is it, Felipe?" Raul asked.

"Ortega is strong in Nuevo Laredo, but if we let him have it, he will control Juarez and Laredo, two of the major entries into Texas. I think it would be wise to risk sending men from Monterrey into Nuevo Laredo from the south and take them by surprise. Ortega would never expect that."

Raul thought about it, then nodded. "No, he wouldn't. Especially if we pressured him from Laredo to the north. Do it, Felipe. Put it in place, then get to Houston and reinforce it."

"Consider it done, Raul."

"But keep in touch, Felipe. We need to remain flexible. We don't know what Ortega is going to do, so we need to be prepared to adjust our tactics."

"I have both phones with me, Raul. Call on either one at any time."

～

Houston, Texas

Felipe called Raul two hours after getting to Houston. "I know it's early, Raul, but nothing is happening. None of Ortega's men have attacked anything."

"Don't let that fool you. His men may be delayed, or he may be playing a game of some sort. Tell everyone to stay alert."

"I told everyone to be on guard, but we haven't seen anything. Have you heard from Dallas? Anywhere else?"

"We're having trouble in Dallas already; in fact, we've lost two men, but we managed to surprise him in Nuevo Laredo. He didn't expect us to come up from the south."

"Good," Felipe said. "We don't even have to take Laredo; if we can disrupt his operations enough, we'll mess with his smuggling system."

"Exactly," Raul said. "And Laredo would give us direct access to San Antonio. It would kill Ortega to lose control of that."

Raul was about to hang up when he thought of something. "Felipe, while you're in Houston, check on Rodrigo. Make sure he is being taken care of, and that he wants for nothing."

Dallas, Texas

Eliondo had verified that San Antonio was secure, then did the same with Austin. Afterward, he took a dozen men, and they headed to Dallas.

"What are the plans," Rubio asked as they drove up I-35.

"Don't worry so much, Rubio. When we get there, you'll know. Until then, you have no need to know."

Antonio chimed in from the back seat. "Is Ortega sending anyone else, or are we the only ones?"

"Ortega is swamping the place," Eliondo said. "We have men from Tyler coming in from the east; we're coming up from the south; and Lubbock and Wichita are approaching from the west. Raul's men will be taken completely by surprise. Before two days go by, Dallas will be ours."

Rubio turned in his seat and looked back at Antonio. "Once we have Dallas, it is only a matter of time before Austin falls. Then, with three of the four major cities in Texas, plus El Paso, we will own the market."

Eliondo smiled. "So true. Raul won't be able to hold Houston for long once we control the rest."

For three days, men from Ortega's operation and men from Raul's fought, mostly in Dallas and Nuevo Laredo. After ten bodies dropped, the police in both cities swarmed the known drug locations and made dozens of arrests.

Before long, drug traffic in both cities slowed to a crawl.

Juarez, Mexico

Ortega called Manuel to his side. "Manuel, can you get a number for Raul? I want to call him."

"I can try, señor, but Ortega is no different than the rest of us. He changes phone numbers all the time. We might be better off trying to reach his men and have them contact him."

"I don't care how it happens, just see if you can get him. If you have to, give my number to one of his men and ask him to call."

~

H ours later, Ortega received a call. "Olla?"

"It's me," Raul said. "I understand you wanted to talk about surrender."

Ortega laughed. "Hardly that, but I did want to talk. We need to put an end to this nonsense before the police see to it that we have nothing to fight over."

"And how would you suggest we do that? I didn't start this, you did."

"Me? I started nothing."

Raul took a few deep breaths. "You first tried dealing drugs in Houston, then you killed three of my men, not to mention stirred up law enforcement by killing a prominent citizen *and* a priest."

"I did none of those things," Ortega said. "Not the drugs or the killings. And I would *never* harm a priest. If someone is saying I did this, they're lying."

Raul thought for a moment. "All right. I'm going to look into this. In the meantime, suppose we return things to the way they were before this began? I know you made headway in Dallas, but you lost territory in Nuevo Laredo. Nothing changed in San Antonio or Houston."

"I'm waiting to hear what you say," Ortega said.

"You take the west and north parts of Dallas, and I take the east and south parts. We keep to our territories, no matter what. Your men don't sell in my territories, and my men don't sell in your territories."

"And Laredo?" Ortega asked.

"You can have Laredo back, but you need to allow us safe passage for distribution."

"I have no problem sharing passage into Texas, but if you get caught too many times, it will put more pressure on my operations there, and that would make it more difficult for me to conduct business."

"Would you rather give me access to El Paso? I'd take that."

"Raul, it seems as if I'm giving up a lot. I already had half of Dallas, but I also had Laredo. If I agree to your proposal, I'd still only have half of Dallas, but I would be giving up some of Laredo."

"Ortega, I believe we're both concerned with the same things, and that is money. There is more than enough business in Texas for us to split. I know you have a stronger smuggling operation in Laredo, so if your concern in Laredo is me getting caught, how about I give you ten percent of whatever I take over—successfully. That gives you incentive to help me get my product across the border, and it gives us both reason to work together."

"Raul, I will agree, but you must agree to find out who killed the priest in Houston. I won't have my name ruined in such a way."

"Consider it done, Ortega. As of now, I will issue orders to my men in both cities."

"And I'll do the same," Ortega said. "All that remains is for you to solve the mystery in Houston."

❧

Houston, Texas

Felipe let the phone ring several times before he answered. "Yes?"

"Felipe, where the hell have you been?" Raul asked.

"Right here," Felipe said. "What do you need?"

"Keep alert for things, but don't make it your main concern. I want to know what happened to our men in Houston, and I want to know what happened to that priest who was killed."

"The one who was killed? Or the one who was beaten?"

"Find out about both of them. And find out about Rodrigo while you're there. He was in the hospital the last time I spoke to him. Someone tried killing him as well. Before today, I suspected Ortega. Now, I'm not so certain."

"I'll find out, Raul. Give me his number."

~

Felipe called Rodrigo, who answered right away. "Hello?"

"Rodrigo, it's Felipe. Raul is having trouble with Ortega, and we need to talk. Are you still in the hospital?"

Rodrigo hesitated, then said, "I am, but you can come here. We'll be free to talk."

Rodrigo gave Felipe directions to the hospital and told him what room he was in. Half an hour later, Felipe showed up.

He entered the room, went to Rodrigo's side, and sat alongside the bed. "How are you, Rodrigo? You look like shit."

Rodrigo grinned. "Why, thank you, Felipe. I appreciate the compliment."

"Who did this?" Felipe asked. "Was it Ortega's men?"

Rodrigo shook his head. "I don't know. I wish I did, but I

don't. And worse, I don't know why either." Rodrigo took a sip of the water from his table. "What are you doing up here? I never knew you to come to Houston."

Felipe nodded. "I usually don't, but Raul is in a frenzy. He and Ortega are at war, and he sent me to secure Houston since you were in the hospital."

Felipe snapped a picture of Rodrigo with his phone. "He'll want this. It will provide more motivation to get even with Ortega."

Rodrigo appeared upset at first, but then he nodded. "Just make sure nobody but Raul sees it. I don't like my picture out there."

"No problem," Felipe said. "I feel the same way."

"What is Raul doing? Is he going after Ortega in other cities?"

"I can't discuss his plans, Rodrigo, but be comfortable knowing he plans to get revenge for what Ortega did to you," Felipe said.

"That's good," Rodrigo said. "But I wish he waited until I got out, so I could take part."

Felipe laughed. "Unless you plan to nurse it, you'll have plenty of time. This isn't ending overnight."

"Then save Ortega for me," Rodrigo said. "I want his ass badly."

"Will do," Felipe said, then he patted Rodrigo on the arm and scooted his chair closer. "I can tell you this much . . ."

∼

Two hours later, Felipe left the hospital and drove to the house he used for a safe house. On the way, he texted a picture of Rodrigo along with a message to Raul.

He doesn't look great, but he's not as bad as we were led to believe. Here's a picture of him as of tonight.

Raul looked at Rodrigo's face and scowled. "Ortega will die for this," he said.

~

Raul dialed Ortega. When the call was answered, he spoke. "You said you had nothing to do with it, but as you see, someone did. Help me understand who might have done it, if not you."

"Give me a few hours," Ortega said. "In the meantime, think of the proposal on the table."

Ortega called his top men to the room. When they were all there, he showed the picture to everyone. "Does anyone here know what Rodrigo looks like?"

Hidalgo's brother answered immediately. "That's him. He's beaten badly, but there's no question, it's him."

"Anyone else recognize the man in the picture?" Ortega asked. When no one replied, Ortega dismissed them.

Houston, Texas

My cell phone rang, and I picked up. "Hello?"

"Detective, this is your friend, Ortega, from Mexico."

I almost spat. "I have no friends named Ortega. For that matter, I have no friends in Mexico."

"Fine, but at least allow me to help you solve one of your mysteries. We spoke last time about a priest who was beaten, and you suspected it was me, or possibly Raul. I want to send you a picture. See what you think."

A moment later, my text message sounded and a picture came through, with the heading:

This is Rodrigo. And I didn't do this.

"What kind of bullshit is this?" I asked. "This is Father Burns, the priest who was beaten."

"I'm sorry, Detective, I sent the wrong picture, but regardless, you have restored my faith in mankind. Have a good evening."

"Lunatic," I said, then I began thinking. "Why would Ortega call me with that if it was nothing?" I drove a few more miles, then turned left and headed toward Ribs's house as I dialed Marissa. "Babe, I am going to be late. I've got to stop and talk with Ribs."

"Fine by me, but if you drink too much wine, spend the night."

I knocked on Ribs's door, then waited for an answer. Rosalee opened it in a moment. "Gino, what are you doing here? Is Marissa with you?"

I shook my head. "By myself, Rosalee. I need to brainstorm with your husband on a case."

She stepped aside and invited me in. "Take a seat. I'll get him."

Ribs walked in a moment later. "Talk about surprises—cousin Gino, at this time of night."

Before sitting down, he asked, "Beer or wine?"

"Red wine, Ribs. You know that."

He brought in a full bottle and set in on the table between us, along with glasses for both of us, then he poured. "Feel privileged, cuz. This is the almost-ten-dollar bottle."

I smiled. "I'm impressed, Ribs. Thank you."

"So what are you here for?" Ribs asked.

I handed him my phone. "Look at the last text. It's from Ortega."

Ribs looked, then handed me back the phone. "What does he mean by 'this is Rodrigo.'?"

"Good question, isn't it? And note that when I said it was Father Burns, his response looked like bullshit too."

Ribs drank a sip of his wine, then he took another sip. "Are you thinking what I'm thinking? That Burns is Rodrigo?"

"I don't know what else to think," I said. "The question is, why?"

Ribs yelled to Rosalee. "Darling, we may need another bottle of wine, if you don't mind."

Chapter Thirty-Seven

GINO AND RIBS FIGURE IT OUT

Houston, Texas

At three a.m., they finished the second bottle of wine. While Ribs got another one, I thought out loud. "Assuming we buy into this bullshit, and that's a big *if*, why would someone hide as a priest?"

Ribs sat down, placing another bottle between us. "Are you kidding me? There's not much better. Hell, a priest is better than a cop."

"In what way?" I asked. "I wouldn't cut him any slack."

"But recognize that you're the exception to the rule, cuz. Most people would, which means he'd avoid initial suspicion. He'd have access to almost anyplace. And if we listen to Connie's Uncle Dominic, he could launder money without being scrutinized."

"Now you're starting to sound like me," I said. "But continue being the devil's advocate and let's assume he was laundering money. What proof do we have?"

Ribs shook his head. "Not a damn bit of proof, not real proof, but we have Burk and Nickles, not to mention Julie, saying he was a good fundraiser in San Antonio."

"That's what a good priest does," I said. "It's part of the job."

"It is also part of the job for a money launderer," Ribs said. "Drugs bring in huge amounts of money, cash money, and they need a way to clean that money. That's where the church comes in."

"All right, let's back up a minute," I said. "If we're going to buy into this, we first have to believe that Burns is Rodrigo. Do you believe that?"

"In order for that to be true, I'd have to believe he ordered his men to beat him and beat him badly."

"Let's back up a minute," I said. "There are only two scenarios here. Either Rodrigo is Burns, and he ordered the beating, or Burns really is a priest, and he was beaten for another reason."

"So we have to believe the cartel screwed up and didn't finish the job, if he's really Burns, or they did as ordered if he's Rodrigo?"

"That's the way I see it," I said. "Either Rodrigo ordered the hit on Burns, and his men screwed up, or he ordered the hit on himself and all went as planned."

"If I were a betting man—and you know I am—I'd wager the man in the hospital *is not* Father Burns, nor was the priest in San Antonio, nor was Father Sebastian."

"I wouldn't take that bet, Ribs. But it does raise a few questions."

"Such as?" Ribs asked.

"If we presume Burns is Rodrigo, why did he call in the plates and car description after Pablo was killed?"

"That's easy," Ribs said. "Because the plate number was wrong, and it had us looking for days for the wrong car. He later gave us the proper number, but it was after the fact."

"I don't know, Ribs. Then why did he kill Jorge and Ranza? We weren't even close to finding them."

"I think he wanted to put the blame on Ortega so it would start a war—which it did. Killing Jorge and Ranza fit right in," Ribs said. "It looked as if Ortega was taking revenge for them killing Pablo and the others."

"But why would he want a war between Raul and Ortega?" I asked.

"To make a play," Ribs said. "It's a classic move. Get both sides fighting, and when they are both weakened enough, make your move. I'm guessing Rodrigo was looking to control the Monterrey cartel or the Juarez one, or both."

"All right," I said. "Just to be safe, let's call and put a couple of uniforms on his hospital room, with orders that he's not to leave."

"I agree," Ribs said. "And let's do it now. The damn night shift never has anything to do anyway."

Ribs called the shift commander and asked him to assign a couple of uniforms to watch Burns, or Rodrigo, or whoever the hell he was. He gave him the hospital and room number, then hung up. "Okay, cuz, we're all set."

He leaned forward and poured another glass of wine. "Now let's enjoy ourselves."

"Is it okay if I stay here?" I asked. "If I'm having more wine, I don't want to drive."

"Sure, you can stay," he said, "But you can't sleep with Rosalee."

I shook my head. "God, you need to be partnered with Tip."

~

Ribs woke me at the ungodly hour of six a.m. "Cuz, get up."

"What? What's the matter?"

"I just called the shift commander. The hospital room is empty. He's gone."

"What? Why didn't he let us know?"

"He did, but we must not have heard the text. He texted me about four in the morning. Come on. Let's get some breakfast and then go catch this son of a bitch."

"You do realize, we don't have a damn thing anyway," I said. "We have no proof the man we know as Father Burns is Rodrigo, and even if we did, we don't have a damn thing we can charge him on. Neither Burns nor Rodrigo have any warrants on them."

"You're right," Ribs said. "All we've got is the word of a drug dealer in Mexico, one we'd never be able to bring here to testify to begin with."

"So why go over there? Any reason you can think of? Any *good* reason?"

Ribs seemed to give it thought. "We can go over and bother him. Let him know we're on to his game," Ribs said.

"And what good will that do, Ribs? I'm of the opinion we should leave him alone and find a way to nail him. We know it won't be long before he does something."

"Let's talk to Coop and see what she says. We'll have to run it by her anyway," Ribs said.

I nodded. "All right. Let's go. You know she gets in early."

~

We got to the station, climbed the stairs, and walked down the hallway to Coop's office. When we turned the corner, we faced that long, straight walk before we got to Cindy's desk. I always felt uneasy making this walk, and I wondered if this was how prisoners walking to their death felt.

"You two are in early," Cindy said. "What did you do wrong?"

"What makes you think we did something wrong?" Ribs asked. "Maybe we just wanted to bring Coop some doughnuts."

"If that's the case, you forgot the doughnuts," Cindy said.

She stifled a laugh, then said, "Go on in. The captain's in there."

We walked in and sat. "Good morning, Captain," Ribs said. "How are you this morning?"

"What do you two want? I know it's not good."

"Actually, I came here to bring you doughnuts, but Gino said you didn't need the extra sugar, so I ate them before we got here."

Coop lowered her head and shook it. "Just tell me what you want and let me have a peaceful day."

"Pay no attention to that idiot, Captain. We came to see about getting a warrant for Father Burns, and we wanted to run it by you."

"A warrant? For the priest? Have you lost your mind? The chief and the mayor both would be crawling up my ass in minutes."

"At least that would keep them busy," Ribs said.

Coop glared at Ribs but maintained her cool. "Delgado, I'll pretend I didn't hear that. And while I forget what I did hear, tell me what made you think it was a good idea to get a warrant on the priest."

Ribs shifted in his seat. "It's where the investigation led, Captain. You've always told us to go where the investigation leads."

"Delgado, *investigations* don't lead, or at least they shouldn't; they should be *led*. *Detectives* are supposed to do the leading."

"So you want us to lay off?" Ribs asked.

"Not by any means," Coop said. "But I told you early on that this case would be a hot one, that the chief had a special interest in it. That means you have to conduct the investigation *without* stirring up a lot of shit if possible. If you're telling me that it's inevitable that we have to get a warrant for the priest, so be it. I'll get one. But no matter what, get this damn case solved."

"Who do you think we should try for the warrant?" Ribs asked.

"Hell, I don't know," Coop said. "What do you even have to substantiate it? Do you have *anything?*"

"We've got the ID from a Mexican drug lord that Father Burns and Rodrigo are one and the same," Ribs said.

"Good God," Coop said. "And I suppose he's going to waltz into the courtroom and testify?"

"I doubt it," I said, "But we've also got a solid parishioner in San Antonio who will swear the same, and he *will* testify."

"That's something," Coop said. "Not enough, but something."

"We also have the circumstantial that the mysterious Father Sebastian disappeared from Holy Rosary—never to be heard from again—at the same time Father Burns showed up at St. Joseph's."

Coop seemed to relax a little more. "Still not ideal, but better," she said.

I cleared my throat and leaned forward. "There is another possibility," I said.

Coop looked over. "I'm listening."

"Let me have someone go undercover, and we might be able to get more to use for a warrant."

"No way. No way in hell. The last time you got undercover clearance, you got the person killed."

"Bullshit," Ribs said. "That wasn't us. It was Tip and Connie."

"Six of one and half dozen the other," Coop said.

"And what the hell does that mean?" Ribs asked. "Is that one of Tip's sayings, 'cause it sounds like one."

"No, it means you're all just criminals with badges," Coop said.

Ribs shook his head. "I don't think it means that, but you're still full of it. Gino and I had nothing to do with getting that cop killed, but if you insist, we can use Gino's wife. I'm sure she'll do it."

"Like hell," Coop said, jumping up from her seat behind the desk. "That's all I need is a civilian killed. The chief would have my ass for breakfast."

"For sure, he'd be filled," Ribs mumbled.

Coop glared. "*What the hell* did you say, you Mexican pervert?"

"I said, I'm sure he'd be thrilled," Ribs said.

I held back laughter while Coop continued staring. "Just get your asses to work and find some way to arrest him so we don't need an undercover person. I don't want any civilians, and I don't want rookies; in fact, I don't want an undercover person, period. We've got enough damn bodies as it is."

I stood up and leaned on her desk. "All right, then help us out with the warrant. Get somebody to write one so we can serve the son of a bitch right away. I don't care if he's saying mass when we get there, either."

Coop nodded. "You two write it up, and I'll get it. But make sure it's written up perfectly. And make sure to include the church, the rectory, and his private property."

"Will do," Ribs said. "One set of church books coming up."

Coop stood and hollered as we left. "That better read two sets of church books, or your ass is mine."

GET YOUR DUCKS IN A ROW

Ribs and I finished out the day writing the warrant. We wrote it three times, and each time, Captain Cooper found something wrong with the wording. Finally, she approved it and said she'd take it to a judge.

We got together that night, and Marissa and I played cards with Ribs and Rosalee. We played canasta and got our ass beat, then we switched to pinochle, but we still got our ass beat. Rosalee was damn good.

By eleven, Ribs and Rosalee left, and Marissa and I sat around and chatted.

"Are you all set for tomorrow?" she asked.

"I think we're as set as we can be," I said. "Coop said she'll have a warrant in the morning, and it will be for the church, the rectory, and his car as well. I can't imagine where else he'd keep a second set of books."

Marissa sipped on her wine and thought. "How about if he keeps the books in a safe-deposit box? Will that be covered?

How was the warrant worded? Do you have to know the location of the safe-deposit box?"

I jumped up from the sofa. "Shit. You're right, Marissa. I didn't think of that. I dialed Coop's home number and let it ring until she picked up."

"Gino, this better be a damn emergency."

"It is," I said. "Suppose he has the second set of books in a safe-deposit box? Are we covered with the warrant on that?"

"I don't think we would be, Gino. Good thinking. Let's hold off until I check. See me in the morning."

Marissa and I relaxed the rest of the evening, spent a romantic night together, then I got up early and drove in with Ribs. I filled him in on my discussion with Coop on the way in.

"Damn, cuz, you could have called me," Ribs said.

"I would have if I wasn't afraid you'd come over," I said. "I needed time alone with Marissa."

"Why? You two having trouble?" he asked.

"No, Ribs, we're not having trouble. Every now and then we enjoy spending time with each other, and doing . . . things."

Ribs smiled. "What kind of things?"

"Shut the hell up, Ribs. You have seven kids. I think you know what kind of things."

"All right, pervert. Enough about sex. What are we going to do about this safe-deposit box? How do we find it?"

"I figure we can serve the warrant on the banks where he and the church do business and see if either one of them has a safe-deposit box. If they do, we seize them and look for the books or any illegal money. If they don't, we're back to square one."

~

It was easy enough to find out where the church banked, and, coincidentally, Father Burns banked the same place. The problem was that neither one had a safe-deposit box. "What now?" I asked.

"Now, we're screwed," Ribs said. "We need to know the location of the box."

"Yeah, and there are too many banks in Houston to just call each one and ask if Father Robert Burns has a safe-deposit box located there."

Ribs snapped his fingers. "Rodrigo," he said. "We check Rodrigo."

"What are you talking about? You think he put the box in Rodrigo's name?"

"It would be the smart thing to do. If no one knew Burns was Rodrigo, no one would look."

"That brings up the same problem," I said. "We can't very well call every bank and ask if a Rodrigo has a box there. Hell, it's worse. We don't even know his last name."

Ribs lost none of his excitement. "No, we don't. But I'll bet Julie can find it. He flew to see Raul on a regular basis, which means he had to use an ID of some sort. Considering he wasn't wanted, I'd bet he used his own."

Ribs had me excited now. "Let's get her on it, then. Call her."

Ribs called Julie and explained what we wanted in detail. "And we need this as soon as possible, Julie. It'll make the case for us."

"You got it, Ribs. I'll call as soon as I get something."

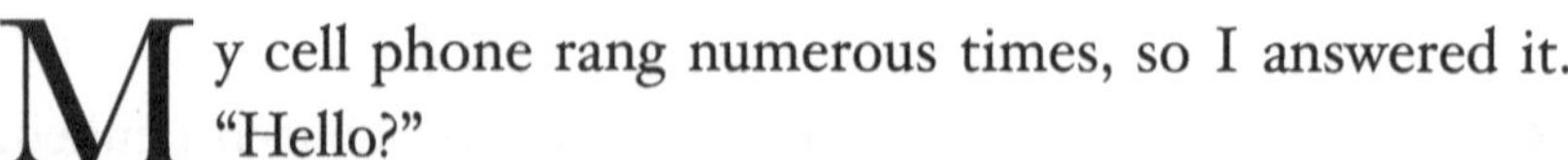

My cell phone rang numerous times, so I answered it. "Hello?"

"Gino, it's Julie. Where the hell have you two been? I've been trying to reach you."

"Damn, sorry, Julie. We had our phones off for a while. We were on a stakeout. What's up? You get anything?"

"A lot," she said. "I found records of a Rodrigo Borrejo, who flew from Houston to Monterrey every couple of months for the past two years, and when I checked the bank he used to pay his tickets with, he had a safe-deposit box in a local branch. He's had it for ten years."

"Son of a bitch, that's great. Which bank, and which branch?" I asked.

"It's Frost Bank, whose headquarters are in San Antonio, no less. And the box is located in the Memorial City branch, which isn't far from Sage Street.

"And it's under the name of Rodrigo Borrejo?" I asked.

"And has been for many years," Julie said.

"Thanks, Julie. You're a doll."

"I know that," she said. "But I still like hearing it."

I turned to Ribs. "Julie came through. We've got the box, and it's in Rodrigo's name."

Ribs didn't seem as happy as I thought he'd be. "Let's just hope we can tie Rodrigo to Burns," he said. "So far, all we have is a possible ID from a very, very old man in San Antonio. One who has a vendetta against a certain Father Sebastian, I might add."

"We'll worry about that later," I said. "For the time being, let's just get this new information typed up and put in the warrant so we don't have issues."

"If we have issues, I'm blaming it on you, cuz. And if that happens, Coop will go through your ass like a swarm of termites through a two-by-four."

"I looked at him and shook my head, then I shook it again. Are you listening to yourself? You sound like Tip junior, and that's not a compliment. Go back to your Mexican sayings and stop trying to copy Tip. At least when you used the Mexican sayings, people didn't understand you due to a language barrier, not because the sayings were plain stupid."

~

We rushed to Coop's office and asked her to amend the warrant to include the new information, which she agreed to do. "I'll have it ready in the morning," she said. "But check your shit and make sure I don't need to make any more changes. Judges don't like that."

"This should be it," I said.

"*Should* be?"

"It's done," Ribs said. "Count on it."

~

We had to wait till the morning, but when we got in, a note was on our desk. "Warrant is ready. See me before you go."

We walked to Coop's office and checked in. "You wanted to see us?" I asked.

"Only to remind you that things *have* to go right," she said.

"The chief and the mayor both have eyes on this operation, and they're waiting for something to go wrong."

"Don't worry," Ribs said. "We've got the *I*'s dotted on this one. We're ready."

"But do you have the Ts crossed as well?" Coop asked. "I can't afford *any* mistakes. None."

"There won't be any, Captain," I said. "We'll nail him, and it will be clean."

TIME TO SERVE THE WARRANT

Houston, Texas

As we turned on to Sage Street, I looked over at Ribs. "You ready, Ribs? This is it. It's do or die."

"Shit, cuz. I've been ready for this for a long time. Let's get this son of a bitch. I hate scum-sucking drug dealers, but one posing as a priest is even worse."

"What do you think? Should we take him in the rectory? Or wait until he's saying mass?"

"I say we take him wherever the hell he is. If it's mass, so be it. If not, the rectory."

"You got the warrant?" I asked.

He tapped his shirt pocket. "Right here, amigo. And I can't wait to serve it. I want to see the look on his face when I do."

We parked in front of the church and entered the front doors. Father Burns wasn't in there, so we walked through to the side door and knocked on the rectory entrance.

Father Burns answered in a moment. "Detectives, what a surprise. Come in," he said, and stepped aside.

Ribs reached in his pocket and pulled out the warrant. "Father, we have a warrant to search the premises for a set of books listing the financial transactions of St. Michael's church for the past ten years. These transactions deal with both local and overseas projects."

Father Burns appeared stunned. "Of course, but why? We have nothing to hide."

"Not even in your second set of books?" I asked.

Burns looked even more dumbfounded. "I don't know what you're talking about. But please, look all you want; in fact, I'll save you some time and show you the books." He walked toward the back of the rectory, but Ribs hollered for him to stop.

"Slow down, padre, and keep your hands clear of your body. I don't want to have to shoot a priest, but I will if it's necessary."

Father Burns raised his arms and slowed his pace. "No need for hasty actions, detectives. I've had enough violence to last a lifetime. I was simply showing you where we keep the books."

"Both sets of books?" I asked. "Or just the ones for the government?"

Burns turned very slowly. "I don't know what you mean by that," he said.

"Then how about you get us this set of books, then we'll take a ride to Memorial City and look at the other set?" Ribs asked. "Would that be good?"

Burns looked left and right, as if searching for an escape route, but there was none available. "Fine by me," he said.

We took the books from the rectory, sealed them in a

plastic bag, labeled them, then went to the car. Burns sat in the back seat. I drove. Ribs rode in the passenger seat and kept an eye on the prisoner.

"So tell me why McLaughlin had to die," Ribs asked.

"I have no idea," Burns said. "I assume some psycho drug dealer killed him."

"You mean someone like you, Rodrigo?" Ribs asked.

"Rodrigo? What are you talking about? Have you lost your mind? I'm Father Burns."

"We'll see," Ribs said. "It won't be long."

I called and asked the team to meet us at Frost Bank in Memorial City. When we pulled up, they were waiting. Ribs, Burns, and I walked inside with two officers holding warrant in hand. They took it to the manager who led us to the safe-deposit boxes.

The manager stood before us, staring at Father Burns, a.k.a. Rodrigo.

I snapped my fingers to catch the manager's attention. "Is this the man you know as Rodrigo, the one who has been accessing this box?"

He nodded. "That's him," he said, "but he wasn't wearing a collar."

I turned to Father Burns and said, "You can hand over the key, Burns, or we can have them drill the lock. It's up to you."

Burns seemed to give it some thought, then he reached into his pocket and handed us a key.

Within moments, the manager had used his own key along with Burns's, and soon handed us the contents of the box.

- *One set of financial records for St. Michael's the Archangel.*
- *Deeds for several houses.*

- *Fifty thousand dollars in cash.*

Ribs tugged harshly on Burns's handcuffs. "Odd bunch of items to be in a priest's box," he said.

"Fuck you," Burns said.

"Odd language for a priest, too."

We locked him up with extra security, and we petitioned the judge to expedite the trial to avoid problems. Within three weeks, he was in the courthouse. He had good lawyers, but so did we.

His lawyer presented every excuse you could think of, but he found it difficult to fight the eyewitness testimony of Miguel Reynosa, the parishioner from Holy Rosary, and the bank manager, not to mention the firsthand testimony from Felipe, who claimed to have attended meetings with Rodrigo —the man known as Father Burns—when he was in Monterrey.

We also had videos from the bank showing him both depositing and removing items from the box, and the video showed him as clear as could be. There was no denying who it was.

Combined with the circumstantial evidence, it was more than enough to put him away: twenty to life. Best of all, because the money laundering crossed international boundaries, he was sentenced to serve in a federal prison.

As he turned to exit the courtroom, he said to Ribs, "Be careful, my friend. I have many who do my bidding."

Without missing a beat, Ribs leaned closer and said, "And

I'd watch my back too, Rodrigo. I know a lot of people in the federal system, and many of them owe me favors."

As Rodrigo walked away, Ribs said, "Oh, and don't think you've gotten away with the murders. We're still working on those."

~

We had a note to see Coop when we returned, so we leisurely made our way to her office, knowing we hadn't done anything wrong.

"What's up, Coop?" I asked when I entered.

"You two did a good job on these murders. I was impressed, and so was the chief. He sends his regards."

"Thank you, Captain, that means something," I said.

"It should," she said. "And he gave you both a week off too, so enjoy yourselves, and do something fun."

"No shit," Ribs said. "A week? Rosalee and I are going to take the kids somewhere."

"And you, Gino?" Coop asked.

"I don't know," I said. "I'll have to talk to Marissa. Maybe San Francisco. She loves it there."

Coop stood and smiled. "No matter. Wherever it is, have fun. And come back refreshed because Tip and Connie are on a tough one, and they may need some help."

"Oh God, no," I said. "Come on, Coop."

"Shut up, Cataldi. I know you love working with Tip. And I know Ribs likes staring at Connie's ass. So go have fun, but be prepared when you get back."

ACKNOWLEDGMENTS

It is with great honor that I give eternal gratitude to my wife and all four of my grandkids. They give me the inspiration to keep going.

ABOUT THE AUTHOR

Giacomo Giammatteo is the author of gritty crime dramas about murder, mystery, and family. He also writes non-fiction books including the No Mistakes Careers series, No Mistakes Publishing, No Mistakes Grammar, and No Mistakes Writing.

When Giacomo isn't writing, he's helping his wife take care of the animals on their sanctuary. At last count, they had forty-five animals—eleven dogs, a horse, six cats, and twenty-six pigs.

Oh, and one crazy—and very large—wild boar, who takes walks with Giacomo every day and also happens to be his best buddy.

nomistakespublishing.com
gg@giacomog.com

ALSO BY GIACOMO GIAMMATTEO

You can see all of my books here.

And you can buy them on the platform of your choice.

This brings up a thought: with more than eighty books out now, it is becoming difficult to try to update the list at the back of all of them. If you want to know what books I have out, use the link above, which takes you to my website, or download the latest copy of my GG recommended reading list, which is free.

Nonfiction

Careers

No Mistakes Resumes, Book I of No Mistakes Careers

No Mistakes Interviews, Book II of No Mistakes Careers

Grammar

Misused Words, No Mistakes Grammar, Volume I

Misused Words for Business, No Mistakes Grammar, Volume II

More Misused Words, No Mistakes Grammar, Volume III

Visual Grammar (this is a compilation of volumes I–III with a bit of new information added. It also includes pictures and is the world's first visual grammar book)

Misused Words and Then Some, No Mistakes Grammar, Volume V

Simply Put: The Plain English Grammar Guide

Publishing

How to Publish an eBook, No Mistakes Publishing, Volume I

How to Format an eBook, No Mistakes Publishing, Volume II

eBook Distribution, No Mistakes Publishing, Volume III

Print on Demand—Who to Use to Print Your Books, No Mistakes Publishing, Volume IV

Other Nonfiction

Uneducated

Whiskers and Bear—Volume I, Sanctuary Tales

A Collection of Animal Stories, Volume II, Sanctuary Tales

More Animal Stories, Volume III, Sanctuary Tales

Surviving a Stroke—Or Two

Life and Then Some

Fiction

Friendship & Honor Series:

Murder Takes Time

Murder Has Consequences

Murder Takes Patience

Murder Is Invisible

Murder Is a Promise

Murder Is Immaculate (coming soon)

Blood Flows South Series

A Bullet for Carlos: A Connie Gianelli Mystery

Finding Family, a Novella

A Bullet from Dominic

The Good Book

The Ranger

Redemption Series

Necessary Decisions: A Gino Cataldi Mystery

Old Wounds

Promises Kept, the Story of Number Two

Premeditated

The Ranger

Rules of Vengeance Series (Fantasy)

Light of Lights (the beginning, a novella)

A Promise of Vengeance

Undeniable Vengeance

Consummate Vengeance

Vengeance Is Mine (2019)

Note: The Light of Lights is a novella. It's about 100 pages long and sets the stage for the series. The other books in the series are between 650 and 850 pages long.

OTHER BOOKS

You can always see the current and coming-soon books on my website.

Fiction

***Memories for Sale* (mystery/sf)**

***The Joshua Citadel* (SF novella)**

Children's Books

No Mistakes Grammar for Kids, Volume I—Much and Many

No Mistakes Grammar for Kids, Volume II—Lie and Lay

No Mistakes Grammar for Kids, Volume III—Bring and Take

No Mistakes Grammar for Kids, Volume IV, "Would've, Should've"
and "Your and You're"

No Mistakes Grammar for Kids, Volume V, "There, They're, and
Their" and "To, Too, and Two"

Shinobi Goes to School—Life on the Farm for Kids, Volume I

Fiona Gets Caught, Life on the Farm for Kids, Volume II

Coco Gets a Donut, Life on the Farm for Kids, Volume III

Squeak Gets a Home, Life on the Farm for Kids, Volume IV

Biscotti Saves Punch, Life on the Farm for Kids, Volume V

The Adventures of Adalina, Volume I, Adalina and the Five Tiny Bears

Coming Soon

The Adventures of Adalina, Volume II, Adalina and the Underwater Bears

Get on the mailing list and you'll be sure to be notified of release
dates and sales.

Mailing list

And don't forget to leave a review!

9 781949 074628